LOVE IN A WYCH ELM

HE Bates
Herbert Ernest Bates lived from 1905 to 1974. A prolific writer, he is best known today for his short stories and his novels *My Uncle Silas*, *Fair Stood the Wind for France* and, of course, *The Darling Buds of May*.

Peter Conradi is an author and journalist. A graduate of Brasenose College, Oxford, he is the author of, among other books, *Hitler's Piano Player*. Formerly a foreign correspondent in Brussels, Zurich and Moscow, Conradi became deputy foreign editor of the *Sunday Times* in 1998. He lives in London.

Tim Bates is a literary agent in London. He previously worked as an editor at Penguin. He lives in North London with his wife and three young daughters.

D1375415

Love in a Wych Elm
and other stories

Love in a Wych Elm
and other stories

_____

HE Bates

FOREWORD BY PETER CONRADI
SELECTION BY TIM BATES

CAPUCHIN CLASSICS

First published:
The Harvest (1927), The Gleaner (1932), The Bath (1934), The Plough (1934),
Cut and Come Again (1935), The Case of Miss Lomas (1937),
Something Short and Sweet (1937), Château Bouganvillea (1938),
I Am Not Myself (1939), Shot Actress—Full Story (1939), Old (1939),
The Ferry (1940), Time Expired (1945), A Christmas Song (1950),
The Evolution of Saxby (1953), Go, Lovely Rose (1953), The Watercress Girl (1953),
Love in a Wych Elm (1954), Now Sleeps the Crimson Petal (1958),
Where the Cloud Breaks (1961)

This edition published by Capuchin Classics 2009
2 4 6 8 0 9 7 5 3 1

© 2009 Evansford Productions Limited

Capuchin Classics
128 Kensington Church Street, London W8 4BH
Telephone: +44 (0)20 7221 7166
Fax: +44 (0)20 7792 9288
E-mail: info@capuchin-classics.co.uk
www.capuchin-classics.co.uk

Châtelaine of Capuchin Classics: Emma Howard

ISBN: 978-0-95557312-9-7

CONTENTS

A Note on the Selection

HE Bates published his first story in 1926 when he was just twenty and his last, exactly fifty years later, in his final posthumous collection. In between he wrote ceaselessly, producing over 300 stories and novellas. This is the first collection of his short stories selected from the entire span of his writing career since Bates' own selection, *Seven by Five*, in 1961, and the first new selection of any kind since the early 1980s.

Like *Seven by Five* it does not include any of the stories in the *Uncle Silas* or *Flying Officer X* series because I share Bates' own view that those stories belong to entirely different and separate categories.

I have attempted to illustrate the full range of Bates' short fiction, from the very early impressionistic sketches written in the 1920s, and the critically acclaimed stories of the 1930s, to the fully realized narrative pieces he published after the enormous international successes of his post-war novels. In each instance, those of the stories are based on the texts of the first volume publication.

Tim Bates

Foreword

Although Bates' novels, after *Fair Stood the Wind for France* in 1944, were often bestsellers, it was as a short story writer that he truly excelled. Interestingly here the story 'Time Expired' rehearses a misandrist, sadistic lesbian Irish nurse (Miss Burke) whom Bates would wheel out again in his novel *The Purple Plain*; but the story is entirely satisfying in itself. Now we can measure his growth as a short-story writer.

'Harvest', from 1927, when Bates was still a struggling unknown writer, evokes the pregnancy of an un-named mother of four, in terms that are faintly menacing, and full of wonderful atmosphere. The harvest of the title refers to autumn plenitude, to the new baby, and to the fact that actions have consequences. Yet Bates, unlike DH Lawrence, never bullies the reader with a moral which, if he has one, he is likely to lose in his own lyricism.

'The Gleaner' is personification as much as portrait. Here Bates captures a way of life going back to Ruth who is described gathering grain in the Old Testament. Bates observed grinding poverty in rural Northamptonshire during his childhood through and after the Great War. His gleaner, struggling to carry her heavy load of victuals, is the last of her breed. Yet the old ways of life died hard. And so perhaps 'Old' and 'The Plough' explore archetypes, as does 'The Ferry' with its wonderful rendering of apocalyptic Fenland flooding which has driven the landlady in the tale to religious madness.

In 'The Bath', published in 1934 but set earlier, Bates evokes the strange atmosphere in the countryside of Weimar Germany, with occupying British troops (who left four years earlier) fraternizing with defeated Germans, and all uniting in their love of creature comforts. Probably the 'British troops' in this story are based on Bates and his friends, who made a trip to Germany in the late 1920s (Charles Lahr the German bookseller and Rhys Davies were among the party), recounted in the novella *The Hessian Prisoner* and in his *Autobiography*.

He is good at awkward, complex, tense relationships ('Cut and Come Again'), as at shock-endings ('The Case of Miss Lomas') in which the person you did not expect to, dies; as on alienation and estrangement ('Château Bougainvillaea', 'I am not Myself'). 'Shot Actress—Full story' concerns press-sensationalism, but renders the costs of this in entirely individual and believable terms.

In a study he first published on *The Modern Short Story* during the war, Bates compared the short story to cinema. Both stand outside tradition, are free, and both can use small vivid details to convey emotion. Indeed Bates's method is strikingly cinematic – which is to say, rendered visually immediate and alive – and it is unsurprising that so much of his work has been adapted for film and television, not just for example *Uncle Silas*, but also the riotously successful adaptations of *The Darling Buds of May*.

From impersonal birds-eye view to close focus, a number of these stories show you a whole world that looks at first impersonally romantic or exotic, only to move in the end towards disenchantment. The Arnoldsons in 'I am not Myself' live more grandly than the narrator, and have at first sight the glamour of wealth, until their daughter appears to be a fabulator, and very possibly unhinged.

Similarly in 'Now Sleeps the Crimson Petal', the protagonist, who delivers meat to the owner of a grand country house during the austere years after the war comes slowly to see how sterile and bitchy this world is. The gentrified world in 'A Christmas Song' is bullying and philistine, while 'The Evolution of Saxby' presents a couple who restore these houses in order to sell on, and are seen to lack moral substance.

In the comic Larkin novels HE Bates showed considerable sympathy for the old gentry (or New Poor), emerging as they did into a harsher post-war world of death duties and high taxation. Little of that is shown here. The title story, 'Love in a Wych Elm', concerns a family who present themselves as To the manor born, so that the narrator admires their apparent scope and ease and confidence. The interest of the tale, however, lies elsewhere, in the romances of childhood itself and in the countryside which Bates so loved, where 'a sense of honeyed rotten quietness spread under the lurching trees' shut in by the boundary line of tapering wych elms.

Bates was a modest man, apparently content with the gift of being able to 'put the English countryside down on paper'. His parents were chapel-going Northamptonshire cobblers who, in true Midlands fashion, ate pudding before the main course. Leather-workers were famously independent-minded and HE Bates was blessed (and also limited) by being a son of this Little England who, despite having good writer-friends and liking to eat well at the Caprice, had no time for literary London, and remained an outsider. His stories show that this a not a bad vantage from which to write if, like Bates, you happen to be richly gifted too.

Peter Conradi
September 2008

Harvest

On most evenings between April and September she had chosen this walk for her children, choosing it because from the top of the lane the colours of the surrounding land, from the time of fresh greens and yellows to the time of harvest, were soft and pleasant to her eyes.

This evening, as on all others, she rested her arms on the gate while regaining her breath after the journey. It was later than usual, though not yet dusk, and sultrily warm with the true oppressiveness of autumn. The air was so still she fancied now and then she could hear the rustle of her children's feet in the grass of the adjoining field. Even if they had never spoken, had never occasionally called to her 'Mother! Mother! here we are!' she would have been aware of their presence because of this sound, heavy and swishing, like the sea.

In the middle of the summer she had often played with the children in this field. It had not once seemed childish or beneath her dignity to lie in the grass and let them hide their faces in her skirts, then scream in her ears and half-suffocate her with hay. She had never been able to reproach them for these things, had never been able to look into any one of their young smiling faces and utter an angry word. She remembered this had been so from the very spring of the year, through the time of daisies, celandines, buttercups and hay, thyme and clover. She remembered looking forward with a naive eagerness, as if she had been a child herself, to this time, each day, of irresponsible joys, of absurd laughter. Sometimes, on the journey back again, she remembered, she had shut her eyes and simply followed the voices before her in her great joy.

They had not once failed to refresh her in spirit. Now, for some days, for a reason she dared not let intrude upon her too often, she had not played with them. Not understanding this the children had showered uneasy questions upon her.

'But why? why won't you come? Mother! Mother!—come now!'

But each time, with a heaviness of her heart, she had refused them without ever giving her reason.

These refusals and the emptiness they made in her daily life, hurt her deeply. This evening more than all others, she felt the lack of their companionship, their soft voices, their faces hiding in her skirts. They had come to gather mushrooms. They had talked excitedly about it since morning. To miss such a simple thing as this and to feel sad about it seemed absurd, she knew, yet she was disappointed and depressed by it, without being able to explain, even to understand why.

From the gate her eyes roamed over the field where the children were. Their four little figures wandered tirelessly among the grass, searching diligently. Behind them, and on all sides, extended cornfields, sloping upon the single dark square of pasture like the sides of a golden frame, enclosing it securely there as a painting worth much to her.

On these slopes she could see figures too. Now and then reached her the sound of a reaper working very late and the low rumble of wagons up and down the hill. The sounds came through the air heavily, as if of another world. Sometimes, as with the dark, still trees above her, it seemed that the wagons and the reaper laboured under a great burden, too heavy for them, which made them groan.

About her it began to grow twilight. Across the field one of the children came running to her.

'The basket, Mother—please—quickly! We've found something!'

He ran off again, hugging it to his breast. It was too big for him.

'Don't be long—come back soon, remember—soon!' she called after him.

He did not answer. It seemed to her most likely he had not even heard her. It was foolish—but she had not the heart to call him again.

She slipped back into a mood of reflection when he had gone. Now, as the twilight took a stronger possession of the trees, of the distant slopes and of the sky, where there would soon be stars, she began to think more and more of the reason why now she never played with her children. She hugged herself for a long time silently, with closed eyes. This reason hurt her even to think about—it seemed so cruel, so unfair, imposing upon her so much.

For a moment she had a fleeting illusion that it did not exist. She opened her eyes and looked up. This illusion became suddenly replaced by a second: it seemed to her that there was another child in the field with the rest. She counted them feverishly: in her haste she counted five, then only four, then five again.

Suddenly it was immaterial to her whether there were four or five. The presence of this fifth one, a presence that had been for so long like a shadow, a burden, and a blessing by turns, was no longer part of an illusion. In a week or two she knew that the other children would be saying among themselves, with simple, incredulous delight: 'We have a little baby!' She saw them being led into her bedroom to peer at it against her breast.

In a day or two she would no longer be able to bring the children up the lane in the evening. Before long she would be forced to move about quietly, to live through a horror of expectation, an oppression of fears, to deny herself, yet to appear calm and fearless, as if nothing were about to happen. She knew this with an unclouded understanding. For her it was an experience not to be dreaded because unprecedented, because unknown, but for the simple reason that it had happened to her before. She was aware so certainly what fears it brought, what remembrances, what agony, even the sounds, the silences—every detail, even the odours, even the attention of the nurse to her bodily needs.

Sometimes the thing more awful than all these, the inevitability of it all, made her cold with fear. It would be as if the night dew had fallen with unnatural heaviness on her alone, so that she felt cold in a world of sultry airs, of luxurious scents, of warm fruits and leaves. It became so that she was never deceived—that there were no illusions of miraculous escape from this new presence.

Dusk began to cover everything, like an oppressive, luxuriant bloom. The trees weighed down heavily beneath it, the grasses shone dimly with wetness. From a great distance came the sound of the wagons rumbling uphill. The reaper had ceased. Clouds with a dim amber light behind them had risen from beyond the hill, and in a little while the moon would be up.

She was very silent. Suddenly she recalled some words spoken to her long ago.

'My little one, I promise you—no burdens, no troubles—only happiness.'

She remembered also the speaker's face with the same clearness. It seemed that if she had said in return, 'I promise you, I will keep a perfect image of you,' she could not have been more faithful. Now it seemed to her changed: in those days it had been not merely a face but the embodiment of all her tenderest, most feminine ideals. She remembered not only this circumstance, but others when she had believed just so utterly in her husband's kindness, his trust, his magnanimity, and when she had even, in this rapturous faith, invented for him fresh and more wonderful virtues.

And this was so no longer: she thought of him now as her husband, a being from whom she no longer expected promises and assurances.

Dusk kept falling about her, the trees hung like dark curtains against the sky. The heart of the evening gave up its sounds: the cries of her children, the rumble of wagons, sometimes the stir of leaves and the late voice of a grasshopper.

She began to whisper to herself, 'No burdens, no troubles.'

She got no further. It seemed to her suddenly that both this thought and the promise which had given rise to it were futile and unnatural. Not all these wishes, she thought, could upset the inevitability of what was about to happen to her. Dreamily, as if she had begun to wander in her mind, she thought of the orchards she had passed in the lane, the damson-trees, the apples, the long ropes of pears, the plums she had seen in the grass.

The weight of these on the uncomplaining arms of the trees made her think slowly, 'It doesn't matter, it doesn't matter.'

What was it that didn't matter? she asked herself. She did not know. She bent her head on the gate.

Then, knowing how late it was, she aroused herself. The dusk had grown heavier and heavier. An orange light pervaded the ease; minute by minute there were more stars.

She raised her voice and called her children. She thought that on no other night had she stayed so long.

'It's late!—quickly, quickly!'

Their indistinct figures seemed to move with terrible slowness across the darkened field. She remembered suddenly the things she must do before bedtime: little George had torn his shirt, a button had come off Edith's chemise. She must see that each of the children washed themselves and ate something and went to bed.

Out of the gloom, with the ominous glow from the east spreading through it, she saw them coming slowly. She called half-frantically:

'Quickly! Quickly! Where have you been?'

The excitement caused a pain in her side. For a moment she held herself quite still, watching the children advance just as before. She felt weak. Everything about her seemed heavy and still, a world unexpectedly overburdened with its own luxuriance and fruitfulness.

Suddenly the children paused not far off. Something showed white on the ground between them. It was the basket, she thought.

'It's too heavy!' they called to her. 'It's full—we can't carry it!'

She hurried to them and lifted the basket with its burden of wild apples, blackberries and mushrooms. The children seized her skirts, her free hand and the handle of the basket.

'You carry it, Mother!'

Their voices fell loudly into the world of autumnal softness and gloom, disturbing echoes that ran from the heavy trees to the cornfields afar off. 'You carry it, Mother, you carry it!'

The Gleaner

She is very old, a little sprig of a woman, spare and twisted. The sun is hardly past its noon. She has climbed uphill out of the town, up the hot, white road, with curious fretting footsteps, half-running, half-walking, as though afraid that some other gleaner will have come up before her. But as far as she can see, into a distance of mellow light under a sky as mild and wonderfully blue as the stray chicory-stars still blooming among the stiff yellow grasses by the roadside, the world is empty. She is alone, high up, insignificantly solitary in a world of pure untrembling light that pours straight down, washing away the summer-green gloom from the tops of the still trees. There is not even the stirring of a sheep over the land or the flickering of a bird in the sky; nothing to alarm or rival or distract her. Yet she goes on always with that fretting eagerness, as though afraid, not resting or satisfied until she sees the wheatfield before her, empty like the rest of the earth except for that downpour and flood of golden light upon its stubbled slope.

She pushes open the gate, clicks it shut behind her, flaps open her sack, takes one swift and comprehensive glance at the field, and bends her back. Her fingers are rustling like quick mice over the stubble, and the red wheat ears are rustling together in her hands before she has taken another step forward. There is no time for looking or listening or resting. To glean, to fill her sack, to travel over that field before the light is lost; she has no other purpose than that and could understand none.

Long ago, in another century, she also came up to this same field, on just such still, light-flooded afternoons, for this same eternal and unchanging purpose. But not alone; they would glean then, in families, occasionally in villages, with handcarts and barrows, from early morning until evening, from one gleaning-bell to another. Since it meant so much, since corn was life—that law was as old as time itself—they gleaned incessantly, desperately. Every ear on the face of every field had to be gathered up, and she can remember her mother's fist in her back harrying her to glean faster, and how, in turn, she also urged her children to go on and on, never to rest until the field was clear and the light had died.

She is already away from the gate, moving quickly out into the field away from the ruts that the wagons have cut and the ears they have smashed into the sun-baked soil. She moves with incredible quickness, fretfully, almost as fearfully as she came up the hill. In her black skirt and blouse, and with her sharp white head for ever near the earth, she looks like a hungry bird, always pecking and nipping at something, never resting, never satisfied.

Her sleeves are rolled up, showing her thin, corn-coloured arms, with the veins knotty and stiff about her bony wrists. Her hands seem to be still young in their quickness and vitality, like the young tips of an old tree, and the intent yet tranquil look on her face is eternal. It is a little, sharp, fleshless, million-wrinkled face; it is like a piece of wood, worn down by time, carved down pitilessly and relentlessly, the softness of the cheeks and mouth and eyes scooped out to make deep hollows, the bone of the cheeks and chin and forehead left high and sharp as knots in the wood. As though years of sun-flooded days in gleaning fields had stained it, the flesh is a soft, shining corn colour. Even the blue dimness of her eyes has become touched by the faintest drop of this corn-coloured radiance—the colour of age, of autumn, of dying, almost of death itself.

In the open field the sun is very hot. Beating down from an autumn angle the force of its light and heat falls full on her back or into her eyes as she zigzags up and down or across the stubble-rows. She appears to move carelessly, without method, gleaning chance ears as she sees them; she moves, in reality, by instinct, to some ancient and inborn system, unconsciously, but surely as a bird. Miraculously she misses scarcely an ear. She moves incessantly, she looks tireless. Sometimes she glances quickly over her shoulders, across the field, into the sky, with brief unconscious anxiety about something, but the world is empty.

It is as though there is no one in the world except herself who gleans any longer. She is not merely alone: she is the last of the gleaners, the last survivor of an ancient race. Nevertheless, moving across the field under the mellow sun, nipping up the ears in her quick hands, shaking her sack, dragging it over the stubble, she looks eternal. She is doing something that has been done since the beginning of time and is not conscious of it; she is concerned only with the ears, the straws, the length of the stubble, the way she must go. She scarcely notices even the flowers, ground blooming and creeping flowers that the binder cannot touch, little mouse-carpets of periwinkle and speedwell, purple coronets of knapweed, trumpets of milk-coloured and pink convolvulus, a scabious bursting a mauve bud, bits of starry camomile. Occasionally she is impatient at something—at the straggling length of the stubble, the riot of thistle and coltsfoot that chokes the rows. Nowadays the binder leaves the straw so long and shaggy. Nobody hoes any longer, nobody gleans, nobody troubles. The crop is poor and uneven, and she comes across wastes of thin straw and much green rank twitch where the earth is barren of corn and she scarcely picks an ear, though she never straightens her back and never ceases that mouse-quick searching with her brown hands.

But later, in the heat of the afternoon, with her sack filling up and the sun-heat and bright light playing unbrokenly upon her, she begins unconsciously to move more slowly, a little tired, like a child that has played too long. She will not cover the field, and as she moves there, always solitary, up and down the stubble, empty except for herself and a rook or two, she begins to look smaller and the field larger and larger about her.

At last she straightens her back. It is her first conscious sign of weariness. She justifies it by looking into the sky and over the autumn-coloured land sloping away to the town; briefly she takes in the whole soft-lighted world, the effulgence of wine-yellow light on the trees and the dove-coloured roofs below and a straggling of rooks lifting heavily off the stubble and settling farther on again.

She stoops and goes on once more; and then soon, another rest, another glance into the sky, and then another beginning. Very soon there is a thistle pricking her hand, and she is glad to stop and pull it out and suck the place with her thin lips.

Ahead of her there is a hedge of hawthorn and blackberry, with great oaks that throw balloons of shadow across the field. She moves into the oak shade with relief; it is cool, like a drink of water, like a clean white sheet; and the coolness fills her with a new vitality, so that she goes on gleaning for a long time without needing to rest.

By and by she is working along the hedge. Straws have been plaited and twisted by wind among the hawthorn and blackberry and wild clematis and sloe, and she goes along picking them off, twisting them together and dropping them into her sack, her body upright. It is easier. She can smell the darkening blackberries, the first dying odour of leaves. She stops to gather and eat a dewberry, squeezing it against her palate like a dark grape; to rub the misty purple-green bloom off a sloe with her fingers.

There are many straws on the hedge. The sack is heavy. She walks very slowly, dragging it, wondering all the time why she does not lift it to her shoulder and start for home, but something stronger than herself keeps her picking and gleaning, missing nothing.

It is not until the light begins to fail that she thinks of departing. She has begun to carry the sack in her arms, hugging it to her chest, setting it down at intervals and gleaning the stubble about it. There is no need to go on, but some inherent, unconscious, eternal impulse keeps her moving perpetually. But still she glances up sometimes with the old fear, wondering if some other gleaner will come.

She has worked towards the gate and there she sets down the sack and rests a moment. It is late afternoon; dark crowds of starlings are flying over and gathering in invisible trees, making a great murmuration in the late quietness. Before she can depart she must lift the sack to her back or lift it to the gate and bend her back beneath it. She is very tired. She might leave the sack under the hedge; she might come again tomorrow; but she suddenly catches the sack in her arms, hoists it to the gate with an immense effort as though her life depended upon it.

Her strength is not enough. The sack, very full, half falls back upon her, but in a moment she makes a tremendous effort and, as she makes it, lifting the sack slowly upright again, she feels her eyes, for some reason, fill with the stupid tears of age and weakness.

In a moment it is all over, forgotten. She makes a great effort to lift up the sack. She succeeds. The sack falls across her back, bearing her down, and she catches at its mouth, holds it and staggers away.

Her tears have stopped and she has not thought of wiping them away, and as she staggers off down the road towards the sunset they roll down among her million wrinkles and find their way to her mouth. She goes on without resting. She looks more than ever eternal, an earth-figure, as old and ageless and primitive as the corn she carries.

As she goes on, the light dies rapidly until there is only an orange glow in the western sky like the murky light of a candle. The air is cool, still, autumnal. Her tears have dried on her cheeks, and now and then she can taste the salt of them still on her lips: the salt of her own body, the salt of the earth.

The Bath

As we struggled with our bags up the little German road in the August heat, leaving the camp of English soldiers-of-occupation in the valley to the left of us, we were all wondering if there would be a bath at the end of the journey. And when was the end of the journey? We must have asked that question of Karl a thousand times. 'Soon,' he would say carelessly, 'soon.' But we were afraid of mentioning the bath, for at heart we all felt that we were going into some lost and legendary German world so isolated and primitive that baths would be as unknown as Englishmen.

It was beautiful country, lost and peaceful. The roadside was starred with many stiff blue chicory flowers and milk-yellow snapdragons and scarlet poppies, the flowers drifting thinly back into hedgeless crops of potatoes and ripening wheat and rye that had old pear-trees planted among them in wide lines, the lines gapped here and there where a tree had died. Along the road-side there were again lines of pear-trees, with odd apple-trees interplanted, and the same breaks where a tree had gone. Beyond the crops of corn and potatoes, the land rose gently, always a pale sand-colour, to the vineyards that gleamed a strange bluish-green in the straight sunlight. To the left was the valley with its broad river flowing between the many-coloured crops, and the English soldiers' tents grouped by the water like chance mushrooms. The road climbed continually, always farther and farther away from that river where we might have bathed and on towards the vineyards that we never quite seemed to reach.

'Where is this village, Karl? How much farther? Can't we stop and rest? Let's stop and get some beer. Karl, let's stop.'

But it made no difference to Karl. He and I walked in front, setting the pace, with chicory flowers stuck in our buttonholes, while Wayford and Thomas came behind us, together, and after them the two brothers Williams. It was the Williams, the one like a little rosy pig and the other like some thin provincial photographer dressed to photograph a funeral, who wanted to rest continually. It seemed that they had once spent a week in Paris and had drunk champagne there; and now it gave them a sort of melancholy amusement to compare the boulevards with the little German road winding up to the vineyards, and the champagne with the lager. But Karl was deaf. The country was his native land, the little road with the poppies and chicory flowers had not changed since his childhood, and he was the prodigal returning after many years.

So he led us implacably on in that August heat until, very late in the afternoon, we came to his native village, a lost and beautiful place, full of old white houses with green jalousies and great courtyards shut off from the narrow shadowy streets by tall wooden doors, a forgotten place, as legendary as we had half-imagined it, lying up there between the forests and the vineyards like a village out of some old German fairy tale.

When we arrived there was great excitement, a sort of explosive excitement, all the fat German fräuleins who were Karl's sisters or aunts or cousins popping off shrieks and cackles of hysterical laughter, and the heavy German men booming thunderously in their round bellies and slapping themselves and Karl on the back in their immense joy. When we were introduced there was a great shaking of hands and a babbling of voices and a running hither and thither, together with all the pantomimic signs with hands and eyes and lips that pass between men who do not speak each other's language. And over and above it all, hysterically and incredulously:

'Karl! Karl! Karl! Karl!'

From that moment our visit became a kind of festival. Day and night there was an incessant pouring of wine and coffee in that old farmhouse with the great courtyard, a babbling arrival and departure of visitors, a cracking and frizzling of a thousand eggs over the great wood fire in the dark and lofty kitchen. We lived for three days the luxurious and pampered life of a conquering army under the roofs of a conquered people. In the mornings we lazed about the courtyard in the hot sunshine, and in the afternoon walked up to the vineyards to watch the peasants thinning and spraying the vines for the last time; or we strolled off into the forest, the breathless pine forest that shut us off from the outer world, and then came back to photograph the peasants cutting the patches of wheat and rye with ancient reapers drawn by even more ancient oxen. We could go where we liked and do what we liked and drink what we liked. We were the English, which seemed to mean that we were the favoured, the elect. Wherever we went in that village some old man or woman or child or young girl would come out to speak and laugh with us and make all the eternal pantomimic signs of gladness and friendship. If we were tired we could walk into the nearest house and sit there and rest; and there would be wine and coffee, talk and laughter, and diffident respect and a sense of quivering happiness. Everywhere there was that feeling of relief and joy that comes between two people who have quarrelled and are friends again, and want only to forget their bitterness.

But there was no bath. And perhaps because of the bath, or perhaps because the elder brother Williams had chased a litter of pigs out of the courtyard with a broomstick, we began to notice a subtle change of feeling towards us on the third day.

We were still welcome; and there was still the same flow of wine and coffee, and still the same air of great respect for us. But now we began to sense the faintest air of suspicion, of unrest, as though we had stayed too long. We began to notice that the peasants would spy on us from half-curtained windows as we walked along the streets. We noticed that the women gossiping in two's and three's became silent as we passed.

'Let's go to Berlin,' the Williams kept saying. 'We could at least get a bath there. Let's get away from this hole.'

'Go,' said Karl. 'Do what you like.'

But they were reluctant. Perhaps the fare was too much? We saw them counting their money in corners.

Then, next day, Williams the elder made a great shine over some cream at lunch.

'This isn't cream,' he whispered.

'Then what the hell is it?' said Karl.

'It's tinned milk.'

Karl sat furious, too hurt and angry to speak articulately. But at last he turned to me:

'Is it cream? You tell them. You're from the country. You tell them. Is it cream or not?'

'It's lovely cream,' I said.

'It's tinned milk!' said the elder Williams excitedly. 'Any fool can tell you that. It's tinned milk, I tell you!'

Across the table the peasants were watching the scene, suspicious. We were their guests. They must have detected the note of dissatisfaction in Williams' uplifted voice. Karl was miserable and furious.

'At least wait till we get outside!' he whispered. 'At least do that.'

The meal was finished in silence, in a silence of suspicion and unhappiness.

Afterwards, in the courtyard, it all broke out again:

'We're off to Berlin!' the Williams shouted.

'And good riddance!' shouted Karl.

'What time is there a train?'

'Find out.'

'We can't speak the language.'

'Learn it.'

They went indoors at last to pack their bags, furious. Coming downstairs again they stood in the courtyard and pored over their little red pocket dictionary in silence, anxious, but independent.

Karl, quieter now, went to them:

'You know the nearest station is four miles off?' he said.

'We can walk,' they said.

'It's a branch line.'

'We know that.'

'Hadn't you better wait? It's seventeen hours to Berlin.'

'We're going to Paris.'

Karl gave it up. Standing on the far side of the courtyard, I could see the peasants standing unrestfully at doors and windows, watching the scene. They must have sensed the cause of the quarrel, that they and their food and their ways were no longer good enough for us, and the air was tense.

It was a wretched situation. Again Karl tried to make it easier:

'Wait till tomorrow. We'll all go then. We'll all go on to Berlin in the morning.'

'We're going to Paris,' said the Williams fervently.

'Wherever you're going, there's no train till four o'clock.'

They condescended to wait, sitting on their bags by the doorstep in the sunshine, so that every peasant going in or out of the house had to step over them. The atmosphere grew more tense and wretched.

Karl had vanished. But suddenly, ten minutes later, he came running back into the courtyard:

'A bath!' he was shouting. 'A bath! We can have a bath.'

The Williams tried to look uninterested.

'Schmidt, the richest farmer in the village, invites us all to his house tonight,' said Karl, 'to have a bath.'

'All of us?'

'All of us. It's a new bath. It's never been used. He's invited us over to use it for the first time. He's the only man for fifty miles round who has a bath. It's a great honour.'

We were at once excited. The mosquitoes had been devilish, the heat and sweat of the days very trying and for a long time we had ached for a bath. Moreover, the news seemed suddenly to dispel the air of suspicion created by the quarrel. Everyone began to act more freely. Only the Williams continued to sit on their suitcases in the courtyard, dismally waiting for the time when they should depart.

But at eight o'clock that evening, when we set off towards the house of Herr Schmidt, for the bath, together with all the girls and women who are Karl's sisters or aunts or cousins, and all their fat husbands or sweethearts, we noticed that the Williams were still with us. They walked a little sheepishly, behind us or apart from us, and the peasants never spoke to them.

The bath of Herr Schmidt was already a legend. Karl translated for us the peasants' ecstasies, and now and then a man would stop and throw out his fat arms to indicate the size of the bath of Herr Schmidt, the colossal wonder of the countryside. Karl's sister Maria was very fat, and once her father paused and urged us to look upon her.

'So!' There was great laughter. 'So!' he said again, as though to indicate that even Maria would be lost when she sat in that bath. Even Herr Schmidt, too, would be lost. Even Herr Schmidt! There was still great laughter.

When we arrived at Herr Schimdt's house, a big farmhouse set in a spacious courtyard, just as the summer dusk was falling, Herr Schmidt himself stood in the doorway, waiting to receive us. Seeing him, we saw at once the reason for the peasants' laughter and the bath's immensity. Herr Schmidt stood on his threshold like the traditional innkeeper in a German opera, so fat that he could scarcely waddle forward to greet us, his laughter so rich and powerful that it rumbled like operatic thunder.

He was in a state of great excitement, greeting us with a thousand explosive invitations to enter the house, laughing mightily whenever he spoke, waving his arms, bowing, shaking our hands with his immense obese paws until we were pained and weary.

'Ender. Pliz go in!' he shouted delightedly. 'Ender!'

We all followed him into the house and he bowed us into the drawing-room. 'Ender. Pliz come in.' It was a great honour, a great honour. He was overwhelmed, overjoyed to have us bathe with him. He could think of no greater honour. And were we in the War? We were too young? Yes? But he, Herr Schmidt, was in the War, and was wounded. Ah! but let us not talk about it. 'Ender! Pliz come in. Pliz come in!'

He rushed away excitedly, excusing himself elaborately. Left in the drawing-room we all became conscious of a strange thing.

The drawing-room was like a boiler house. The heat was terrific, a thick steaming heat that had condensed on the walls and on the pictures and the old polished furniture. As we sat there the memory of the sultry summer evening outside seemed cool and delicious. And now and then we heard strange squeaks and guttural rumblings overhead and about us, like the sound of water bubbling hotly in hidden pipes, and at intervals the sound increased to a great stuttering grunt, as though the pipes must burst.

But Herr Schmidt, carrying many bottles of hock under his arms, came puffing in to reassure us. Had we heard anything? Anything we might hear was just the bath water. It was just beginning to get hot. Beginning! We sat in a mute sweat of alarm at that word. Only a little while and the water would be hot and the bath would be ready. Until then, we must have a little wine. Yes? Herr Schmidt brandished the bottles excitedly.

We were too hot to speak. Herr Schmidt uncorked the bottles loudly and poured out the pale green wine. We sat about weakly, too limp from that steamy heat to talk or move. All the time the subterranean squeaks and grumblings went on in the pipes about us, like the grunting of a litter of pigs, and each time there was some louder and more ominous growling Herr Schmidt would laugh with stentorian excitement, proud as a father at the chucklings of a new baby, drowning the sound of the boiling water with his own enormous voice.

During all this the Williams sat in silent discomfort, bathed in uneasy sweat. They never spoke, and the peasants sat apart from them, as though remembering the quarrel and its causes.

All the time the room grew hotter and the growlings in the pipes more alarming. When we felt that we could bear it no longer, Herr Schmidt rushed out of the room and back again and shouted that the bath was ready.

'Who'll go first?' said Karl.

But Herr Schmidt was not ready. First we must view the bath. It was, after all, unique, a virgin among baths, and ours were to be the first bodies to enter it. So with the peasants eyeing us enviously we all trooped out after Herr Schmidt to the bathroom.

'Ender! Pliz come in. Pliz ender!'

He bowed us into the bathroom. Inside, the heat was infernal, and there, with an immense ten-foot stove of flowered tiles built against it, was the wonder, the virgin bath. We gazed in awe. It seemed to us that that bath could have held an elephant, or that a man might have used it with safety as a boat on the high seas.

Herr Schmidt was almost hysterical with joy at our silent wonder. He dusted the tiniest flecks of dirt off the white porcelain and turned on the tap with a flourish, letting out a volcanic stream of hissing water that set all the pipes in the house growling ominously again.

We murmured in admiration, and Herr Schmidt thundered his laughter.

Ten minutes later I was standing in the bath, the water burning my feet like acid. We had drawn lots for the bath and I was first. But the water was so hot that I could not bear it and the water in the cold tap had grown lukewarm from the violent heat of the stove. I washed myself tenderly and got out of the bath quickly and went back to the drawing-room.

And one by one the rest took their baths and came out quickly, as though they had been through fire. It happened that the Williams had drawn the last places, and by the time they went into the bathroom the grumblings and squeakings in the pipes were already dying away.

'How was it?' we said when they appeared. They had gone in together to scrub each other down. 'Was it too hot?'

'It was beautiful,' they said.

They were radiant.

'Could you get down in it?' we asked. None of us had been able to sit in that infernal water.

'It was grand,' was all they could say. 'It was worth waiting for. It was perfect.'

They were smiling, their faces pink from the fresh warm water. And as they sat down to drink the wine that Herr Schmidt had poured out for them they seemed like different men. The bath seemed to have washed away their sulkiness and misery, their air of condescension, the memory of all their petty grievances. It was so plain in their faces that even the peasants could see it.

We stayed in Herr Schmidt's house all that evening. The wine and the coffee flowed endlessly again, there was good German food, and Herr Schmidt sang songs for us. We also sang songs in return and danced heavily round the room, clumping our feet, with the German women. Even the Williams danced, and all the old feeling of suspicion, and all the deeper feeling that our countries had once been enemies, vanished completely. It was as if the bath had washed them away.

We did not leave till early morning and perhaps because of the wine there seemed to be many more of us to go home than there had been to come. The night was very still and soundless; a big summer moon half-way to setting, a warm gold, in the clear and colourless sky, the corn white in the moonlight, the old pear-trees among it as still as the distant forest and the hills.

As we walked down the road we linked arms with the peasants, making a chain across the road. The girls rested their soft heads on our shoulders, and we all sang at the tops of our voices, not knowing quite what we were singing, in the common language of joy.

The Plough

The boy and the old man were ploughing the field that lay on the valley-slope. The plough was drawn by a single horse, an old bony chestnut. It was early March, but already the weather was beautiful, and it was like an April day. Great clouds of white and grey and stormy blue kept sailing in endless flocks across the bright sky from the west, into the face of the morning sun. The cloud-shadows, travelling at a great pace down the sloping field, vanished and then reappeared on the other side of the valley, racing across the brown and green of the planted and unplanted fields. There was a feeling everywhere of new light, which created in turn a feeling of new life. The light was visible even in the turned land, which lay divided into regular stripes of shadow and light at every furrow. The earth, a dark clay, turned up in long sections which shone in the sun like steel, only a little duller in tone than the ploughshare itself.

The slope of the field made ploughing awkward. It meant that whenever the plough went down the hill the man had to hold the plough-lines taut and keep up a constant backward pull on the handles; and that when the plough came up the slope he had to keep up an endless shout at the single horse and lash his back with the loosened lines in order to make him go at all.

At the end of each upward journey the man and the boy paused to wind the horse. 'Lug the guts out on him. Wind a minute.' Blowing with great gasps the horse would stand with his head down, half-broken, staring at the earth, while the man rested on the plough-handles and the boy stood and carved new spirals in an ash-stick.

The man, half-broken like the horse, would sit silent, staring at the earth or scratching his whitish hair. But the boy would talk.

'Ain't it about time we lit on a skylark's?'

'We'll light o' one. Don't whittle. It's early yet.'

Or he would bring up an old question. In other fields he had seen men at plough with two, three and sometimes four horses. Tremendous teams.

'Why don't we plough with more horse 'n one?'

'Ain't got no more. That's why.'

At the lower end of the field they would pause again, but more briefly. Under the hedge, already breaking its buds, the sun was burning.

'It's that hot,' the boy said, 'I'll ha' me jacket off.'

'Do no such thing! Only March, and stripping—you keep it on. D'ye hear?' The old man glanced up at the vivid spaces of sky, wonderfully blue, between the running clouds. 'Don't like it. It's too bright to last. We s'll ha' wet jackets afore dinner.'

Like this, struggling up the hill, then resting, then half-running down the hill and resting again, they went on turning up the land. As the morning went on the clouds began to grow thicker, the white clouds giving way to grey and purple, until the distances of sky seemed to be filled with sombre mountains. The intervals of sunshine grew less, so that the fresh lines of yellow coltsfoot flowers, turned up by the plough and pressed down between the furrows, no longer withered like those turned up in the earlier day. And very shortly it was not the shadows of clouds that ran over the sunny fields, but patches of sunlight, brief travelling islands of softest yellow, that ran over a land that was in the shadow of unending clouds.

About eleven o'clock the wind freshened, quite cold, and rain suddenly began to fall in driving streaks across the fields. It was spring rain, sudden and bitter. In a moment it seemed like winter again, the distant land dark and desolate, the furrows wet and dead.

The old man and the boy half-ran across the upper head-land to shelter in the bush-hovel that stood by the gate of the field. As they stood under the hovel, listening to the rain on the bush-roof, they heard the sound of wheels on the road outside, and a moment later a thin long-nosed man, wearing fawn gaiters, a check cap and a white smock, came running into the hovel out of the rain.

He shook the rain-drops off his cap and kept saying in aristocratic tones: 'Demn it. The bladdy weather,' and the old man kept speaking of him as Milk, while the boy sat in a corner, on an old harrow, taking no part in the conversation, but only watching and listening.

A moment or two later there were footsteps outside the hovel again, and in came a second man, a roadman, a large, horse-limbed man holding a sack round his shoulders like a cape. He moved with powerful languor, regarding the milkman with extreme contempt. He seemed almost to fill the hovel and he lounged and swaggered here and there as though it were his privilege to fill it.

'The bladdy weather,' the milkman said.

'We want it,' said the big man. It was like a challenge.

'Who does?'

'We do. Joe and me. More rain, less work. Ain't that it, Joe?'

'That's it,' said the old man.

'Be demned,' Milk said. 'It hinders my work.'

'Get up earlier,' said the big man. 'Poor old Milk. All behind, like the cow's tail.'

The milkman was silent, but his face was curiously white, as though he were raging inwardly. It looked for a moment as though there must be a quarrel. And from the corner the boy watched in fascination, half hoping there would be.

Then, just as it seemed as if there would be a quarrel, the big man spoke again.

'Heard about Wag?' he said. 'Wag Thompson.'

'About Wag?' said the old man.

'He's dead.'

'Dead?' said Milk. 'Dead? I see him this morning.'

'You won't see him no more,' said the big man. 'He's dead.'

The old man stared across the field, into the rain, half-vacantly, looking as though he did not know what to say or think, as though it were too strange and sudden to believe.

'It's right,' the big man said. 'He's dead.'

'How?'

'All of a pop. Dropped down.'

The men were silent, staring at the rain. It was still raining very fast outside and clay-coloured pools were beginning to form in the furrows. But strangely the larks were still singing. The men could hear them above the level hiss of the rain.

'It whacks me,' the old man said. 'Strong man like Wag.'

'That's it,' Milk said. 'He was too strong. Too strong and fat.'

'Fat?' said the big man. 'No fatter'n me. Not so fat.'

'His face was too red. Too high-coloured.'

'It's a licker,' said the big man.

He took a snuff-box from his waistcoat pocket, flicked it open, and handed it first to the old man, then to Milk. In silence they took pinches of the snuff and then he took a pinch, the sweetish smell of the spilt snuff filling the hovel.

'Rare boy for snuff,' said the big man. 'Old Wag.'

'Boy. I like that,' Milk said. 'Must have been sixty.'

'Over.'

For almost the first time the old man spoke.

'Wag was sixty-five,' he said. 'We went plough together. Boys, riding the for' ardest.'

He broke off suddenly, drawn back into memory. It was still raining very fast but the men seemed to have forgotten it. It was as though they could think of nothing but the dead man.

'Ever see Wag a-fishing?' the big man said. 'Beautiful!'

'Times,' said the old man. 'He was a don hand. A masterpiece. I bin with him. Shooting too. When we were kids once we shot a pike. It lay on the top o' the water and Wag let go at it. Young pike. I can see it now.'

'And mushrooms,' Milk said. 'You'd always see him with mushrooms.'

'He could smell mushrooms. Made his living at it,' said the big man. 'That and fishing, and singing.'

'He *could* sing,' said the old man. 'Ever hear him sing *On the Boat that First took me Over*?

'I thought every minit
'We should go slap up agin it.'

The old man broke off, tried to remember the rest of the words, but failed, and there was silence again.

In the corner the boy listened. And gradually, in his mind, he began to form a picture of a man he had never known, and had never even seen. It was like a process of dream creation. Wag took shape in his mind slowly, but with the clarity of life. The boy began to feel attached to him. And as the image increased and deepened itself he felt as though he had known Wag, the plump, red-faced, mild-hearted man, the fisherman, the snuff-taker and the singer, all his life. It affected him profoundly. He sat in a state of wonder. Until suddenly he could bear it no longer. He burst into tears. And the men, startled by the sound of them, gazed at him with profound astonishment.

'Damned if that ain't a licker,' the big man said.

'What's up with you? What're crying for?'

'Something frit him.'

'What was it? Something fright you? What're you crying for?'

'Nothing.'

'What you think o' that? Nothing.'

'Whose boy is it?'

'Emma's. My daughter's. Here, what're you crying for?'

'Nothing.'

'He's tender-hearted. That's how kids are.'

'Here, come, dry up. We've had enough rain a'ready. Come, come.'

And gradually, after a few tears, the boy stopped crying. Looking up through the film of his tears he saw that the rain was lessening too. The storm-clouds had travelled across the valley.

Milk and the big man got up and went outside.

'Blue sky,' said Milk.

'Yes, and you better get on. Folks'll get milk for supper.'

Milk went through the gate and out into the road and a moment later the big man said 'So long' and followed him.

Patches of blue sky were drifting up and widening and flecks of sunlight were beginning to travel over the land as the man and the boy went back to the plough. In the clay-coloured pools along the furrows the reflection of the new light broke and flickered here and there into a dull silver, almost as light as the rain-washed ploughshare. The turned-up coltsfoot flowers that had withered on the ridges had begun to come up again after the rain, the earth gave up a rich fresh smell and the larks were rising higher towards the sunlight.

The man took hold of the plough handles. 'Come on, get up there, on, get up.' And the plough started forward, the horse slower and the share stiffer on the wet land.

Walking by the horse's head, on the unploughed earth, the boy had forgotten the dead man. Skylarks kept twittering up from among the coltsfoots and he kept marking the point of their rising with his eyes, thinking of nothing but the nests he might find.

But all the time the man kept his eyes on the far distance of cloud and sunlight, as though he were lost in the memory of his dead friend.

And the plough seemed almost to travel of its own accord.

Cut and Come Again

The man cutting the hedge between the roadside and the field of winter wheat was quite young and slight. But he was wearing gloves: large hedger's gloves, having deep gauntlets scarred and ripped by thorns of bramble and haw, and for some reason they gave him an appearance of greater age and muscularity. The hedge, old and wild, branched high up with great trunks of ash and hawthorn dwarfed and thickened and misshapen by long confinement with each other. And the young man was laying it: half-splitting the boughs at the foot and bending them prostrate and staking them into a new order. He worked slowly, but with concentration, rather fiercely, and almost at times with anger. In the mild February air the sweat broke out on his fair skin abundantly, renewing itself as soon as he had wiped it away. He would take off his right glove repeatedly in order to wipe his face with his hand; and once he dropped it and it lay on the ground like a flat dry pancake of cow-dung. He picked it up, swore, and flapped it across his knee with exclamations of anger that were really against himself.

Then, at intervals, he stood still and looked down the road. It was almost noon, the sun was quite high, and the road, seen across the new prostrate hedge and in the quiet sunshine, would surprise him. It gave him a fresh sense of space; it was part of a new world, vanishing to a new horizon.

And he seemed to be angry even with that. He stared always as though expecting to see someone, but the road remained empty. And he would vent his anger at that emptiness on the hedge, slashing the hawthorn trunks almost clean through, hooking out the brambles viciously with the point of the bill, his quick sweat filling the wrinkles that ran across his forehead like ploughed furrows.

Then, at last, as he paused to wipe off the sweat and look down the road again, he saw someone coming. It was a young woman. He had no sooner sighted her than he was slashing the hedge again, with great deliberate blows of concentration, in an energetic pantomime of indifference.

In another moment or two the girl was quite near. He behaved as though he did not see her, as though he did not want to see her. But every now and then, furtively, with a kind of cross-glance, he would watch her. And each time she was walking as though he did not exist, looking at the wide winter fields of bare earth and corn stretching away in the sunshine.

Then he was angry again at her display of indifference. And automatically he increased his own. So that as she came nearer he kept up a pretence that she was going farther away; and she in turn walked as though she wanted to make the pretence a reality.

But suddenly he was aware of her standing there, close to him, in the grass, beyond the barricade of bushes he had thrown down. She was younger even than he was; and her gloves of thin creamy cotton, in contrast to his own, made her look still younger. She was very dark, her black hair only half-covered by her red woollen hat, her lips very small and tight, so that she seemed to be for ever biting them.

He looked up quickly, saw the basket she was carrying, and then looked away again. For a moment he did not know what to do with this pose of preoccupied indifference. He felt a fool. And then suddenly he dropped it. He muttered to her:

'Thought it looked like you.'

She did not speak. She was staring at the bushes. They formed a barricade so that she could not pass.

"I'll move 'em,' he said.

'You needn't bother yourself!'

She was already walking along the grass again, towards the gate into the field. He threw down the bill-hook, furious. Then he picked it up again and stood helpless against his sudden anger. He heard the gate click, and then the girl's feet in the dry hedge-grass. Slowly he took off his gloves, his anger evaporating, the sense of foolish embarrassment coming back again.

Then, for the first time, as the girl halted and set the basket on the ground, he looked full at her, but sullenly.

'What's the matter?' he said.

'Nothing.'

The word was like a bubble: very light and airy and careless. He broke if abruptly, almost savagely:

'I wonder you come at all.'

'I wonder.'

The sudden retaliation, quicker even than his own, silenced him. He picked up the basket, lifted the napkin, looked in, and then stared at the girl again.

'Had yourn?'

'No.'

'Better stop.'

'I don't want none.'

As he sat down, under the hedge that was still uncut, with the basket on his knees, she was looking across the wheatfield as though fascinated by some object afar off.

'Stand up there like somebody half-sharp,' he muttered.

'I can go!' she flashed.

He seemed not to hear.

'You don't want me!' she said.

'Who said so? Who said so?'

'Well . . .'

'I never said so. When did I say so? When did I say it?'

He waited for an answer; and when she said nothing it was almost a triumph for him; as though his words were irrefutable.

'You don't want *me*,' he said. 'That's what it is. That's the drift on it.'

Once again she said nothing. But now her face had lost its look of mock preoccupation, and was in pain, filled with thoughts and miseries too complex for her to express. When she did not answer again he took out the knife from the basket and then the food: the bread and cheese and onion and meat.

He sat for a moment waiting, as though for her. Then he began to eat, sullenly, staring at the food, not really tasting it. He tried to think of something to say. Then while he was still thinking she came and sat down. And they sat for a moment or two in silence, waiting for each other to speak, but as though at peace with one another, in the warm half-spring, half-winter sunshine under the shelter of the great hedge.

'Better have a mite o' summat,' he said.

'I don't want nothing.'

'All right. Be different.'

The silent antagonism renewed itself. He ate heavily. Looking up, he saw her staring at the earth, lost in reflection. And unable to tell what she was thinking, he was troubled. She looked as though she wanted to let it pass, to forget it. He wanted to thrash it out, get to the bottom of it, find the reason of it all. And he challenged her:

'We allus going on like this?'

She seemed indifferent.

'I don't know.'

'Don't you want me?'

'What do you think I married you for?'

'Ah, start that again. I thought we had all that out last night.'

They were silent again, waiting for each other to speak. He started to peel the onion, the dry sun-brown outer skin crackling like scorched paper. Then she spoke quite quietly:

'You want too much,' she said.

'Who does? Who does?' He was consumed with a fresh flame of anger. 'Prove it, prove it.'

'I don't want to prove it. It don't need to be proved. You're jealous as well.'

'That's it, you see, that's it. You say things and can't prove 'em. Jealous. My God!'

'You know you want too much. Look at last night.'

'What about last night?'

'Just because you couldn't have—.'

'A trifle. That's all. A bloody trifle.'

'It hurt, any way.'

That silenced him; but he kept up the pose of arrogance, this mouth stubborn, as he peeled and sliced the onion.

'You know,' she said, 'we shall never get on. Not like that. Not if you don't give way, sometimes. We've only been married five minutes. We shall be everlasting at logger-heads.'

He kept his eyes lowered; they were beginning to smart, sharply, with the juice from the onion. And he did not speak.

'You lose your temper over nothing. Don't you? You said it yourself.'

He was still sullen and silent, and would not look up at her. And now the pain in his eyes was blinding, as though he were weeping tears of vinegar. He was too proud to wipe them, and the smarting water ran down his cheeks.

Then she saw what was the matter with him. And suddenly she laughed. She could not help it. In an instant he swung out his hand blindly, to hit her. She lurched and his hand struck her shoulder, and then he could see nothing for the pain in his eyes, the tears running down his cheeks like a child's. Then as he sat there trying to press the smartness from his eyes with his knuckled hands he became aware that she was crying. They were real tears, bitter and half-suppressed, and she let them fall into her cotton gloves. Hearing her cry, he wanted to do something, but could not. And they sat there together for five minutes, he weeping with the stinging false onion tears and she in reality, until at last he spoke:

'Shall we chuck it? Afore it's too late?'

'What? How do you mean?'

'Finish. You go and live with your mother.'

He did not mean it. He felt cold and numb. And it was a relief to speak.

'All right,' she said.

He was staggered. Did she mean it? His heart gave a great upward pound of fear.

'All right,' he said. And then he saw the fresh opportunity for bitterness. 'I thought that'd suit you. Damned if I didn't.'

'Is that what you think of me?' she said.

He was sullen and silent, not wanting to commit himself. But she insisted:

'Is it? Is it?'

'You know what I think of you,' he said.

'What do you think? What do you?' The words flowed out quickly, with her tears, and bitterly. 'Tell me what you think. Tell me.'

He sat for a moment in a state of wretched embarrassment, staring heavily, sick of himself and the argument and even the sight of the field stretcing out before him, until suddenly she was overcome by extreme tenderness for him.

'You do love me?' she said, 'don't you? don't you?'

'You know I do,' he said. 'You know that.'

He stretched out one hand and embraced her and they sat in a silence of retribution; at peace with one another, not thinking, only staring at the bright green wheat and feeling the sun tenderly warm on their hands.

Until at last he knew it must be time to start again.

'I s'll ha' to get on,' he said. 'No use.'

'All right. I'll get back.'

'You needn't. Walk round the field and seek for a primrose or two.'

'No. I'll get back.'

'Have it your own way.'

Almost, but not quite, the old antagonism broke out again. But she seemed played out, too weary to accept the challenge again, and the moment passed. He picked up his gloves and she began to pack up the basket, wrapping the half-eaten food in the napkin.

'Don't storm out without your dinner again, will you? It's a long drag up here.'

'All right.'

He drew on his gloves, and the old appearance of age and muscularity returned. He seemed much less volatile in the great scarred gloves, and more sure of himself. And she in turn seemed less troubled by him.

'It's a funny old hedge,' she said.

'Ah.'

'Looks as if it could never grow up again, the way you're laying it.'

'Ah, it'll grow up. And be as bad again as ever.'

They stood talking a little longer until, without a definite parting but only 'I'll be going I think now,' she went through the field-gate and began to walk along the grass by the roadside. At first the tall uncut hedge cut her off from him, and when she appeared at last he was watching her in a stillness of expectation.

She smiled at him. 'Don't be late,' she said.

'All right. So long.'

As she began to walk away he attacked the hedge as though it were the cause of all their differences, a tangible barrier that cut them off from one another. She walked slowly and he could see her stopping now and then, by the hedgerow, to look for a chance primrose. He paused at intervals, waiting for her to turn, but whenever he paused she was engrossed in walking or searching for the flowers, and finally he could see her no longer.

And even then he would cease his attack on the hedge and still look after her, unsure about it all, lost in a conflict of doubt and tenderness and some curious inexpressible pain.

The Case of Miss Lomas

In the dining-room of the Bellevue Boarding House Miss Lomas and Mr. Sanderson ate their fish in silence. They sat at separate tables. They were the only guests. Miss Lomas was somewhere between thirty-five and forty: a woman of medium height with pale brown hair and a reserved, almost apologetic manner, who looked as though keeping to the medium, even the unhappy medium, had been her life's most constant ambition. She had a habit, never varied, of staring out to sea as she ate. Today the rain was coming down in a thin curtain between great islands of cloud shadow and vast blue storms lying over the coast of France. It was already late October, and it looked as if the weather were breaking up at last.

Mr. Sanderson felt that he might say so. He had been at the Bellevue, now, for three days, but Miss Lomas, except to say 'Good morning,' or 'Good afternoon,' had not spoken to him. She had not even got so far as saying 'Good night.' She looked in some way pre-occupied with melancholy, with herself, with some indefinable and perhaps even unmentionable grievance or difficulty. He himself was not feeling too cheerful either; he had lost his wife, he had not been over-grand all summer. He was rather an upright, handsome man of fifty-two, though he felt, if anything, a little order. Nor was the Bellevue too cheerful. The smell of stale food was so thick and almost sickening everywhere that it was like an anaesthetic. It was perhaps hardly the place, after all, to put him on his feet again.

At last he spoke. 'Well,' he said, in a deliberate voice, 'I rather think. . .'

He got no further. The maid, at that moment, came in to clear the fish plates. He sat silent, playing with the salt. The girl took Miss Lomas's plate. She came over to take his own. It was just then that he made up his mind to say to her what he had wanted to say to Miss Lomas.

'Well,' he said, 'I rather think it looks as if the weather has broken.'

'Oh! you never know,' the girl said. 'The autumn goes on a long time here.'

She spoke in a friendly voice, and Mr. Sanderson felt cheered. She was not much more than a girl. He watched her go out of the dining-room, eyes fixed on her slim legs.

She came back with plates of boiled mutton, and then dishes of potatoes and cabbage. All the time Miss Lomas gazed out of the window. They both are in silence. Miss Lomas's mouth, while she ate, was a mouth with no expression of emotion on it at all—no hunger, no pleasure, no distaste, no annoyance, no weariness, nothing. It seemed to express a personality that was at once upright and negative. So that Mr. Sanderson could not help wondering about her. What was she, what was she doing, why was she so standoffish? She was negative almost to a point of mystery.

And then the pudding came. Before he had realized it Miss Lomas had refused it. Her only sign of refusal was to walk out. She was gone before he could make a gesture.

It began to rain before the girl brought in the coffee. The sea was turned by rain into a stormy expanse of steel, and the afternoon seemed suddenly almost dark, with rain sweeping along in dark gusts that splintered white on the deserted promenade.

'Nice how-d'ye-do,' he said.

'Were you going out?' the girl said.

'Well, I was and I wasn't. I didn't really know what to do. What can I do? You know more about this place than I do?'

'Go to the pictures. Or if it clears up you could walk over to the Flats. It's grand out there. I love it. It's always so grand and windy out there.'

Somehow that didn't seem like a waitress. She spoke nicely, easily, with some sort of refinement.

'Been in service long?' he said.

She stood and grinned at him, openly, almost pulling a face. 'Me? I'm Mrs. Harrap's daughter.'

'Well, I'm blowed.'

'I left school at August. I'm waiting to get a job.'

'Well.' He looked at her. She was pretty, with short yellow hair cut straight, and strong bare arms, and rather a fine high forehead. 'Now I've come to look at you, you're like your mother.'

She laughed; and Mr. Sanderson, less depressed, laughed too, and they were intimate.

'Like being a waitress?'

She just grinned. 'Would you?'

'Don't you get out?'

'Oh! yes. But what can you do in a place like this?'

'That's what I want to know.'

He drank his coffee. The girl watched the rain. Suddenly he thought 'Oh! damn it, why not?' and said:

'If I went to the pictures would you come with me?'

'I would. I'd love it.'

'Good.' He felt suddenly light-hearted. 'That's more than I dare have asked Miss Lomas. Even at my age.'

'She wouldn't come if you asked her.'

'Why not?'

'I don't think she believes in it. In relationships, I mean—man and woman. Even if it's platonic. I think she lives it all in books.' Then suddenly she said. 'If I'm coming with you I'd better fly. I'll meet you at the cinema, shall I? We needn't broadcast it from the house-tops that we're going together.'

'I don't know that we need,' he said.

When he went to get his mackintosh Miss Lomas was just going across the hall and into the drawing-room, with a novel in her hands. She did not speak. She carried herself with the same upright negation as ever. Looking straight before her, she seemed to be looking always towards some kind of spiritual but empty horizon. Her medium spiritless brown eyes had some sort of subdued pain in them. 'Perhaps she suffers from indigestion,' he thought.

Later he said this to the girl. When they met at the cinema the rain had ceased. It was windy, with sudden acres of blue sky and, under the shelter of the white boarding houses on the promenade, an almost hot sun. 'It seems too good to go to the pictures,' she said, and he agreed. 'Let's walk over to the Flats instead.'

'All right,' he said, and they walked eastwards out of the town, into a gusty bright afternoon. As they walked, the wind and sun cleared the sky above the sea until the air shone with a kind of lofty radiance. And then, beyond the town, the marsh-land stretched out, yellowish green, the grass still summer-dried, in places almost white with salt. Tufts of sea-pink, half seed, half flower, were still blooming in the drifts of shingle. The girl walked fast. She had no hat, and her hair blew all about her face. She talked a lot, exuberantly, girlishly. She would stop sometimes and point out headlands along the coast, or sea-birds, or churches beyond the rim of marshland. 'I adore it,' she would say. It was her favourite word. And she seemed to carry him along on a succession of flights of adoration.

And then they talked of Miss Lomas. 'She has indigestion,' he said. 'That's her trouble.'

'I don't know,' the girl said. 'She comes to us every winter. This is the fourth winter. She comes when the summer people have gone, and stops till Easter.'

'Is that all?'

'Yes. She just sits and reads, that's all. That's all I ever saw her do.'

'I still think it's indigestion,' he said.

After that, they forgot her. Mr. Sanderson walked along with a great sense of exhilaration. At home he was a draper. It was fine to feel free, to smell sun and sea instead of serge and calico. 'This walk is doing me good,' he said. And then: 'By the way, you never told me your name?'

'Freda,' she said.

'And what's Miss Lomas's name?'

'I never heard it,' she said.

In the late afternoon they rested. They sat down on the very edge of the shore, where hollows of sand were fringed with thin dune-grass and still blue sea-thistle. The girl lay down. He half sat beside her, resting on one elbow. Her hair was almost the colour of the sand. She lay with arms stretched out, her dress tight across her body, her eyes opening and shutting in what seemed to be an ecstasy of mental drowsiness. She seemed to lie there in deliberate invitation to him, so that he felt some kind of stupid eagerness, almost an ache, grow up in him. By that time the afternoon was going quickly. The tide was coming up and the sea losing its light. For two or three minutes he lay and watched the vague passage of ships. Then he turned and looked at the girl again. She looked back, straight, with a frankness of invitation that made him feel almost shocked.

'You're slow,' she said.

Rather stupidly he bent down then and she put her arm up to him. He felt in some way passive, impelled by her. In the end he kissed her, not very well and with a feeling of being out of practice, with consequent stupidity. 'Come on,' she said softly. 'Again. Better than that. A long one. A real one.' She held her lips still and slightly apart and shut her eyes.

All the way back across the marshland in the sudden twilight, he was troubled by a constant notion that he ought to be careful. 'She's only a kid,' he would think. All the way he walked with his arm round her, closely. It was she who had put it there.

And then, in the town, they separated. He felt rather old and a little tired. Walking in that strong air, with intervals of unexpected passion, had been almost too much for him. He was glad to get back to Bellevue and have a bath and a rest before dinner.

And at dinner only Miss Lomas, as usual, was there; and, as usual, she did not speak. To his disappointment also, there was no sight of Freda. Mrs. Harrap, a jolly, rather assertive woman with ear-rings, brought in the dishes herself. Even for her Miss Lomas had no conversation. And now, since she could not look out to sea, she looked at the venetian blinds, drawn down over the window. There was no difference in her manner. If the horizon itself had been shut out, the spiritual horizon remained, to be everlastingly affixed by her medium brown eyes, with their air of spiritless martyrdom.

He did not see Freda until much later. Miss Lomas had gone to bed and he was in the hall, reading the amusement guide before going himself. The girl came in as he stood there. The house was very quiet and for some moments she not speak. She stood and smiled and then opened the door of the drawing-room and they went inside. It all happened without a word. It was dark and she put her arms about him and kissed him. It was literally she who kissed him. He stood passive, holding her tightly. 'Again,' she would say. 'Tighter, hold me tighter. Please. Tighter.' And he held her and kissed with something of the old feeling of inadequacy, rather stupidly, feeling some-how that he was no match for her.

Then, as they came out of the dark drawing-room, they heard a sound on the stairs above. It was as though someone had moved suddenly away.

'What's that?' he said. 'Somebody watching?'

'It's nothing. What does it matter, anyway?'

After another moment, they said good night. The girl seemed careless, impish. And then going upstairs, he saw that the door of Miss Lomas's room was ajar.

II

It was not until two days later that Miss Lomas spoke to him. In the interval he had twice taken the girl out again, once to the cinema, in the afternoon, and once to the pier, late in the evening. Coming out of the cinema, he had been surprised to see Miss Lomas. With umbrella and mackintosh on her arm, she had been walking rapidly along the promenade, as though in a great hurry to get somewhere. He got ready to raise his hat. And then, suddenly she crossed the street and did not see them at all.

Then, the following day, she spoke to him. He was sitting in the drawing-room, after lunch, reading the paper. He was feeling better in health. He could read and lose himself in what he was reading. And it was pleasant to think of flirting with the girl after all. Suddenly, there was Miss Lomas. She was standing in front of him, ready to speak.

Then, before she spoke, he noticed an odd thing. Her hands were tightly clenched. And she seemed to be looking beyond him. She seemed extraordinarily nervous, and it made him nervous. As he got up he kicked the chair-leg and dropped his newspaper and then hurriedly took off his reading glasses.

'I would like to speak to you,' she said.

'Oh! yes, Miss Lomas,' he said. 'Oh! yes. Good. What was it?'

She was silent. He waited. And then she said, with a kind of righteous, almost comic abruptness.

'I saw you out with that girl.'

He got ready to reply. She went on at once:

'I don't think it right. Secretly. She's only a girl.' She repeated it, as though to convince him. 'I don't think it's right. Your meeting her like that, secretly. It's not right.'

'You mean you don't think it's right,' he said.

'It's the same thing. I don't think it's right.'

'What do you want me to do?' he said.

For a moment she stood still, silent. She was breathing fast, in agitation. There was some kind of explosive dignity about her.

Her eyes were no longer in any way medium. They were passionately, almost comically indignant. She was a little short-sighted and it was as though her eyes were not strong enough to sustain any such ferocity of emotion. Then suddenly she burst out. 'Do you expect me to tell you what to do?' and went out.

The whole thing made him feel perverse. He was not more than momentarily angry. That afternoon he went out with the girl again, arranging it deliberately. He told her about Miss Lomas. 'Interfering old cat,' she said, and they had a good laugh about it together.

Then, after dinner that evening, something else happened. He took the evening paper into the drawing-room, prepared and even anxious for trouble. Miss Lomas sat there with her eternal book. He had hardly sat down when she got up and did an extraordinary thing. She apologized.

'I'm sorry about this afternoon,' she said.

He could think of nothing to say. She was very earnest and it was almost comic. He simply stood still and listened while she made efforts, by repetition, as she had done earlier, to convince him.

'I shouldn't have said what I did. I'm very sorry. It was not my business.'

Then he did feel, for the first and only time, momentarily angry with her.

'If it was not your business why did you do it? There's no need to spy on people.'

She just stood silent, as though it were true and as though she accepted it. Her eyes did not change their look of medium stupidity. Except that now it was painful. He could not look at her.

After that there seemed nothing he could say and he left the room and got his mackintosh and went for a walk along the promenade. It was a squally cold evening, with a sharp wind off the sea, and when he got back to the boarding house the drawing-room was empty and he rang for some coffee. Freda brought it.

'I must tell you about Miss Lomas,' he said. 'By the way, where is she? Gone to bed?'

'She went up some time after eight.'

'I must tell you about her. She apologized tonight.'

They went on to talk about it and they had another laugh about her.

'She's not a bad sort,' he said. 'She suffers from indigestion, that's all.'

'She's all right,' the girl said. 'Why don't you ask her to the cinema—just to see what happens. Just to see how she takes it.'

'I thought you said she didn't believe in it?'

'Well, ask her. Just for fun. For a joke,' she said. 'Ask her for fun.'

He put it to Miss Lomas on the following day, casually, rather off-hand. Very much to his astonishment she accepted, and they went in the evening, after dinner. On the way he said something about life being short and there being no reason why they should not be good friends and she said yes, she agreed except that sometimes life seemed rather long. He thought it an odd remark but after that they did not speak much. She had dressed up a little for the occasion: a brown and mauve hat and, underneath her coat, a mauve silk dress. In the cinema she took off her coat and he could see her flat, unbecoming chest that had no shape about it at all. It was a cold evening, but once or twice during the performance she said how hot it was. He thought she seemed restless and afterwards at the boarding house he said so.

'Oh, I'm like that,' she said. 'It was really wonderful.'

And then, as she shook hands before going upstairs to bed, he was amazed to find out how really hot she was. Her hand was damp with sweat. It was as though it had been a kind of exquisite ordeal for her.

And when, after lunch on the following day, Freda wanted to know all about it, he said, joking: 'I think it was a bit too much for her. She got all hot and bothered.'

'She fell for you,' the girl said. 'That's all. You made a hit. She thinks you're Valentino. Very nice.'

They were in the dining-room alone. The girl took a quick look round.

'Kiss me,' she said. 'Now. Quickly.' She kissed him, rapturously, with devilry, and then said: 'And tell me something. Valentino or no Valentino, that's the last time? Or else *I* shall get jealous.'

'Don't worry,' he said. 'Once with Miss Lomas is enough for a lifetime.'

Almost before he had said it he felt curiously uneasy. He turned quickly round and looked at the doorway. Miss Lomas was standing there. Caught in the very act of listening, she did not move or speak. She made no kind of protest, and after a moment she turned and went quickly back to the drawing-room.

'That's the limit!' the girl said. 'That *is* the limit. That shows what she is.'

'Yes, that finishes it,' he said.

From that day until he left, a fortnight later, Miss Lomas did not speak to him. It was even, sometimes, as though he did not exist. She lived constantly in that medium spiritless brown world in which he had first found her, looking out to sea as she ate, reading eternal novels, gazing at her spiritual horizon beyond the drawn venetian blinds in the evenings. He saw a change only once. Looking up from his paper, unexpectedly, one evening in the drawing-room, he caught her looking at him. She was looking at him with the oddest conflict of emotions: hatred and doubt and despair and what he felt was also a kind of religious devotion. It was as though she were trying to hypnotize him. It filled her ordinarily emotionless eyes with a painful complexity of tenderness and jealousy.

Two days later he left. He said goodbye to Freda on the previous evening. She took it badly. The weather had turned warm, with real soft autumnal humidity, and they lay on the dark beach and kissed a lot until, at last, the girl cried. 'It'll be rotten when you've gone,' she said. 'What shall I do? Why don't you stay? Oh! I'll drown myself or something.'

'Look here, don't talk silly.'

'I will. It'll be so rotten. Why do you have to go?'

'I work for my living. I've got a business. I'll come back. I'll see you again.'

'You won't. You'll forget me.'

'I won't. I'll come. Now be a good girl and kiss me and promise you won't do anything silly.'

There was passion in her kisses, but no promise. All the way home in the train he was worried by stupid fears. She was a dynamic girl and he felt as though he had left her in suspense. Over-charged with passion, she might very well go off into some tragic explosion. Girls did silly things and even, sometimes, killed themselves. He felt, all along, that he had been something of a fool.

A week later he got a letter. It was from the girl herself. It was a long letter, and she enclosed a cutting from a newspaper.

It was Miss Lomas, not she, who had killed herself. It was an awful thing, the girl said, and she did not understand it.

Nor did he understand it himself.

Something Short and Sweet

The car was stationary, by the wood-side, under snow-wet beeches. The man and the young woman sat in the front seats. They were also quite still. Outside nothing moved except the snow, which fell wetly, a slither of watery whiteness on the wind-screen, a wet frosting on grass and branches. The car hood was ripped and some snow had feathered in on the piles of books on the back seat. They were all red books, all the same book. The man had one of them, open, in one hand, with the other hand palm downwards on the flattened page, so that momentarily he looked like a man expounding a sermon.

'What is it you don't understand?' he said.

The girl looked anaemically at the snow, without speaking. She was about twenty. Her face reflected the dull whiteness of the snow, making her eyes snow-glassy.

'Is it anything in the book?' the man said. 'In here? If it is I can explain it. Don't be afraid. Tell me. Is it the book?'

'Partly.'

'Which chapter?' He waited for her to speak. She said nothing. In the intervals of speech he twitched his weak eyes, as though his spectacles were troubling him. He was about forty, with very dark hair that was greasy, and his coat collar shone at the edges with a sort of lead-coloured wax, the result of years of rubbing. He had many raw pimples on his face. 'Tell me which part, which chapter?' he said. His hat sat low on his ears, giving him an almost fanatical look of correctness. 'The Displacement of Self by God?' he said. 'Is that it? Is it that which is troubling you? I admit it's difficult to understand. Is it that?'

'I don't know what it is,' she said.

She sat huddled up, cold to the bone, simply looking at the snow.

'You're not losing faith?' he said.

She shook her head. Waiting for her to speak, he twitched his weak eyes rapidly.

'You need vision,' he said earnestly.

'I know, I know,' she said. 'But people are so rude!' she burst out. 'They're so rude. They treat you like dirt.'

'They don't know,' he said blandly. 'They don't understand. Vision hasn't been granted to them as it has been to us. Vision isn't granted to everybody. It's just what happened to Christ. When you've been in the mission as long as I have you'll understand. You're new to it. We must bear the burden. It's our task. It's our mission. Don't you believe it?'

'I believe it when you say it,' she said. 'But I'm not so sure when I say it myself.'

He wetted his thumb and began turning over the leaves of the book. Looking at him, she saw suddenly that he had a button off his overcoat.

'You've lost a button,' she said. 'I'll sew it on. Where did you lose that, I wonder?'

'Where? What button?' he said. 'Don't worry. Here, this is it. Here—'

But she was out of the car. Merely to get out was a blessed, almost hysterical relief to her. She went round to the back of the car quickly. It was snowing fat wet blots. She undid the suit case strapped to the luggage-grid and foraged in it and found a needle and cotton. Above the grid, on the back of the car, was chalked 'Galilee Gospel. Prepare to Meet Thy God.' The snow was beginning to wash the words out a little.

Back in the car she tried to thread the needle, but her hands were numb. She tried and tried again, until she outdid the man in extreme earnestness of expression. And all the time, as she vainly wetted and screwed and pointed the thread, he was expounding from the book on his knees.

'So long as the self dominates there can be no God,' he read out. 'And until there is God we shall know no fulfilment of true happiness. The worship of self means the rejection of Our Lord. Vice versa the acceptance of our Lord means the burying of the graven image of self. God is with us for ever, but the self is not and must perish.'

He left off reading and blinked. 'Surely that's clear?' he said.

His voice startled her. By a great effort she had almost threaded the needle. When he spoke her fingers trembled and she felt suddenly upset. She looked for a second as if she would cry out. But she just did nothing. The man also did nothing, taking no notice of her. In a moment she took up the thread again and he went on expounding and saying: 'That's clear, isn't it? You understand, don't you? You must see. It's vision you need. That's all.'

As he was speaking she felt painfully hungry. It was long after midday. That morning they had come about thirty miles out of Oxford, from headquarters. In other districts other workers for Galilee would have covered the same distance, for the same purpose. It was part of the spring campaign. Clear of the town, the man would stop the car every mile or so and the girl would get out and with a large piece of chalk would print the symbols of the creed on field-gates and telegraph poles, while the man kept a look out and waited. 'In the Midst of Life we are in Death,' she chalked, or 'The Kingdom of Heaven is at Hand.' At the top of hills she chalked, 'Prepare to Meet Thy God,' in the biggest letters of all. It had been savagely cold from the very beginning. Then the snow came on, her hands got frozen, and she made the journeys in absolute misery, in slush up to her ankles. Once he had a brainwave. 'The Canker of Self is Eating your Soul,' he said. 'Put that.' She had to chalk the words on two gate bars. The snow blinded her. She felt the snow go right through her heart. Then whenever they came to houses or a village he stopped the car again and she took a bundle of books and went the round of doors and chanted what was really, for her, a meaningless rigmarole:

'I speak for the Galilee Mission. In this great book you will find the solution to the problem of our existence here on earth. God is at hand. At any moment he may strike you down. Have no fear. Find God in this book. We are offering it at our special price of half a crown. Normally it is ten shillings. You will never see such a chance again. Make your peace with God before it is too late.'

Sometimes, often, she never got as far as that. She stood on the doorstep and, after a moment found herself speaking to space. It was that which crushed not only her but the meaning of it all too. Malfry was always telling her to emulate him, to have vision, to be inspired. But what was the use of being inspired if nobody listened?

'Shall we have something to eat?' she said.

'Do you feel clear about it?' he said. 'Until you believe it yourself how can others believe it?'

His voice was impersonal, hare as bone. She stuck the unthreaded needle absently into the dashboard and looked all the time at the snow. The she got out some food from among the books on the back seat: four beef sandwiches and an apple. She ate ravenously. The man ate without pleasure, ascetically. Afterwards there was a little tea, in a thermos flask. All the time, as they drank, the girl kept looking at the man, expectantly, waiting for some kind of softening and change in him. Nothing happened. He kept turning over the pages of the book, reading odd paragraphs, making pencil notes, his earnest eyes blinking.

Then, when the food was finished, she was still cold. The wind came through the slit canvas hood and made a continuous mournful draught. The snow slithered everlastingly down the windows and the girl shivered.

'I think I'll put another jumper on,' she said. 'Do you mind?'

'No, I don't mind.' He did not look up.

She got out of the car again and fetched in the suit-case. The snow was almost yellow on the road, the tyre-tracks a dirty orange. In the car, kneeling on the seat, she opened the suit-case and found a dark green jumper. Then she put the suit-case back among the books and took off her coat. Underneath it she had on a brown jumper.

Suddenly she gave one look at the man and took it off. Her heart was thumping. Her small breasts were just visible above the skirt top.

'Mr. Malfry, shall I look best in the green one or the brown one?' she said.

'Eh?' He looked up, blinking, with open mouth. 'Oh! which you like.'

She waited for him to do something. She turned the green jumper right side out and sat there almost stupidly expectant, her heart pounding.

'I never showed you my birth mark, did I,' she said. 'Look here at it, on my shoulder. It's like a walnut.'

She let down her right shoulder strap. The man just looked at the birth mark, blinking his eyes, as though he could not see it properly.

'Isn't it funny?' she said. 'I've always had it. It's just the shape of a walnut.'

'So it is.' He laid his hand on the book. 'I've marked all the passages in the Displacement of Self by God which I think are obscure. You can have a look at them tonight. It's only vision you need. It's only faith.'

She sat forward, so that the whole of her skirt fell loose, the shoulder strap down, her small apple breasts as nearly visible as she dare let them be.

'We'd better get on,' the man said.

'Yes. Don't you think it funny about my birth mark?' she said.

Hè did not speak. He started the car. Very slowly she pulled on first the green jumper and then the brown and then, just before the car started, her coat. Putting on her coat she half stood up and when she sat down again her skirt was pulled up over her knees and she did not put it back again.

In a minute the car moved off into the snow. She sat quiet, her anaemic face intent.

'Don't worry if people are rude,' he said. 'You've got to suffer that. That's our mission. You've got to suffer many things before people see as you do.'

Ten minutes later he pulled up. The gate was black. Far off a cyclist was coming, a dark spot in the snow.

'Quick,' he said. 'Something short. God is love. Something short and sweet.'

She got out of the car and staggered through the snow to the gate. Slowly, with bitterly cold hands, she chalked the words on it, though by that time she could hardly see.

Château Bougainvillaea

The headland was like a dry purple island scorched by the flat heat of afternoon, cut off from the mainland by a sand-coloured tributary of road which went down past the estaminet and then, half a mile beyond, to the one-line, one-eyed railway station. Down below, on a small plateau between upper headland and sea, peasants were mowing white rectangles of corn. The tide was fully out, leaving many bare black rocks and then a great sun-phosphorescent pavement of sand, with the white teeth of small breakers slowly nibbling in. Far out, the Atlantic was waveless, a shade darker than the sky, which was the fierce blue seen on unbelievable posters. Farther out still, making a faint mist, sun and sea had completely washed out the line of sky.

From time to time a puff of white steam, followed by a peeped whistle, struck comically at the dead silence inland. It was the small one-line train, half-tram, making one way or the other its hourly journey between town-terminus and coast. By means of it the engaged couple measured out the afternoon.

'There goes the little train,' he would say.

'Yes,' she would say, 'there goes the little train.'

Each time she resolved not to say this stupid thing and then, dulled with sleepiness and the heat of earth and sky and the heather in which they lay, she forgot herself and said it, automatically. Her faint annoyance with herself at these times had gradually begun to make itself felt, as the expression of some much deeper discontent.

'Je parle Français un tout petit peu, m'sieu.' In a voice which seemed somehow like velvet rubbed the wrong way, the man was talking. 'I was all right as far as that. Then I said, "Mais, dites-moi, m'sieu, pourquoi are all the knives put left-handed dans ce restaurant?" By God it must have been awfully funny. And then he said—'

'He said because, m'sieu, the people who use them are all left-handed.'

'And that's really what he said? It wasn't a mistake? All the people in that place were left-handed?'

'Apparently,' she said, 'they were all left-handed.'

'It's the funniest thing I ever heard,' he said. 'I can't believe it.'

Yes, she thought, perhaps it was a funny thing. Many left-handed people staying at one restaurant. A family, perhaps. But then there were many left-handed people in the world, and perhaps, for all you knew, their left was really right, and it was we, the right, who were wrong.

She took her mind back to the restaurant down in the town. There was another restaurant there, set in a sort of alley-way under two fig-trees, where artisans filled most of the tables between noon and two o'clock, and where a fat white-smocked woman served all the dishes and still found time to try her three words of English on the engaged couple. From here they could see the lace-crowned Breton women clacking in the shade of the street trees and the small one-eyed train starting or ending its journey between the sea and the terminus that was simply the middle of the street. They liked this restaurant, but that day, wanting a change, they had climbed the steps into the upper town, to the level of the viaduct, and had found this small family restaurant where, at one table, all the knives were laid left-handed. For some reason she now sought to define, this left-handedness did not seem funny to her. Arthur had also eaten too many olives, picking them up with his fingers and gnawing them as she herself, as a child, would have gnawed an uncooked prune, and this did not seem very funny either. Somewhere between olives and left-handedness lay the source of her curious discontent. Perhaps she was left-handed herself? Left-handed people were, she had read somewhere, light-brained. Perhaps Arthur was left-handed?

She turned over in the heather, small brown-eyed face to the sun. 'Don't you do anything left-handed?'

'Good gracious, no.' He turned over too and lay face upwards, dark with sun, his mouth small-lipped under the stiff moustache she had not wanted him to grow. 'You don't either?'

For the first time in her life she considered it. How many people, she thought, ever considered it? Thinking, she seemed to roll down a great slope, semi-swooning in the heat, before coming up again. Surprisingly, she had thought of several things.

'Now I come to think of it, I comb my hair left-handed. I always pick flowers left-handed. And I wear my watch on my left wrist.'

He lifted steady, mocking eyes. 'You sure you don't kiss left-handed?'

'That's not very funny!' she flashed.

It seemed to her that the moment of temper flashed up sky high, like a rocket, and fell far out to sea, soundless, dead by then, in the heat of the unruffled afternoon. She at once regretted it. For five days now they had lived on the Breton coast, and they now had five days more. Every morning, for five days, he had questioned her: 'All right? Happy?' and every morning she had responded with automatic affirmations, believing it at first, then aware of doubt, then bewildered.

Happiness, she wanted to say, was not something you could fetch out every morning after breakfast, like a clean handkerchief, or more still like a rabbit conjured out of the hat of everyday circumstances.

The hot, crushed-down sense of security she had felt all afternoon began suddenly to evaporate, burnt away from her by the first explosion of discontent and then by small restless flames of inward anger. She felt the growing sense of insecurity physically, feeling that at any moment she might slip off the solid headland into the sea. She suddenly felt a tremendous urge, impelled for some reason by fear, to walk as far back inland as she could go. The thought of the Atlantic far below, passive and yet magnetic, filled her with a sudden cold breath of vertigo.

'Let's walk,' she said.

'Oh! no, it's too hot.'

She turned her face into the dark sun-brittled heather. She caught the ticking of small insects, like infinitesimal watches. Far off, inland, the little train cut off, with its comic shriek, another section of afternoon.

In England he was a draper's assistant: chief assistant, sure to become manager. In imagination she saw the shop, sun-blinds down, August remnant sale now on, the dead little town now so foreign and far off and yet so intensely real to her, shown up by the disenchantment of distance. They had been engaged six months. She had been very thrilled about it at first, showing the ring all round, standing on a small pinnacle of joy, ready to leap into the tremendous spaces of marriage. Now she had suddenly the feeling that she was about to be sewn up in a blanket.

'Isn't there a castle,' she said, 'somewhere up the road past the estaminet?'

'Big house. Not castle.'

'I thought I saw a notice,' she said, 'to the château.'

'Big house,' he said. 'Did you see that film, "The Big House"? All about men in prison.'

What about women in prison? she wanted to say. In England she was a school-teacher, and there had been times when she felt that the pale green walls of the class-room had imprisoned her and that marriage, as it always did, would mean escape. Now left-handedness and olives and blankets and the stabbing heat of the Atlantic afternoon had succeeded, together, in inducing some queer stupor of semi-crazy melancholy that was far worse than this. Perhaps it was the wine, the sour red stuff of the *vin compris* notice down at the left-handed café? Perhaps, after all, it was only some large dose of self-pity induced by sun and the emptiness of the day?

She got to her feet. 'Come on, m'sieu. We're going to the castle.' She made a great effort to wrench herself up to the normal plane. 'Castle, my beautiful. Two francs. All the way up to the castle, two francs.' She held out her hand to pull him to his feet.

'I'll come,' he said, 'if we can stop at the estaminet and have a drink.'

'We'll stop when we come down,' she said.

'Now.'

'When we come down.'

'Now. I'm so thirsty. It was the olives.'

Not speaking, she held out her hand. Instinctively, he put out his left.

'You see,' she said, 'you don't know what's what or which's which or anything. You don't know when you're left-handed or right.'

He laughed. She felt suddenly like laughing too, and they began to walk down the hill. The fierce heat seemed itself to force them down the slope, and she felt driven by it past the blistered white tables of the estaminet with the fowls asleep underneath them, and then up the hill on the far side, into the sparse shade of small wind-levelled oaks and, at one place, a group of fruitless fig trees. It was some place like this, she thought, just about as hot and arid, where the Gadarene swine had stampeded down. What made her think of that? Her mind had some urge towards inconsequence, some inexplicable desire towards irresponsibility that she could not restrain or control, and she was glad to see the château at last, shining with sea-blue jalousies through a break in the mass of metallic summer-hard leaves of acacia and bay that surrounded it. She felt it to be something concrete, a barrier against which all the crazy irresponsibilities of the mind could hurl themselves and split.

At the corner, a hundred yards before the entrance gates, a notice, of which one end had been cracked off by a passing lorry, pointed upwards like a tilted telescope. They read the word 'château,' the rest of the name gone.

'You see,' she said, 'château.'

'What château?'

'Just château.'

'You think we'll have to pay to go in?'

'I'll pay,' she said.

She walked on in silence, far away from him. The little insistences on money had become, in five days, like the action of many iron files on the soft tissues of her mind: first small and fine, then larger, then still larger, now large and coarse, brutal as stone. He kept a small note-book and in it, with painful system, entered up the expenditure of every centime.

At the entrance gates stood a lodge, very much dilapidated, the paintwork of the walls grey and sea-eroded like the sides of a derelict battleship. A small notice was nailed to the fence by the gate, and the girl stopped to read it.

'What does it say?' he said. 'Do we pay to go in?'

'Just says it's an eighteenth-century château,' she said. 'Admission a franc. Shall we go in?'

'A franc?'

'One franc,' she said. 'Each.'

'You go,' he said. 'I don't know that I'm keen. I'll stop outside.'

She did not answer, but went to the gate and pulled the porter's bell. From the lodge door a woman without a blouse on put her head out, there was a smell of onions, and the woman turned on the machine of her French like a high pressure steam-pipe, scrawny neck dilating.

The girl pushed open the gate and paid the woman the two francs admission fee, holding a brief conversation with her. The high pressure pipe finally cut itself off and withdrew, and the girl came back to the gates and said: 'She's supposed to show us round but she's just washing. She says nobody else ever comes up at this hour of the afternoon, and we must show ourselves round.'

They walked up the gravel road between sea-stunted trees towards the château. In the sun, against the blue sky above the Atlantic, the stone and slate of it was burning.

'Well,' she said, 'what do you think of it?'

'Looks a bit like the bank at home,' he said. 'The one opposite our shop.'

Château and sky and trees spun in the sunlight, whirling down to a momentary black vortex in which the girl found herself powerless to utter a word. She walked blindly on in silence. It was not until they stood under the château walls, and she looked up to see a great grape vine mapped out all across the south side, that she recovered herself and could speak.

'It's just like the châteaux you see on wine-bottles,' she said. 'I like it.'

'It doesn't look much to me,' he said. 'Where do we get in?'

'Let's look round the outside first.'

As they walked round the walls on the sun-bleached grass she could not speak or gather her impressions, but was struck only by the barren solitude of it all, the arid, typically French surroundings, with an air of fly-blowness and sun-weariness. To her amazement the place had no grandeur, and there were no flowers.

'There ought to be at least a bougainvillaea,' she said.

'What's a bougainvillaea?'

Questioned, she found she did not know. She felt only that there ought to be a bougainvillaea. The word stood in her mind for the exotic, the south, white afternoons, the sea as seen from the top of just such châteaux as this. How this came to be she could not explain. The conscious part of herself stretched out arms and reached back, into time, and linked itself with some former incarnation of her present self, Louise Bowen, school-teacher, certificated, Standard V girls, engaged to Arthur Keller, chief assistant Moore's Drapery, sure to become manager, pin-stripe trousers, remnants madam, the voice like ruffled velvet, seventy-three pounds fifteen standing to credit at the post office, and in reaching back so far she felt suddenly that she could cry for the lost self, for the enviable incarnation so extraordinarily real and yet impossible, and for the yet not impossible existence, far back, in eternal bougainvillaea afternoons.

'Let's go inside,' she said.

'How they make it pay,' he said, 'God only knows.'

'It has long since,' she said mysteriously, 'paid for itself.'

They found the main door and went in, stepping into the under-sea coldness of a large entrance hall. Now think that out, now think that out, now think that out. Her mind bubbling with bitterness, she looked up the great staircase, and all of a sudden the foreignness of her conscious self as against the familiarity of the self that had been was asserted again, but now with the sharp contrast of shadow and light. She put her hand on the staircase, the iron cool and familiar, and then began to walk up it, slowly but lightly, her hand drawn up easily, as though from some invisible iron pulley, far above her. She kept her eyes on the ceiling, feeling, without effort of thought, that she did not like and never had liked its mournful collection of cherubim painted in the gold wheel about the chandelier. For the first time that day, as she mounted the staircase and then went on beyond into the upstairs corridor, and into the panelled music-room with its air of having been imported as a complete back-cloth from some pink-and-gold theatre of the 'seventies, her body moved with its natural quietness, accustomed, infinitely light, and with a sense of the purest happiness. All this she could not explain and, as they went from music-room to other rooms, ceased to attempt to explain. Her bitterness evaporated in the confined coolness just as her security, outside on the hot headland, had evaporated in the blaze of afternoon. Now she seemed incontestably sure of herself, content in what she knew, without fuss, was an unrepeatable moment of time.

She did not like the music-room but, as she expected, Arthur did. This pre-awareness of hers saved her from fresh bitterness. As part of her contentment, making it complete, she thought of him with momentary tenderness, quietly regretting what she had said and done, ready now to make up for it.

'Shall we go up higher,' she said, 'or down to the ground-floor again?'

'Let's do the climb first,' he said.

To her, it did not matter, and climbing a second staircase they came, eventually, to a small turret room, unfurnished, with two jalousied windows looking across to the two worlds of France and the Atlantic.

She stood at the window overlooking the sea and looked out, as from a lighthouse, down on to the intense expanse of sea-light. Her mind had the profound placidity of the sea itself, a beautiful vacancy, milkily restful.

'Funny,' Arthur said. 'No ships. The Atlantic, and not a ship in sight.'

'You wouldn't expect to see ships,' she said, and knew that she was right.

Looking down from the other window they saw the headland, the brown-lilac expanse of heather, the minute peasants scribbled on the yellow rectangle of corn, the estaminet, the one-eyed station. And suddenly also, there was the white pop of steam inland, and the small comic shriek, now more than ever toy-like, pricking the dead silence of afternoon.

'Look,' he said, 'there's the little train.'

'Yes,' she said, 'there's the little train.'

Her mind had the pure loftiness of the tower itself, above all irritation. She felt, as not before in her life, that she was herself. The knowledge of this re-incarnation was something she could not communicate, and half afraid that time or a word would break it up, she suggested suddenly that they should go down.

Arthur remained at the window a moment longer, admiring points of distance. 'You'd never think,' he said, 'you could see so far.'

'Yes you would,' she called back.

Now think that out, now think that out, now think that out. Her mind, as she went downstairs, sprang contrarily upwards, on a scale of otherwise inexpressible delight. Arthur engaged her in conversation as they went downstairs, she on one flight, he on one above, calling down: 'It may be all right, but the rates must be colossal. Besides, you'd burn a ton of coal a day in winter, trying to keep warm. A six-roomed house is bad enough, but think of this,' but nothing could break, suppress or even touch her mood.

Downstairs she went straight into the great reception hall, and stood dumb. At that moment she suddenly felt that she had come as far as she must. Time had brought her to this split second of itself simply in order to pin her down. She stood like an insect transfixed.

Arthur came in: 'What are you looking at?'

'The yellow cloth. Don't do anything. Just look at it. It's wonderful.'

'I don't see anything very wonderful,' he said.

At the end of the room, thrown over a chair, a large length of brocade, the colour of a half-ripe lemon, was like spilled honey against the grey French-coldness of walls and furniture. Instantaneously the girl saw it with eyes of familiarity, feeling it somehow to be the expression of herself, mood, past and future. She stood occupied with the entrancement of the moment, her eyes excluding the room, the day, Arthur and everything, her self drowned out of existence by the pure wash of watered fabric.

Suddenly Arthur moved into the room, and ten seconds later had the brocade in his hands. She saw him hold it up, measure it without knowing he measured it, feel its weight, thickness, value. She saw him suddenly as the eternal shopkeeper measuring out the eternal remnants of time: the small tape-measure of his mind like a white worm in the precious expanse of her own existence.

'If you bought it today,' Arthur called, 'it would cost you every penny of thirty-five bob a yard.'

'Let's go,' she said.

Half a minute later she turned and walked out of the door, Arthur following, and then past the wind-stunted trees and on down the road, past the estaminet. It was now herself who walked, Louise Bowen, Standard V girls, certificated, deduct so much for super-annuation scheme, tired as after a long day in the crowded chalk-smelling classroom. As they passed the estaminet, the place looked more fly-blown and deserted than ever, and they decided to go on to the station, and get a drink there while waiting for the train. As they passed the fig trees her mind tried to grasp again at the thought of the Gadarene swine, her mood blasted into the same barrenness as the tree in the parable.

'Well, you can have your château,' Arthur said. 'But I've got my mind on one of those houses Sparkes is putting up on Park Avenue. Sixteen and fourpence a week, no deposit, over twenty years. That's in front of any château.'

She saw the houses as he spoke, red and white, white and red, millions of them, one like another, sixteen and fourpence a week, no deposit, stretching out to the ends of the earth. She saw herself in them, the constant and never-changing material of her life cut up by a pair of draper's scissors, the days ticketed, the years fretted by the counting up of farthings and all the endlessly incalculable moods of boredom.

'Two coffees please.'

At the little station café they sat at one of the outside tables and waited for the train.

'Well, we've been to the château and never found out its name,' he said.

'It ought to be Château Bougainvillaea.'

'That's silly,' he said. 'You don't even know what a bougainvillaea is.'

She sat stirring the grey coffee. She could feel the sun burning the white iron table and her hands. She looked up at the château, seeing the windows of the turret above the trees.

'Now we can see the château,' she said, 'as we should have seen ourselves if we'd been sitting down here when—'

It was beyond her, and she broke off.

'What?' he said.

'I didn't mean that,' she said.

'What did you mean?'

'I don't know.'

'Well, in future,' he said, 'mind you say what you mean.'

The future? She sat silent. Inland the approaching train made its comic little whistle, cutting off another section of the afternoon.

And hearing it, she knew suddenly that the future was already a thing of the past.

I Am Not Myself

I

It was summer when the Arnoldsons first asked me to go and stay with them. I could not go. I did not go until the following winter, on January 5th. It was bitterly cold that day, with thin drifts of snow whipped up from the ground like fierce white sandstorms, and there was snow on the ground almost every day until I left, four days later.

The Arnoldsons lived about seven miles from the nearest town. The house is quite ordinary: plain red brick, double-fronted, with large bay-windows and a large brass-knockered front door and a spotless white doorstep. It is the colour of a new flower-pot and at the back in the garden there is a long pergola of bay-trees which is like a tunnel leading to nowhere.

Before that day in January I did not know any of the Arnoldsons except Laurence. We were at school together but we had not seen each other for fifteen years. He was an architect and I had written a letter to a paper about country architecture and he had seen it and that was how the invitation to stay with them had come about. Laurence Arnoldson is a man of medium height, with straight dark hair brushed back. He wears plain ascetic-looking gold spectacles and is a man of meticulous habits; always paring his finger-nails, polishing his glasses, splitting life into millimetres. His craze for exactitude and his contempt for people who have no time for it have made him a prig. He holds his head very high and you can see him looking down his nose at the world. The best thing about him are his eyes: they are weak but they are a deep, rather strange shade of brown. There is something remote about them.

Laurence met me at the station that day in a fairly old but carefully kept Morris-Oxford, a four-seater. His father was with him. He sat in the front seat, huddled in a black rug, with a large shaggy grey scarf muffled round his head. The scarf covered almost all of his face except his eyes. As Laurence introduced me I saw that his father's eyes had exactly the same deep remote brownness as the son's. It was snowing a little at the time and Laurence had left the windscreen wiper working and I could see the man's eyes mechanically following its pendulum motions. They slid to and fro like two brown ball-bearings moving in grey oil, fascinated by the clear glass arc made by the wiper in the furred snow.

Laurence's father did not speak to me and neither he nor Laurence exchanged a word as we drove slowly out into the frozen country. Their silence depressed me. I felt it had something to do with myself. Now and then I made a remark and once, about half a mile from the house, we passed a pond frozen over and I said something about skating, and Laurence said:

'Oh! Yes. That's the pond where my sister saw a fox walk across the ice yesterday.'

The Arnoldsons' house stands on what was formerly a private estate and there is a private gravel road half a mile long leading up to it through fenceless fields that are planted with groups of elm and lime.

There is no Mrs. Arnoldson. She has been dead for thirteen years, and the house has been run for all that time by her sister, aunt Wilcox. It was aunt Wilcox who met us at the front door that afternoon, a dumpy woman with white hair scraped back sharply from her soap-polished face. She came out of the house briskly, shook hands with me without waiting to be introduced and then helped Mr. Arnoldson out of the car. I thought at first he had been ill, but then as he stood upright I could see that there was nothing wrong with him and that he was really a big and rather powerful man. His hands were very large-boned and his head, hugely swathed in the great scarf, had a kind of ill-balanced power about it. It swayed slightly to and fro as he walked, as though it were loose on the spine. He did not speak to me.

Aunt Wilcox spoke with a strong Yorkshire accent. The Arnoldsons themselves are Yorkshire people and the house is furnished in Yorkshire fashion: a rocking-chair in every room, big dressers, patchwork cushions, heavy pink-and-gold tea services. In the large drawing-room the curtains are of some claret-coloured woollen material, with plush bobbles, and they hang from great mahogany rods by mahogany rings that are like the rings on a hoop-la. On the mantelpiece stand two large china dogs, spaniels, black and white. They face each other and they appear to be looking at the same thing. They are extraordinarily lifelike.

I had been upstairs to unpack my things and had come down again and was looking at these dogs when Laurence came in to say that tea was ready. We went across the hall into the opposite room. It was about four o'clock and the white reflected light of the fallen snow was prolonging by a few minutes the fall of darkness. We sat down to tea in this strange snow-twilight, aunt Wilcox and Mr. Arnoldson opposite each other at the ends of the table, Laurence and I opposite, I myself opposite the window. The room was the exact reflection of the other. At the windows were the same sort of heavy woollen-bobbled curtains and on the mantelpiece stood what might have been the same pair of china spaniels watching with extraordinary lifelike fixedness some invisible object between them.

We sat there eating and drinking, without saying much. Aunt Wilcox poured tea from a huge electroplated pot that might have held a gallon. The cups were like pink and gold basins.

I drink my tea very hot, and suddenly, as aunt Wilcox was taking my empty cup, I saw someone coming up the road towards the house. I knew at once, somehow, that it was Laurence's sister.

She was wearing a big brown coat, but no hat. Every now and then she stepped off the road on to the grass and wandered off, as though looking for something. She was like someone playing follow-my-leader with herself. Once she wandered farther off than usual and in the half-darkness I lost her for a moment. Then I saw her again. She was running. She was running quite fast and all at once she fell down on her knees in the snow and then ran on again. She was still running when she came to the house.

Two minutes later she came in. Her knees and the fringe of her coat were covered with snow where she had fallen down and there was a small salt-sprinkling of snow on her hair. She was about twenty-three, but she looked much younger, and I shall never forget how she came in, out of breath, to look at us with the same remote brown eyes as Laurence's, intensely excited, with a stare that had nothing to do with earth at all.

'I saw him again,' she said.

For a moment no one spoke. Then Laurence said:

'Who? The fox?'

'Yes. I saw him run over the pond again and then I chased him up through the park and then just as I got near the house I lost him.'

No one spoke a word.

II

That evening, after supper, she told me more about the fox. She described him: how bright he was and how good-coloured and how it was only in snowy or frosty weather that she saw him, and as she described him I saw him, bright, quiet, his back feet slipping from under him a little as he sloped across the ice on the small pond. I saw him as she saw him, as she wanted me to see him.

She told me about the fox in two or three minutes. She talked rather quickly, but all her impressions were in reality created with her eyes; the images of fox and snow and frozen pond were thrown up in them with untarnishable clarity. Unlike a great many people she looked straight at me while talking. Her eyes were full of great candour. They looked straight forward, with natural ardour. You felt that they could never look sideways. They had in them an unblemished honesty that was very beautiful and also very convincing, but also, in some way, empty.

For those two or three minutes we were alone. We had all had supper and we were going to play cribbage. Laurence had gone into his room to finish a letter and aunt Wilcox was in the kitchen. Mr. Arnoldson had gone upstairs to find a new pack of cards.

'I'd like to come out in the morning,' I said, 'and see this fox.'

She did not say anything.

In a little while first Laurence, and then Mr. Arnoldson and then aunt Wilcox came back, and we made arrangements to play. Cribbage was the only card game all of us knew and we decided to play in two pairs, for a shilling a horse, man out scoring. We cut the cards, ace high, lowest out, and aunt Wilcox said:

'It's you, Christiana. Mind now, no edging.'

The girl had cut a two of hearts, and I realized suddenly that it was the first time I had heard her name.

Aunt Wilcox and I played together. We were both rather quick, downright players, quick to sense a hand. We always had the pips counted before we put them on the table. This was not the Arnoldson way. Deliberation, to me an increasingly irritating deliberation, marked everything Laurence and his father did. They weighed up their hands guardedly and put on poker expressions, giving nothing away. Just as the girl spoke with her eyes, they played with their eyes. Between the counting of the hands they did not speak a word.

The game was a near thing and it looked, for a moment, as if aunt Wilcox and I might die in the hole, but we got home and I noticed aunt Wilcox pocketing the shilling. The Arnoldsons were not at all satisfied, and Laurence went over the last hand again, architect fashion, checking up, before giving in.

Mr. Arnoldson looked at Christiana. I forgot to say that he had a large grey sheep-dog moustache. The expression of his mouth was thus hidden. The whole expression of his face was compressed into his eyes. They shone very brightly, with a rather queer glassy look of excitement.

For the second game aunt Wilcox dropped out and Christiana took her place, playing with me. She was the quickest player I had ever seen. Every player gets now and then a hand he cannot make up his mind about, but that never happened to her. She played by instinct, second sight. She hardly looked at the cards. She kept her eyes on me. Yet she made up her mind before we began. I felt that, in some miraculous way, she could see through the cards.

All through the game she sat with her eyes on me. This constant but completely passionless stare had me beaten. It was hypnotic, so that whenever I looked away from her I was conscious of being drawn back. At first I thought it was deliberate, that she was simply trying hard to attract me. Then I got into the way of accepting her stare, of returning it. But where there should have been some response, there was only an unchanged anonymity, a beautiful brown wateriness filled with a remote, quietly hypnotic strength. I saw her as one of those composite pictures of two people. Two personalities are fused and there remains no personality, only some discomforting anonymity that fascinates.

During the game the tension between Christiana and her father increased. She was constantly one leap ahead of us all. She knew; we guessed. She had good cards, twice a hand of twenty-four. All the time I could see Mr. Arnoldson fidgeting, his eyes generating new phases of resentment.

Aunt Wilcox seemed to understand this. The Christmas decorations were still hanging up in the house, sprays of holly, withering now, stuck up behind the pictures, and a wand or two of box and fir. Suddenly aunt Wilcox said:

'Twelfth day tomorrow. We mustn't forget the decorations.'

'Pancakes,' Christiana said.

'Fifteen two and a pair's four and three's seven,' I said. 'Pancakes?'

'A north-country custom,' aunt Wilcox said. 'You fry the pancakes with a fire of the evergreens.'

'I think,' Laurence said, 'I have a pair.' He slowly laid out his cards. 'Mind you don't set the chimney on fire.'

Suddenly Christiana's hand was on the table. She counted it like a parrot saying something by heart. She had three sixes and a nine and a three was up and she rattled it off, running the words together, making eighteen. Eighteen was quite right, but Mr. Arnoldson sprang to his feet, as though he had not heard it.

'Nineteen, nineteen, you can't score nineteen!' he shouted. 'It's not possible in crib!'

'I said eighteen!'

'Eighteen is right,' I began.

'She said nineteen. I heard her. I distinctly heard her. You think I don't know her voice?'

'Eighteen!' she said.

'You said nineteen and now you're lying on top of it!'

He was on his feet, shouting at her, grey with anger. Suddenly he began to shake violently and I knew he had lost control. He turned round and picked up the heavy mahogany Yorkshire chair he had been sitting in and swung it about, over his head. Aunt Wilcox got hold of Christiana and half pushed, half dragged her out of the room, and I automatically went after her, shouting after her as she ran upstairs in the darkness.

When I went back into the room, a moment later, Mr. Arnoldson was lying on the hearth-rug, on his back, in a fit. The chair was lying smashed on the table where he had brought it down. He was clenching in his hands some bits of withered holly he had torn down from one of the pictures. His hands were bleeding and it was a long time before we could get them open again.

III

The next morning Laurence, aunt Wilcox, Christiana and I sat down to a large and healthy breakfast, plates of porridge, lumps of rather fat beefsteak with fried mashed potatoes and eggs, thick toast and very strong marmalade, with the usual basins of tea. It was all very solid, very real. Unlike the behaviour of Mr. Arnoldson on the previous night it was something you could get your hands on and understand. Mr. Arnoldson did not appear at breakfast and no one said anything about him.

During breakfast Laurence read his letters and said he had a couple of hours' work to do and would I mind amusing myself? In the afternoon we could go and look at some houses; there were one or two good stone mansions in the neighbourhood. It was still bitterly cold that morning, but there had been no more snow. The snow of yesterday had been driven, like white sand, into thin drifts, leaving exposed black islands of ice.

I decided to go for a walk, and after breakfast I asked Christiana to come with me. 'We could look for the fox,' I said.

Except for refusing, she did not say much. She was going to help aunt Wilcox. About the fox she was very evasive. It might not have existed. She might not have seen it.

'I'll have a look for it myself,' I said.

She looked at me emptily, not speaking. Her eyes had lost completely the natural ardour and candour, both very childlike, which had infused the picture of the fox with reality and which had made me believe in both it and her. At that moment she could not have made me believe in anything.

I got my overcoat and gloves and went out. It was an east wind, steady, bitter, the sky a dull iron colour, without sun. In the fields the grass had been driven flat by wind. The earth was like rock.

In a scoop of the land a small stream flowed down between squat clumps of alder, catkins wind-frozen, cat-ice jagging out like frosted-glass from the fringe of frost-burnt rushes on both banks. Farther on a flock of pigeons clapped up from a field of white kale, clattering wings on steel leaves, spiralling up, gathering, separating again like broken bits of the dead sky.

I went on until I found the pond. I knew it at once because, a field away, I could see the road, and because of what Christiana had said about it. She had described the black sloe bushes barricading one side, the speared army of dead rushes, and a broken-down, now half-submerged cattle-trough on which the fox, she said, had leapt and sat and stared at her. The pond was covered with ice and the ice in turn with the fine salt snow swept in a succession of smooth drifts across it.

I stood and looked at the pond. Then I walked round it. At the opposite point, by the cattle-trough, I stood and looked at it again. On the cattle-trough the light snow crusts were unbroken, and on two sides of it, away from the water, snow had drifted in long arcs, rippled and firm as lard. On the trough and in the snow drifted round it and all across the pond there were no marks of any fox at all.

IV

When I got back to the house, about twelve, aunt Wilcox and Christiana were taking down the decorations. Most of the evergreens had been hung up in the hall, holly behind the pictures, sheaves of yew tied to the newel-posts of the polished pine staircase, and a very dry spray of mistletoe hung from the big brass oil-lamp. Aunt Wilcox and Christiana were putting the evergreens into a zinc bath-tin.

'You're just in time,' Christiana said.

'Last come must last kiss,' aunt Wilcox said.

'And what does that mean?' I said.

'You've got to kiss us both.'

Laughing, aunt Wilcox stood under the mistletoe and I kissed her. Her lips were solid and sinewy, like beefsteak, and lukewarm wet. As she clasped me round the waist I felt her coopered, with stays, like a barrel. Then Christiana stood under the mistletoe and I kissed her. Just before I kissed her she looked at me for a moment. Her eyes had the same remote anonymity as on the previous day, the same tranquil but disturbing candour. As I kissed her she was quite still, without fuss. Kissing her was like kissing someone who was not there. It was a relationship of ghosts. For one moment I felt I was not there myself. The recollection of this unreal lightness of touch was something I carried about with me for the rest of the day.

That afternoon Laurence and I went for a walk. I asked after his father and he said he was better, but resting. We talked about him for a short time. He told me how he had begun as a pit-boy in a Yorkshire colliery, but had worked himself up, and had later become a schoolmaster. Then the war broke out and he felt suddenly that he was wasted in the class-room and had gone back to the pit, to become under-manager. After about six months there was a disaster in the pit, an explosion that had brought down a vast roof-fall, entombing thirty-five men. Arnoldson went down for rescue work. For two days he could hear the voices of the entombed men quite clearly, then for a whole day he could hear them intermittently, then they ceased. But though they ceased Arnoldson fancied all the time he could still hear them, the voices of the dead, of men he had known, screaming or whispering in his mind more sharply than in life. He went on hearing these voices for weeks, the voices of people who were not there, until they broke him down. Christiana had been born about a year later.

Laurence spoke of his father with a slight impatience. He spoke as though, occupied himself with concrete things, the small matter of voices disturbing the spirit of another man had no material importance for him. It was clear that he did not believe in voices. From the subject of his father we went on to the subject of himself. I walked with head slightly down, mouth set against the wind, saying yes and no, not really listening, my thoughts in reality a long way behind me, like a kite on a string.

When we got back to the house, about four o'clock, I noticed a curious thing as we went past the dining-room. The door of the room was open and I could see that one of the china spaniel dogs was missing from the mantelpiece. At the time I did not take much notice of this. I went upstairs to wash my hands and came down and went into the drawing-room. Christiana sat reading by the fire, but for about half a minute I did not look at her. One of the china dogs was missing from the mantelpiece.

It was only about ten seconds after this that I heard Laurence coming downstairs. His way of coming downstairs was unmistakable. I heard his feet clipping the edges of the stairs with the precision of an engine firing in all its cylinders: the assured descent of a man who knew he could never fall down.

As he came down into the hall Christiana suddenly went to the door and said in a loud voice:

'Tea's ready. You're just right.'

We went straight into the dining-room. Christiana was last. She shut the door of the drawing-room after her. On the mantelpiece of the dining-room the two china dogs sat facing each other.

All through tea I sat looking at Christiana. She sat looking at me, but without any relationship between the eyes and the mind. Her eyes rested on me with a stare of beautiful emptiness. It might have been a stare of wonder or distrust or adoration or appeal: I could not tell. There was no way of telling. For the first time I saw some connection between this expressive vacancy and the voices that Mr. Arnoldson had heard in his mind. Sitting still, eyes dead straight but not conscious, she looked as though she also were listening to some voices very far away.

Just as we were finishing tea, aunt Wilcox said to me: 'I hope you didn't get cold this afternoon. You look a bit peaked.'

'I'm all right,' I said. 'But I never really got my feet warm.'

'Why don't you go and put on your slippers?' Christiana said.

'I'd like to,' I said.

So I went upstairs to put on my slippers, while Laurence went to write his evening letters, and aunt Wilcox and Christiana cleared the table. It was Sunday and aunt Wilcox was going to chapel.

I came downstairs again in less than five minutes. Christiana was sitting by the fire in the drawing-room. The two china dogs sat on the mantelpiece. I looked at the dogs, then at Christiana, with double deliberation. She must have seen I was trying to reason it out, that perhaps I had reasoned it out, but she gave no sign.

I sat down and we began to talk. It was warm; the small reading-lamp imprisoned us, as it were, in a small world of light, the rest of the room an outer darkness. I tried to get her to talk of the fox. There was no response. It was like pressing the buttons of a dead door-bell. Once I said something about her father. 'He's asleep,' she said. That was all. We went on to talk of various odd things. She lay back in the chair, facing the light, looking quietly at me. I fixed my eyes on hers. I had a feeling, very strong after a few minutes, that she wanted me to touch her. All at once she asked me had I ever been abroad? I said: 'Yes, to France once, and Holland once. That's all. Holland is lovely.' She did not say anything at once. She looked slowly away from me, down at the floor, as though she could see something in the darkness beyond the ring of light. Suddenly she said: 'I've been to Mexico, that's all.' I asked her for how long. She looked up at me. Without answering my question she began to tell me about Mexico. She told me about it as she had told me about the fox, speaking rather quickly, telling me where she had been, reciting the beautiful names of the places, talking about the food, the colour, the women's dresses. I had a feeling of travelling through a country in a train, in a hurry, getting the vivid transient panoramic effect of fields and villages, sun and trees, of faces and hands suddenly uplifted. She described everything quickly, her voice certain and regular, like a train passing over metals. She described an episode about Indians, how she had gone up into the mountains, to a small town where there was a market, where thin emaciated Indians came down to sell things, squatting close together on the ground in the cold, with phlegmatic and degenerate eyes downcast. There a woman had tried to sell her a few wizened tomatoes, holding them out with blue old veined hands, not speaking, simply holding the tomatoes out to her. Then suddenly, because the girl would not have them, the woman had squeezed one of them in a rage until seeds and juice ran out like reddish-yellow blood oozing out of the fissures between her frozen knuckles. As the girl told it, I felt rather than saw it. I felt the bitter coldness of the little town cut by mountain winds and the half-frozen juice of the tomato running down my own hands.

She went on talking, with intervals, for about an hour. After a time, some time after she had told me about the Indian woman, I had again the feeling that she wanted me to touch her. Her hands were spread out on her lap. I watched the light on them. I could see the slight upheaval of the white fingers, regular and intense, as she breathed, and this small but intense motion radiated a feeling of inordinate and almost fearful strength. The effect on me was as though I were looking down into very deep, not quite still water: an effect slightly hypnotic, slightly pleasurable, quietly governed by fear. I felt afraid to take my eyes away from her and I felt, after a time, that she did not want me to take them away.

After a time I did something else I knew she wanted me to do. I went and sat by her, in the same chair. I put my arms round her, not speaking a word. As I held her I could feel her listening. Perhaps she is listening, I thought, for someone to come. She did not speak. I could feel her fingers, outspread, clutching my back, as though she were falling into space. After a time she spoke.

'What did you say?' she said. I sat silent. 'What did you say?' she said. 'I thought I heard you say something.'

'No,' I said, 'I didn't speak.'

'Perhaps it was someone else?' she said.

I sat still. I did not say anything. Her breathing was slightly deeper. All the time I could feel her listening, as though waiting for the echo of some minute explosion on the other side of the earth.

'Don't you ever think you hear the voices of people who are not here?'

'Everybody does that,' I said.

'I mean you.'

'Sometimes.'

'Often?'

'Not often.'

The small reading-lamp stood on a table between the chair and the fireplace. I felt her stretch out her hand towards it. About us, for one moment the house seemed dead still. She put out the light. I heard the small click of the switch freeing us, as it were, from the restriction of light. She put her hands on my face, held it. I remember wondering suddenly what sort of night it was, if it were starlight, whether there was snow.

'Can you see me?' she said.

'No.'

'I can see you.'

I felt her withdraw herself very slightly from me. Then I knew why she could see me. I was sitting facing the window and through the slits of the dark curtains I could see blurred snow-white chinks of moonlight.

V

We did not have supper, that night, until nine o'clock. We had Yorkshire ham and pork pie, cold apple tart, with red cheese, mince pies and cheese-cakes, with large basins of strong tea.

Aunt Wilcox had pickles and towards the end of the meal we pulled half a dozen crackers that had been left over from Christmas. Out of her cracker Christiana had a tall white paper hat in the twelfth-century style, pointed, like a cone. As she put it on I got an instant impression that the dark brown eyes, under the white cap, looked darker than ever, and that they were slightly strange, not quite real, and for the first time it hurt me to look at them.

This impression continued until the following day. The moonlight was very strong nearly all night and I did not sleep well. All through the next morning I wanted to be alone with Christiana, but the chance did not seem to come. Mr. Arnoldson came downstairs and sat all day in front of the drawing-room fire, wrapped in rugs, so that the drawing-room was never empty. The two china dogs sat on the mantelpiece there and were not, as on the previous day, changed at all. Once I heard the voices of aunt Wilcox and Christiana coming from the kitchen. They were talking about the dogs. 'It's in my room,' Christiana said. 'I've stuck it with seccotine.' I sat most of that morning in Laurence's study, reading. He went in mostly for technical books and towards the end of the morning I got bored and asked him if he had any books of travel. He said there were a few in his bedroom. I went up to his room and there, on his chest of drawers, I found a book on Mexico. I took it downstairs and in five minutes I was reading the episode about the tomato and the Indian woman in the little cold mountain town.

In the night there had been another fall of snow, but it was a little warmer. The sun was very brilliant on the snow and out of Laurence's study window I could see, high up, peewits flashing like semaphores, white and dark against the very blue winter sky. I felt I had to get out.

I went out and walked across the fields, in the snow, past the brook and over towards the pond. The white of the snow was dazzling and I felt a slightly dazed effect, the light too sharp for my eyes. Along by the brook the snow was beginning to melt a little on the branches of the alders, bringing down showers of bright ice rain. I could see everywhere where rabbits had loped about in the early morning snow and there were many prints of moorhens, but there was nothing that looked at all like the mark of a fox.

The snow had covered everything of the pond and the surface was smoother than water. I stood and looked at it for a moment and then went on. A little farther on I picked up the brook again and I did not come back for half an hour.

Coming back I saw Christiana. I could see where she had walked in the snow. She had walked round the pond and now she was about half a field away, going back towards the house. I called and she turned and waited for me, standing against the sun. She stood with her arms folded, her big coat lapped heavily over her. Her face was white with the strong upward reflection of snow.

We walked on together. She walked with her arms continually folded. 'Have you seen the fox?' I said.

She did not answer. I knew I did not expect her to answer. Farther on we had to cross the brook by a small wooden bridge. On the bridge I stopped her, holding her coat. I put my arms round her and held her for a moment. Holding her, I could feel, then, why she walked with her arms folded. She had something under her coat. She kissed me without speaking. All the time I could feel her holding some object under her coat, as hard as stone.

We stood there, above the sun-shining water, slightly dazzled by the world of snow, for about five minutes, and I kissed her again. She was acquiescent, but it was an acquiescence that was stronger, by a long way, than all the strange remote activity of her spirit had ever been. It was normal. I felt for the first time that she was there, very young, very sweet, very real, perhaps a little frightened. Up to that time we had said nothing at all about affection. I had not thought of it. Now I wanted her. It seemed very natural, an inevitable part of things.

'You like me, don't you?' I said. It was all I could think of saying.

'Yes,' she said.

'Very much?'

'Very much.'

She smiled very quietly. I did not know what to do except to smile back. We walked on. Out in the open snow I stopped and, before she could do or say anything, kissed her again.

'Someone will see us.'

'I don't care,' I said.

I was very happy. At that moment, out in the snow, walking away from the sun, watching our two blue shadows climbing before us up the slight slope to the house, I had no doubts about her. Half an hour before I had wanted to tell her that I knew there was no fox, that she had never been to Mexico, that all that she had told me was an imposture. Now it did not seem to matter. And the voices? They did not seem to matter either. Many people hear the voices of people who are not there, who have never been there. There is nothing strange in that.

I was worried only by one thing: what she was carrying under her coat. Then, when we went in for lunch I knew, for certain, that it was the china dog. And that night I knew why it was.

Mr. Arnoldson went to bed very early that night, about half-past seven, and aunt Wilcox went upstairs with him, to see that he was all right. Laurence had gone down to the post office and I was sitting in the drawing-room, reading the morning paper. From the dining-room, suddenly, I could hear voices.

They went on for five minutes and I could not understand it. At last I got up and opened the drawing-room door. Across the hall the dining-room door was open a little and Christiana was sitting at the dining table, talking to a china dog.

'The fox,' she was saying, 'the fox!'

I stood looking. She was jabbering quite fast to the dog, strangely excited, her fingers tense.

'Christiana,' I said.

She did not hear me.

'Christiana.'

She got the dog by the neck and ran it across the mahogany table, towards a glass fruit dish, in crazy pursuit of something, jabbering, laughing a little, until I could see that the dog had the fox by the neck and that they were tearing each other to bits in the snow.

I saw it quite clearly for a moment, like a vision: the mahogany changed to snow, the fruit dish to fox, the china dog to a dog in reality, and in that moment, for the first time, I felt a little mad myself.

I went away on the following afternoon. Laurence drove me to the station. Nothing much happened. It was snowing fast and Christiana did not come outside to see us off. She stood at the window of the drawing-room, staring out. Except that her face was white with the reflection of the snow, she looked quite normal, quite herself. No one would have noticed anything.

But as we drove away I saw her, for one second, as someone imprisoned, cut off from the world, shut away.

We had not much time for the train and Laurence drove rather fast. 'You look a bit queer,' he said at the station. 'Are you all right?'

'Yes,' I said.

'Are you sure? Let me carry your bag. You don't look quite yourself.'

I could not speak. No, I thought, I am not myself.

Shot Actress—Full Story

There were fifteen thousand people in Claypole, but only one actress. She kept a milliner's shop.

My name is Sprake. I kept the watchmaker-and-jeweller's shop next door to Miss Porteus for fifteen years. During all that time she never spoke to me. I am not sure that she ever spoke to anyone; I never saw her. My wife and I were a decent, respectable, devoted couple, Wesleyans, not above speaking to anyone, and I have been on the local stage myself, singing in oratorio, but we were never good enough for Miss Porteus. But that was her affair. If she hadn't been so stand-offish she might, perhaps, have been alive today. As it is she is dead and she died, as everybody knows, on the front page of the newspapers.

No one in Claypole knew much about Miss Porteus. We knew she had been an actress, but where she had been an actress, and in what plays and in what theatres, and when, nobody knew. She looked like an actress: she was tall and very haughty and her hair, once blonde, was something of the colour of tobacco-stained moustaches, a queer yellowish ginger, as though the dye had gone wrong. Her lips were red and bitter; and with her haughty face she looked like a cold nasty woman in a play. She dressed, just for show, exactly the opposite of every other woman in Claypole: in winter she came out in chiffon and in summer you would see her walking across the golf-course, not speaking to anyone, in great fox furs something the colour of her own hair.

Her shop was just the same: at a time when every milliner-draper in Claypole used to cram as much into the shop-window as possible, Miss Porteus introduced that style of one hat on a stand and a vase of expensive flowers on a length of velvet. But somehow that never quite came off. The solitary hat looked rather like Miss Porteus herself: lonely and haughty and out of place.

The backways of her shop and ours faced on to each other; the gardens were divided by a partition of boards and fencing, but we could see from our bathroom into Miss Porteus's bathroom. You could see a great array of fancy cosmetic bottles outlined behind the frosted glass. You could see Miss Porteus at her toilet. But you never saw anyone else there.

Then one day we did see someone else there. One Wednesday morning my wife came scuffling into the shop and behind the counter, where I was mending a tuppenny-ha' penny Swiss lever that I'd had lying about for months, and said that she'd seen a man in Miss Porteus's back-yard.

'Well, what about it?' I said. 'I don't care if there's fifty men. Perhaps that's what she wants, a man or two,' I said. Just like that.

I was busy and I thought no more about it. But as it turned out afterwards, my wife did. I daresay she was a bit inquisitive, but while she was arranging the bedroom curtains she saw the man several times. She got a clear view of him: he was middle-aged and he had side-linings and he wore a yellow tie.

That night, when I went to bed, the light was burning in Miss Porteus's bathroom, but I couldn't see Miss Porteus. Then when I went into the bathroom next morning the light was still burning. I said, 'Hullo, Miss Porteus left the light on all night,' but I thought no more about it. Then when I went up at midday, the light was still on. It was still on that afternoon and it was on all that night.

My wife was scared. But I said, 'Oh! it's Thursday and she's taken a day off and gone up to London.' But the light went on burning all the next day and it was still burning late that night.

By that time I was puzzled myself. I went and tried Miss Porteus's shop door. It was locked. But there was really nothing strange about that. It was eleven o'clock at night and it ought to have been locked.

We went to bed, but my wife couldn't sleep. She kept saying I ought to do something. 'What can I do?' I said. At last she jumped up in bed. 'You've got to get a ladder out and climb up and see if everything's all right in Miss Porteus's bathroom,' she said.

'Oh! all right,' I said.

So I heaved our ladder over the boards and then ran it up to Miss Porteus's bathroom window. I climbed up. That was the picture they took of me later on: up the ladder, pointing to the bathroom window, which was marked with a cross. All the papers had it in.

What I saw through the bathroom window, even through the frosted glass, was bad enough, but it was only when I had telephoned to the police station and we had forced an entrance that I saw how really terrible it was.

Miss Porteus was lying on the bathroom floor with a bullet wound in her chest. We banged the door against her head as we went in. She had been dead for some time and I could almost calculate how long, because of the light. She was in a cerise pink nightgown and the blood had made a little rosette on her chest.

'Bolt the garden gate and say nothing to nobody,' the sergeant said.

I said nothing. The next morning all Claypole knew that Miss Porteus had been murdered, and by afternoon the whole of England knew. The reporter from the *Argus*, the local paper, came rushing round to see me before seven o'clock. 'Give me it,' he said. 'Give me it before they get here. I'm on lineage for the *Express* and I'll rush it through. Just the bare facts. What you saw. I'll write it.' So I made a statement. It was just a plain statement, and every word of it was true.

Then just before dinner I saw three men with cameras on the opposite side of the street. They took pictures of Miss Porteus's shop, and then they came across the road into my shop. They as good as forced their way through the shop, into the back-yard, and there they photographed Miss Porteus's bathroom window. Then one of the cameramen put a pound note into my hand and said, 'On top of the ladder?' The ladder was still there and I climbed up and they photographed me on top of it, pointing at the window.

By afternoon the crowd was packed thick right across the street. They were pressed tight against my window. I put the shutters up. Just as I was finishing them, four men came up and said they were newspaper-men and could I give them the facts about Miss Porteus?

Before I could speak they pushed into the shop. They shut the door. Then I saw that there were not four of them but twelve. I got behind the counter and they took out notebooks and rested them on my glass show-cases and scribbled. I tried to tell them what I had told the local man, the truth, and nothing more or less than the truth, but they didn't want that. They hammered me with questions.

What was Miss Porteus like? Was her real name Porteus? What else beside Porteus? What colour was her hair? How long had she been there? Did it strike me as funny that an actress should run a milliner's shop? When had I last seen the lady? About the bathroom—about her hair—

I was flustered and I said something about her hair being a little reddish, and one of the newspaper men said:

'Now we're getting somewhere. Carrots,' and they all laughed.

Then another said: 'Everybody says this woman was an actress. But where did she act? London? What theatre? When?'

'I don't know,' I said.

'You've lived next door all this time and don't know? Did you never hear anybody say if she'd been in any particular play?'

'No. I—Well, she was a bit strange.'

'Strange?' They seized on that. 'How? What? Mysterious?'

'Well,' I said, 'she was the sort of woman who'd come out in big heavy fox furs on a hot summer day. She was different.'

'Crazy?'

'Oh! No.'

'Eccentric?'

'No. I wouldn't say that.'

'About her acting,' they said. 'You must have heard something.'

'No.' Then I remembered something. At a rehearsal of the Choral Society, once, her name had come up and somebody had said something about her having been in *Othello*.

I remembered it because there was some argument about whether Othello was a pure black or just a half-caste.

'Othello?' The newspaper-men wrote fast. 'What was she? Desdemona?'

'Well,' I said. 'I don't think you ought to put that in. I don't know if it's strictly true or not. I can't vouch for it. I don't think—'

'And this man that was seen,' they said.' When was it? When did you see him? What was he like?'

I said I didn't know, that I hadn't seen him, but that my wife had. So they had my wife in. They questioned her. They were nice to her. But they put down, as in my case, things she did not say. Yellow tie? Dark? How dark? Foreign-looking? Actor? Every now and then one of them dashed out to the post office. They questioned us all that afternoon.

The next morning the placards of the morning newspapers were all over Claypole. 'Shot Actress—Full Story.' It was my story, but somehow, as it appeared in the papers, it was not true. I read all the papers. They had my picture, the picture of Miss Porteus's shop, looking somehow strange and forlorn with its drawn blind, and a picture of Miss Porteus herself, as she must have looked about 1920. All over these papers were black stabbing headlines: 'Search for Shot Actress Assailant goes on.'

'Police anxious to Interview Foreigner with Yellow Tie.' 'Real Life Desdemona: Jealousy Victim?' 'Eccentric Actress Recluse Dead in Bathroom.' 'Mystery Life of Actress who wore Furs in Heat Wave.' 'Beautiful Red-haired Actress who Spoke to Nobody.' 'Disappearance of Dark-looking Foreigner.'

It was Saturday. That afternoon Claypole was besieged by hundreds of people who had never been there before. They moved past Miss Porteus's shop and mine in a great stream, in cars and on foot and pushing bicycles, staring up at the dead actress's windows. They climbed in over the fence of my back garden and trampled on the flower-beds, until the police stopped them. Towards evening the crowd was so thick outside, in the front, that I put the shutters up again, and by six o'clock I closed the shop. The police kept moving the crowd on, but it was no use. It swarmed out of the High Street into the side street and then round by the back streets until it came into High Street again. Hundreds of people who had seen Miss Porteus's shop every day of their lives suddenly wanted to stare at it. They came to stare at the sun-faded blinds, just like any other shop blinds, as though they were jewelled; they fought to get a glimpse of the frosted pane of Miss Porteus's bathroom. All the tea shops in Claypole that day were crowded out.

We had reporters and photographers and detectives tramping about the house and the garden all that day and the next. That Sunday morning I missed going to chapel, where I used to sing tenor in the choir, for the first time for almost ten years. My wife could not sleep and she was nervously exhausted and kept crying. The Sunday newspapers were full of it again: the pictures of poor Miss Porteus, the shop, the bathroom window, my shop, the headlines. That afternoon the crowds began again, thicker than ever, and all the tea shops which normally did not open on Sunday opened and were packed out. A man started to sell souvenir photographs of Claypole High Street in the streets at threepence each, and it was as though he were selling pound notes or bits of Miss Porteus's hair. The sweet-shops opened and you saw people buying Claypole rock and Claypole treacle toffee, which is a speciality of the town. The police drafted in extra men and right up to ten o'clock strange people kept going by, whole families, with children, in their Sunday clothes, staring up at Miss Porteus's windows, with mouths open.

That afternoon I went for a walk, just for a few minutes, to get some air. Everybody I knew stopped me and wanted to talk, and one man I knew only slightly stopped me and said, 'What she look like, in the nightgown? See anything?' Another said: 'Ah, you don't tell me she lived there all alone for nothing. I know one man who knew his way upstairs. And where there's one you may depend there's others. She knew her way about.'

The inquest was held on the Monday. It lasted three days. My wife and I were witnesses and it came out, then, that Miss Porteus's name was not Porteus at all, but Helen Williams. Porteus had been her stage name. It came out also that there was a conflict of opinion in the medical evidence, that it was not clear if Miss Porteus had been murdered or if she had taken her life. It was a very curious, baffling case, made more complicated because the man with the yellow tie had not been found, and the jury returned an open verdict.

All this made it much worse. The fact of Miss Porteus having had two names gave her an air of mystery, of duplicity, and the doubts about her death increased it. There sprang up, gradually, a different story about Miss Porteus. It began to go all over Claypole that she was a woman of a certain reputation, that the milliner's shop was a blind. 'Did you ever see anybody in there, or going in? No, nor did anybody else. Did anybody ever buy a hat there? No. But the back door was always undone.' That rumour gave cause for others. 'Sprake,' people began to say, 'told me himself that she lay on the floor naked. They put the nightgown on afterwards.' Then she became not only a woman of light virtue and naked, but also pregnant. 'That's why,' people began to say, 'she either shot herself or was shot. Take it which way you like. But I had it straight from Sprake.'

As the story of Miss Porteus grew, the story of my own part in it grew. Business had been very bad and for three days, because of the inquest, I had had to close the shop, but suddenly people began to come in. They looked out old watches and clocks that needed repairing, brooches that had been out of fashion for years and needed remodelling, and they brought them in; they came in to buy watches, knick-knacks, ashtrays, bits of jewellery, clocks, anything. A man asked for an ash-tray with Claypole church on it as a souvenir.

By the week-end I was selling all the souvenirs I could lay hands on. The shop was never empty. I took my meals standing up and by the end of the day my wife and I were worn out by that extraordinary mad rush of business. We rested in bed all day on Sunday, exhausted. Then on Monday it all began again, not quite so bad, but almost. We were besieged by people coming in, ostensibly to buy something, but in reality on the chance of hearing me say something about Miss Porteus's death. I was in a dilemma: I wanted to close the shop and end it all, but somehow it wasn't possible. Business is business and death is death and you've got to live. And so I kept open.

Then the police came to see me again. The man with the yellow tie had not been found and they wanted my wife and me to go to the station to check the statements we had given. We shut the shop and drove to the station in a taxi. We were there three hours. When we got back there was a crowd of fifty people round the shop, murmuring and pushing and arguing among themselves. The rumour had gone round that the police had arrested me.

Once that rumour had begun, nothing could stop its consequences. It was a rumour that never quite became tangible. It drifted about like smoke. It was there, but you could never grasp it. No one would really say anything, but the rumour was all over Claypole that I knew more than I would say. With one rumour went others: it began to be said that my wife and I were busy bodies, Nosy-Parkers. How else had we come to be squinting into Miss Porteus's bathroom? How else had we seen the man with the yellow tie in the back-yard? We were Peeping-Toms. I never heard anyone say this. But it was there. I saw it in people's faces: I felt it. I felt it as plainly as a man feels the change of weather in an old wound.

But there was one thing I did hear them say. I used to belong, in Claypole, to a Temperance Club, the Melrose; we had four full-sized billiard tables and in the evenings I went there to play billiards and cards, to have a smoke and a talk and so on. Next to the billiard-room was a small cloak-room, and one evening, as I was hanging up my coat, I heard someone at the billiard table say:

'Old Sprake knows a thing or two. Think I should be here if I had as many quid as times old Sprake's been upstairs next door? Actress, my eye. Some act. Pound a time. Ever struck you it was funny old Sprake knew the colour of that nightgown so well?'

I put on my coat again and went out of the club. I was trembling and horrified and sick. What I had heard seemed to be the crystallization of all the rumours that perhaps were and perhaps were not going round Claypole. It may have been simply the crystallization of my own fears. I don't know. I only know that I felt that I was suspected of things I had not done and had not said; that not only was Miss Porteus a loose woman but that I had had illicit relations with her; that not only was she pregnant but that I, perhaps, had had something to do with that pregnancy; that not only had she been murdered, but that I knew more than I would say about that murder. I was harassed by fears and counter fears. I did not know what to do.

And all the time that mad rush of customers went on. All day people would be coming in to buy things they did not want, just on the off-chance of hearing me say something about

Miss Porteus's death, or of asking me some questions about her life. It was so tiring and irritating that I had to defend myself from it. So I hit upon the idea of saying the same thing to everybody.

'I just don't know,' I would say. I said it to everyone. Just that: 'I just don't know.'

I suppose I must have said those words hundreds of times a day. I suppose I often said them whether they were necessary or not. And when a man goes on repeating one sentence hundreds of times a day, for two or three weeks, it is only natural, perhaps, that people should begin to wonder about his sanity.

So it crept round Claypole that I was a little queer. One day I had to go to London on business and a man in the same compartment as myself said to another: 'Take any murder you like. It's always the work of somebody half-sharp, a maniac. Take that Claypole murder. Clear as daylight. The work of somebody loopy.'

That was not directed against me, but it stirred up my fears into a great ugly, lumpy mass of doubt and terror. I could not sleep. And when I looked into the glass, after a restless night, I saw a face made queer and wretched by the strain of unresolved anxieties. I felt that I could have broken down, in the middle of that rush of customers and questions and fears and rumours, and wept like a child.

Then something happened. It was important and it suddenly filled the front pages of the newspapers again with the mystery of Miss Porteus's death. The police found the man with the yellow tie. It was a sensation.

The man was a theatrical producer named Prideaux and the police found him at Brighton. The fact that his name was French and that he was found at Brighton at once established him, in the public mind, as the murderer of Miss Porteus.

But he had an explanation. He had not come forward because, quite naturally, he was afraid. Miss Porteus was an old friend and her death, he said, had upset him terribly. It was true that he had seen Miss Porteus just before her death, because Miss Porteus had invited him to come and see her. She needed money; the millinery business was not paying its way. She feared bankruptcy and, according to Prideaux, had threatened to take her life. Prideaux promised to lend her some money and he was back in London early that evening. He proved it. The porter of his hotel could prove it. It was also proved that people had seen Miss Porteus, alive, walking out on the golf-course, as late as five o'clock that day. The hotel-porter could prove that Prideaux was in London by that time.

That was the end. It was established, beyond doubt, that Miss Porteus had taken her life. And suddenly all the mystery and sensation and horror and fascination of Miss Porteus's death became nothing. The papers were not interested in her any longer and her name has never appeared in the papers again.

I no longer live at Claypole. All those odd, unrealized rumours that went round were enough to drive me mad; but they were also enough to kill my wife. Like me, she could not sleep, and the shock of it all cracked her life right across, like a piece of bone. Rumour and shock and worry killed her, and she died just after the facts of Miss Porteus's death were established. A month later I gave up the business and left the town. I could not go on. The first week before her death I had three people in the shop. All that mad inquisitiveness had hardened into indifference. Nobody even stopped to stare up at Miss Porteus's windows.

Poor Miss Porteus. She took her life because she was hard up, in a fit of despair. There is no more to it than that. But nobody in Claypole ever believed that and I suppose very few people ever will. In Claypole they like to think that she was murdered; they know, because the papers said so, that she was a strange and eccentric woman; they know that she acted in a play with a black man; they know, though nobody ever really said so, that she was a loose woman and that she was pregnant and that somebody shot her for that reason; they know that she let men in and up the back stairs at a pound a time and they like to think that I was one of those men; they know that I found her naked in the bathroom and that I was a bit queer and that I knew more than I would ever say.

They know, in short, all that happened to Miss Porteus. They can never know how much has happened to me.

Old

The old man walked slowly up the street, pressing himself against the wind that violently blew open his jacket. It was Sunday afternoon. He had once been rather a tall man, with splendid muscular hands, black hair, and long strenuous legs. Now he took little shuffling steps, and pressed the whole quivering weight of his short body on his walking-stick. He was wearing a rather faded old-fashioned bowler hat and a black muffler folded round his neck and tucked away into his armpits. When the wind struck at him with sudden bursts of violence he seemed to have no contact with earth. It seemed as if the wind would whip him up and scatter him, as it does a piece of fragile charred paper from a fire.

At the top of the street the wind seized him and swung him across to the other pavement. He lifted his head and looked at the numbers of the houses. The wind had beaten tears into his eyes. Presently he grasped the iron railings in front of Number 67, pulling himself up the step which was like a fresh white tombstone, and fumbled his way into the house.

'Wipe your feet!'

The words flew out of the front sitting-room like birds of prey. Aggie's voice—his eldest daughter. The look in his tired wet eyes did not change, but he wiped his boots; not because they were dirty, only out of habit, automatically. Then he shuffled slowly across the passage, down which the linoleum lay like brown bright glass. He was still wearing his hat and muffler. He had not forgotten it: it was only that he liked to sit in the house with his hat and muffler on. Yes, he liked doing that. He liked doing that when they did not stop him.

Now he opened the sitting-room door and shuffled into the room. The tears made by the wind still lay in his eyes and the room was full of people. It was Aggie's house. Aggie had never been married. Thirty years ago they used to say of Aggie that she polished the coal before she put it on the fire. Now in the room there was a great Sunday shine of brass and porcelain. Tea was laid on the big round mahogany table that Aggie had fought so hard for when her mother died, and bright orange firelight shone on the Sunday crockery, the face of the piano, the pictures and on the faces of the family. It shone too into the tired wind-watered eyes of the old man, who saw his family as if they were figures on a bright tinsel postcard. He saw that Emma was there, with her husband, Clem. Clem was a foreman finisher. They had no family; Clem had a good job and they had saved money. Then there was Harry, his son. Once Harry and Clem and Emma hadn't spoken for fifteen months. Then another time Clem and Emma and Gladys hadn't spoken for six months. Clem and Emma were the mischief makers. Gladys, who was there too, was his niece. She was his brother Arthur's daughter, and now she had a daughter herself, a child of seven, who was sitting on the hearthrug. It was quite a large party. Gladys's husband, Albert, had a good job, travelling in washing-machines up and down the country. He had a car and did not often come home at week-ends and Aggie pretty well knew for a fact that during these times he was up to no good.

The greeting that the family started to give to the old man was silenced and snatched away by Aggie.

'Well, if he hasn't come in with his hat and muffler on I'll never!' she said. 'Just like a baby!'

'I'm all right,' he said. 'I want 'em on.'

'Never mind what you *want*,' she said, 'go and take 'em off.'

He went slowly back into the passage and took off his hat and muffler. Without them his neck and head felt strange and cold.

While he was out of the room he heard Aggie say something about she'd bet anybody he'd been street-corner gossiping with Jim Clayton and that he was getting just like a baby again, forgetting things, forgetting his hat and muffler. Next thing they'd hear of he'd be forgetting who he was, then there'd be a nice howdy-do.

'Jim Clayton's bin bad a-bed this last week,' he said when he came back into the room again.

'Well, if it wasn't Jim Clayton,' she said, 'it was somebody else. That I do know.'

He did not ask how or why she knew it, but sat down.

'You needn't go sitting yourself down!' she said. 'Tea's ready, and bin ready this ten minutes. And while you've bin soodlin' along anyhow we've bin wasting good daylight.'

He began to say something about grudging a penny in the gas, but the family had already begun to gather round the table, voices and chairs clattering one against another, and nobody heard him. At the table he found himself between Harry, his son, and the little girl, Jean. She had fair bobbed hair, and a face as open and fresh as a water-lily. He took out his handkerchief and spread it surreptitiously across his lap, as a napkin, and while waiting for his tea he looked out of the window. It was early November and already the daylight was dying quickly, and in the window, like pieces of fired bronze in the fire-light, there were vases of chrysanthemums.

His cup of tea came at last and he began to stir it, tasting it loudly from his spoon, putting the spoon back into his cup.

'Watch him, Harry,' Aggie said, 'you know what happened last week.'

Yes, something terrible had happened last week. He had knocked over his tea on the table-cloth. It had put Aggie into a rare temper and in her anger she had said something which he felt she might have been harbouring in her mind for a long time. She had said something about having had enough, that if he couldn't behave properly they might have to see that he was sent somewhere where he would.

He knew what that meant. Sooner or later they would send him to the Union. He picked up a piece of bread and butter, folding it slowly in his bony hands. He suddenly felt astonishingly hungry and began to cram piece after piece of bread into his mouth, washing it down with tea.

It was only after he had been eating for nearly five minutes that he realized what he had been doing. He had been drinking with his mouth full and more than that, with the spoon in his cup, and now all the family was watching him. They were watching him as if for some reason they felt that the very old ought not to eat and drink with so much pleasure, even perhaps as if they ought not to eat at all.

He looked down at his plate. Like his cup, it was empty. Something now made him look at the little girl beside him. She had bitten her piece of bread and butter into the shape of a dog, and this dog was drinking tea out of her saucer. The little girl had shining yellow hair. For some reason he thought she was very like Aggie had been, and he wondered why people grew up and changed. Aggie with the fair shining hair was now Aggie with a thin soapy face, grey bunned-up hair, slight heart trouble, and a sour jealousy for the lives of others. During the last war she had been fore-woman in a clothing factory. She had saved money. This money was now invested in war-loan and the post-office bank, and everybody in turn was bitterly jealous of Aggie because nobody knew just what the amount was.

He stopped thinking, and looked up. No one was now paying much attention to him, and he took the opportunity to help himself to a heavy slice of plum-cake.

And now, instead of thinking, he sat listening. Emma, who always stuck out her little finger while drinking, was saying how the days dropped in and how soon it would be dark before they'd finished dinner. It was a broad hint for Aggie to light the gas, but Aggie took no notice. Instead she opened up a new line of conversation and said was anyone going to Chapel?

Not if he knew it, Clem said.

Because Clem paid pew-rent at High Street Congregational, and had done so for many years, the remark was a sensation. Clem spoke with a great sense of grievance. He was something of a tenor and made a great show of singing with a tune-book, though he could not read a note. Emma had held a place among the High Street sopranos for thirty years, showing during all that time a misguided passion for descant at the wrong moments.

Well, it was something of a change to hear Clem speak like that, Aggie said.

To which Clem said there had been changes to make him speak like that. Big changes. Changes that he never thought he'd live to see happen.

Well, Aggie said, whatever *had* happened?

Didn't they know, Emma said, that she and Clem hadn't sat in the choir for three weeks?

Well, Aggie said. Well!

Signing on new blood? Harry said. He spoke almost for the first time. He had always been a man of sarcastic, laconic speech, who drank a little, strictly on the q.t., and had no use for chapel.

There was nothing to joke about, Clem said. It was no laughing matter, he went on in an unsteady, sensational voice, when he and Emma had been as good as turned neck and crop out of the choir in which they'd sat for thirty years!

Well, Aggie said, she'd never heard a word until now. Well!

She might well well! Emma said bitterly.

She was about to say how and why it was that she and Clem had ceased to sing in the choir when the old man suddenly felt himself cease listening. It was as if his mind broke away from the mass of bitterness and jealously and fell down like a tired meteorite into the space of age, unable to keep the pace. Still hungry, he helped himself to a second slice of cake. As he did so, he looked again at the little girl. The dog made of bread and butter had gone now, to be replaced by a strange creature bitten out of a biscuit.

'What d'ye call that?' he said.

'It's a tiger,' she said. 'It's very froshus.'

He took a bite out of his cake. It was a nice game, he thought, and he called the little girl's attention to the fact that that was now an elephant on his plate.

'Is that froshus?' she said.

'No,' he said. 'It's just a tame elephant.'

'Where's its trunk?'

'I'm just making it,' he said. 'Here.'

He began to squeeze some of the cake in his fingers, elongating it, making the trunk. He did not feel old or tired any longer. For some time he went on walking the elephant about his plate and the table-cloth, making it at intervals meet the tiger, until at last the conversation carried on by Clem and Aggie and the rest of the family receded to a great distance, bringing only faint echoes of conflict and bitterness out of a real and darkening world to which he did not belong.

Suddenly the little girl got tired of the elephant and the tiger and began to eat the tiger. He came to himself too and began to eat the elephant. For an instant he felt tired, but then the little girl began talking again. She said how much she liked his hair.

'It's nice and white,' she said. 'I'd like to brush it.'

'You eat your tea,' he said, automatically, not knowing why he said it.

'Can I brush it?' she said. 'Can I? Can I?'

He was about to say something else when he saw her slip down from the table. She went out of the room, and he was left to himself. For a few seconds reality beat upon him out of the darkening room. The chrysanthemums were colourless now except in the winks of the firelight. Out in the street the lamps were not yet lit and he could not see very clearly the faces of his family. Aggie was asking if anyone wanted another cup and Clem was saying that it was not as if he and Emma asked for favours or that they grudged anyone else have a chance, but in his opinion some of the old ones could still sing some of the young ones inside out. Anyway, he was saying finally, it had cured him for a bit. If that was chapel and religion, he said, then he'd stop at home.

Funny sort of religion, Harry said.

The remark was taken as a kind of heresy, and Aggie pounced on Harry, starting an argument, so that no one saw the little girl come back into the room. In the confusion of voices the old man pushed his chair back from the table. The little girl sat on his knee and he bent down his head to her. She had found a small white hair-brush, and now she began very gently and slowly to brush his hair. She went on brushing his hair for a long time, talking to him, telling him as if he were a child to keep still, to hold his head this way and that. The repeated, soothing motions of her brushing produced on him a kind of mesmeric peace. There appeared on his face a look of lost and beautiful tranquillity, his eyes no longer wet or tired, his hands placidly at rest.

About him the conversation that he no longer wanted to follow was going on more bitterly. Emma and Harry were arguing loudly as to whether you went to church to worship the minister or whether you went to worship God Almighty, and Gladys, who had not spoken much, was trying to keep the peace. Harry, replying to Aggie, was saying warmly that it would be more sense if someone lit the gas. It was too dark to see your way to your mouth, he said, but Aggie flared back that if he couldn't see he must feel. His mouth was big enough.

Outside in the street, by this time, the lamps were alight. The bright greenish beams of light were coming into the window, turning the edges of the chrysanthemums to curls of tarnished silver. The old man sat staring at the flowers with a gaze of profound stillness, while the little girl tirelessly brushed his thin white hair.

In the conflict of voices no one seemed to be taking any notice of him now. In the falling darkness no one could tell what he was thinking.

The Ferry

Richardson drove his car down to the river, and there a woman of sixty or more ferried him and the car across. The water, chopped by the motion of the crossing, flapped against the low mud banks, the piles of the disused wharf and mournfully against the clumps of dying reed. The sky was dirty over the interminably flat land, very low, with breaks of wintry evening sunlight that were here and there reflected in the dark water of the dykes. When the ferry hit the opposite bank the big woman lumbered off, caught the rope and pulled on it, digging her great gum-booted feet into the turf.

'You can drive off now!'

At that moment something made him turn and look back. He saw on the bank, standing back, the low mud-plastered pub that had perhaps been the ferry-house for more than a hundred years. Three boats were drawn up in the yard. It was November, but they were still not covered for the winter, and on one side the wind had piled up against them like a golden shoal a great drift of fallen willow-leaves.

'Any fishing here?' he said.

'About as much here as anywhere,' she said. 'Pike-fishing mostly. Some tidy roach though.'

'I've been trying all day farther up,' he said. 'Nothing doing at all.'

'Over-fished,' she said. 'When it ain't that it's poison from the tanneries. Nothing left but water-rats and gudgeon.'

She still stood braced on the rope, her heavy feet dug into the earth, while he took one more look at the pub, the boats and the shoals of leaves on the wooden jetty.

'Ain't you coming off?' she said.

'I just wondered if you let rooms,' he said. 'I might stay the night and try a day here tomorrow.'

'We got a room or two,' she said. 'We get a fisherman or two here most week-ends.'

Without surprise, as if it were something that had happened very often before, she began to ferry him back again. On that return journey he noticed the great strength of her thick legs and arms, straining on the rope. Her jaw had the square set of a boat broad and clumsy in the bows. Most of the lines of her face ran vertical, like dry seams opened by weather. Her mouth was thin and fine but not bitter, fixed with a kind of dry smile that she did not know was there.

It began to rain as they went together across the yard. The wind sprang up across the dykes in a sudden dirty burst, and the ferry rocked on the slopping water, banging the chain.

'I'll give you the back room,' she said. 'If there's a mite o' wind you'll hear things slapping about all night'

'You think it'll set in?' he said, 'the rain?'

'The wind's about right,' she said. 'It's bin raining off and on for two days now.'

She took him straight through the small front passage and up the narrow varnished stairs. It was growing darker every moment. Suddenly, as he followed her, he got for an instant the impression of a movement behind him. He turned round and saw at the foot of the stairs a thin pale woman of sixty or so watching him. As he saw her she began to move away, slowly but dead silent. She had in her hands a candle that was not lighted, and for a moment he thought she had the air of someone who resented something but had forgotten what it was.

He went up into his room. The brass bedstead shone cold in the wintry light. The big woman ran her great brown hands across the white quilt, smoothing it, saying she hoped it was all right for him. 'And what about your tea? You'd like something to eat now?' He said he would, and she said she would cook whatever she could, eggs and ham or fish if she had it. 'Sometimes we get a boat coming up from Lynn and they drop in with a little sea-fish. But gen'lly we don't see nobody much, only week-ends.'

She went out of the room, but from the passage outside she called back: 'You can go down and sit in the parlour. There's fire there. The bar ain't properly open till six.'

Rain beat desolately on the windows while he unpacked his things. Looking out, he saw it raking the air far across the endlessly flat landscape of already blackened earth. The bones of willow-trees alone broke the skyline, and stacks of brown reed the empty desolation of fields bound everywhere by dark lines of water.

Going downstairs, he found the parlour by the glow of the fire coming through the open door. He went in, and was startled to see the thin pale woman sitting by the fire, her hands in her lap, her head turned away from him.

'Good evening,' he said.

She did not answer; as far as he could tell she did not move at all.

'Wretched weather,' he said.

She coughed slightly into her hands, once or twice, dryly, almost without a sound. Then she drew in her breath, as if to cough again, but nothing happened. Her body retracted slowly and her hands fell into her lap. He saw then that they were long, bony, inanimate hands, beside which the hands of the other woman now seemed exceeding powerful. For some time he stood there waiting for her to do or say something, but nothing happened and at last he went out of the room.

He stood for a time in the darkening bar, looking seawards through the heavy rain. By the time the voice of the other woman called that his tea was ready he could no longer see even the nearer fields; he could see the ferry rocking and slapping against the bank and the water of the river wildly broken by the bullet hail of rain, but the pub seemed now to be standing on the edge of a vast dark plain that had no end.

He thought as he went in for his tea that no one would come in there that night, and for a long time he was right. He ate his meal of eggs and ham and sausages slowly, by lamplight, alone except at the beginning of it, when for a few moments the big woman stood by, telling him how there was no fish, that the boats had not been by all day. 'I don't know whether you see the papers,' she said, 'but the water's pretty high on the Level. It'll be a high tide tonight with the wind where it is too. We had a big break across here two year back.'

'How far away?' he said. 'How big?'

'Three or four mile down. Big enough to flood a farm or two out. We had everybody working at it as could work. Had seven feet of water here in the cellars.'

'I remember reading about it,' he said. 'It was bad.'

'It was bad, but you get used to it. You're born with your feet in water here. You live on water and you die on water.'

She left him to eat alone and when he saw her again, in the bar, it was as he had expected. She too was alone; no one at all had come in. The continuous crash of rain from far across the immense flat space of land on all sides struck the house with a force that shattered them both, at intervals, into silence. Small tin oil-lamps lighted with a deep yellow glow the varnished walls of the little bar, and the scales of a twenty-pound pike shone with savage beauty in a glass case above the low back-room door. As he looked at this pike, meaning to ask her who had caught it and when, he noticed something else. The spirit bottles on the bar shelves were marked with many small horizontal white lines: the chalk marks of successive drinks. He asked her then if it was a tied house or a free house, and she said, rather proudly but a little wearily too he thought, 'A free house. We own it. We've kept the ferry for thirty years.'

'We?'

'Me and my sister.'

'Was it your sister,' he said, 'that was sitting in the parlour?'

'That was her.'

'I spoke to her,' he said, 'but she didn't seem to hear me.'

'No.'

'You're not much alike,' he said.

'No,' she said. 'No.'

Directly afterwards the door opened and the wind battered into the bar a man in a heavy reefer jacket and high gum-boots. Behind the bar the woman reached for the whisky. 'Evenin,' Dave,' she said.

'Evenin,' evenin',' he said. He looked at Richardson. 'Evenin'.'

'Evening,' Richardson said. 'Have it on me. And you,' he said to the woman. 'Let's all have one.'

'No,' she said. 'No. No thanks.' She poured two whiskies and set them on the bar. 'What's it like Dave?'

'Water's riz a foot,' he said. 'And still rising. Busted the bank a bit on th' old river. I just bin up there. Fast as they bung it up one place it starts in another. They'll want all the help they can get.'

'You'll be getting water in the cellar again,' Richardson said.

The woman did not answer. The man set the empty whisky glass on the bar, looking at Richardson. 'Another? I got to go.'

Richardson said thanks, and they had another whisky. 'You're going back to help?' Richardson said.

'Yeh.'

'Any good if I came?'

'You don't want to go, sir,' the woman said. 'Slopping about in that Fen clay up to your eyes. You be ruled by me, don't you go sir. Don't you go.'

She seemed almost frightened: not for him, but for herself, as if not wanting to be alone.

'I'd like to go,' he said. 'I won't get any fishing anyway.'

'But it's a dirty night. You'd be better here. There's nothing like a dirty Fenland night.'

'I'll just go up and look,' he said. 'I'll go up for an hour and come back. What time do you close up?'

'Ten, sir,' she said. 'But I'll be up until you come.'

It was strange, he thought, that she had suddenly begun calling him sir. He went upstairs to his room and put on his mackintosh and his fishing boots and sou-wester. As he came back through the passage behind the bar he saw a light shining upward from the open door of the cellar. He passed quickly, and did not see if anyone was there. In the bar the big woman watched him go without another word except a low 'Good night.'

Outside, the rain struck with a succession of heavy blasts across the yard above the jetty, smashing the ferry with eternal melancholy janglings of the chain against the wooden piles. He groped his way to the car, blinded by darkness, calling the other man. The reply was snatched up and hammered away by the lash of wind, but finally he reached the car and got in, switching on the headlights. In the interior calmness he heard the voice of the other man now shouting beyond the black glass of the windows and saw a pair of yellow gesticulating hands, the voice and hands both like those of a person trapped and trying to escape. He opened the side-window of the car and shouted 'Get in!'

'You won't get far with a car,' the man shouted. 'There'll be water on the road.'

'Never mind, we'll try. Go as far as we can. How far is it?'

'Two mile or more.'

'All right. Get in.' He started the car and switched on the windscreen wipers, peering ahead through the arc of smoothed black glass. 'Keep a look out for water.'

Driving away from the ferry, travelling for a time in low gear, not nervous but simply tense, not yet used to the light, he felt on both sides of the narrow dyked road a great solidity of darkness out of which wind and rain hammered with heavy violence on the car, beating it like a drum. In this atmosphere there was not much he could say. He slowed down once or twice, imagining he saw water lying ahead, but the man beside him would say, 'It's all right, it's all right. You won't git no water here. I'll tell you when you'll git water.' He saw a light: a moment later a house floated past like a white-washed boat, swiftly drifting away. And then something about the solitary house reminded him of the pub, solitary too by the river edge, and the big woman back there leaning her muscular and yet uneasy body on the bar, suddenly calling him sir and not wanting him to go. It reminded him too of the other woman sitting alone in the parlour, not speaking, thin, strange, inanimate and yet in a way alert. It reminded him of the light in the cellar.

'They'll be flooded out at the pub,' he said, 'won't they, if this keeps on?'

'Ah! they'll cop out. They always cop out. Did y'ever see the flood marks in the cellar? Y' ought to look at'em. Plenty o' times six or seven feet o' water down there.'

Richardson did not speak again. Ahead, now, he could see lights and as they sprang increasingly out of the darkness the man at his side shouted.

'Water!'

Richardson stopped the car. Flowing like a stream, clay-coloured water came up to the front wheels. The man got out, and in the beam of the headlights Richardson saw him wading ahead calf-deep in water. Presently he came back. 'All right. Go on now. But steady.'

'How far?'

'Twenty or thirty yards. It's the water from the break. You can see the lights on the Level.'

They came slowly through the water, drove on a short distance and then stopped. They got out of the car and began to walk towards the lights. Sounds of human voices, disembodied, remote, irregularly driven across the short intervening space of darkness, became louder and more living as Richardson saw the shape of the Level, vaguely marked out by lights, a wall of earth rising thirty or forty feet above the black flat land.

It was some time later, when his eyes became used to the darkness, that he saw what was happening. Figures of men, working in the light of oil-lamps and here and there by an inspection-lamp plugged by a lead to a standing car, swarmed darkly on and about the bank like stooping ants, sucked down into heavy postures of determination by the clay they cut and shovelled and carried. He saw sometimes the steel gleam of a spade as it carved the clay that in turn caught the yellow glow of lamplight; he saw it piled on barrows and wheeled away on the plank-lines and at last effaced by the dark torrent of ceaseless rain. He watched for a time the men coming and going out of the darkness. Then he walked up the road to the point where it bridged the Level. The wind was strong and cold. On the far side he could see for a few yards the ripple of flood-water beaten up by wind and rain, but beyond that nothing. Solid, like a wall of black clay, the darkness shut out whatever lay beyond the ripple of water.

Up there, and again when he came down to the lower point of the road, he began to be aware of the smell of water. It was cold and powerful, and with it rose the sour dead odour of clay. It seemed to rise out of the earth; it rose straight into his nostrils, biting them. He gulped it into his mouth in icy gasps of rain.

After a time he got hold of a spade and began working. At the first stroke or two of the spade the great force of suction pulled at his heart. He realized he was not used to it and made a great effort, stooping and gripping the spade with all his power. And still, even then, the clay and the water under the clay sucked at the muscles of his arms and chest and heart and even the muscles of his neck. It caught at his boots; his feet were held in a trap. For a moment he suffered a spasm of childlike terror, feeling as if something unknown and limitless and powerful were sucking him down. He felt the sudden lifting of the clay, at last, like the tearing away of a piece of his own flesh. He was struck by shock and pain, and then by a shudder of relief, followed by a blank of stupidity.

He worked on for a long time like this, bravely and clumsily carving the grey sour clay out of the darkness, stupid, sucked down, not thinking. The clay he cut and loaded was carried away into the rain along the plank-lines to some point of danger he never saw. Farther beyond still the tide was rising. The land and the water and the darkness and himself were part of a great conflict. The rain stood like a cold sweat on his face. When he wiped it away with his hands his fingers left on his flesh the colder smeared impression of the clay.

Some hours later he struggled to his car and drove back to the ferry. As he went into the lighted bar his weariness took the form of a temporary blindness. He did not know what time it was and he stood by the bar, leaning heavily on his elbows, not seeing. The clay had partially dried on his hands, contracting the skin, so that his fingers too felt dead.

'I'll have a whisky,' he said.

After almost half a minute he looked up to find that no one had answered him. To his surprise the bar was empty. By the clock above the bar-shelves it was seven or eight minutes to ten.

Some moments later he heard voices. They seemed to come from somewhere in the passage behind the bar. After listening a moment he walked into the passage. He could see the light, now, coming up from the cellar; the voices were coming from there too, the voices of the two women, low, hollow, in argument, unconscious of him.

What he saw down there at the foot of the cellar steps, in the lamplight, puzzled and startled him. Water had begun to rise already in the cellar, so that the beer-barrels seemed almost to be floating. The lamplight fell with a cloudy glow on the dark barrels, the white-washed walls and on the still water itself. It case upward the heavy shadows of the two women, who were watching. One, the big woman, was standing on the lowest of the cellar steps, which the water had not yet reached. Her body seemed more than ever huge, anxious and in some way helpless. But it was clear that what she was really watching was not the water. He knew that she must have seen that many times before: many times, and worse, much worse. He remembered the story of the marks on the wall. What she was really watching was the other woman, and it was she, dreadfully thin, thin and worn-out and obsessed by some kind of parsimonious terror, who in turn was really watching the water. And as he stood there looking down, watching the small figure sitting on one of the pub chairs in the middle of the rising water, her feet on the rung, her body thin and frail but tight with a fanatical stubborness, he knew that this too must have happened before, and he knew the reason for the big woman's fear and anxiety. He knew why she had not wanted him to go.

He moved at last and the big woman, hearing him suddenly, turned her startled eyes upward. Seeing him, she scrambled heavily up the steps. Behind her, as if nothing had happened, the little woman did not move.

In the bar he saw the big brown hands trembling as they drew the whisky. 'Won't you have one too?' he asked her.

'No. No sir, no thanks, no thanks.'

She tried to keep her hands still by pressing them together, and he knew she was alarmed by what he had seen.

'Is there anything I can do?' he said.

She shook her head.

'Nothing?' he said.

'No sir, no sir,' She stood silent again, defensive, trembling. He took a drink of whisky, and saw that it was a minute or so past ten o'clock. She realized it too and went across the bar and proceeded to draw the heavy bolts of the door, locking it afterwards.

'You've been working on the Level,' she said as she came back. 'I can see you're tired. You'll want some supper, won't you?'

'I don't think I'll have anything,' he said.

'What time would you like breakfast?' she said. She wanted him to go. He drank his whisky, hesitating. He wanted to say to her, 'Why does she sit down there? What makes her do that?' but some-how he couldn't. It was after all no concern of his: what they did or felt, why even they were there, why one of them should behave in that strange silent way, watching the water.

Then all at once she began to speak. She began to tell him why it was, in a voice unamazed, low, rather mechanical. While she spoke she kept her eyes lowered, and he felt sorry for her: the big hands flat on the bar, the heavy embarrassed face that could not lift itself, the difficult statement of painful words.

'She's got some idea that there'll be a second Flood.'

He did not speak. He let he go quietly on, telling him how the other woman would sit there in the cellar, not only when rain came and the water was rising, but when there was no rain, even in summer: how she would sit there waiting, watching the flood-marks on the wall, and then how she would come up into the bar, obsessed by hours of watching these marks, and begin to make the marks he had seen on the spirit-bottles behind the bar. She was afraid and had been afraid now for many years that the waters would rise and cover them in the night and sometimes, as on nights like this, nothing could make her go to bed. There was nothing so very strange in that, he thought. There were people who lived their lives under the oppression of just such fears, the fear of being drowned or burned or suffocated while they slept. What was so strange, he thought, was that they had not acted about it in the most simple, obvious way.

'Why don't you move and go somewhere else?' he said.

'Us?' she said. 'Move?' She looked up at him at last, explaining. If the water was bad in one way it was good in another. It was their living: the ferry, the boats in summer, the fishing, the pun. 'We couldn't move,' she said. 'We couldn't move. What'd we do, at our age? Start again?'

'You could sell up,' he said.

'No,' she said. 'We can't sell up. It's entailed. We couldn't sell up if we wanted to.'

'But sitting down there, like that,' he said. 'She'll be ill.'

'She is ill,' she said.

He finished his whisky and then stood looking into the empty glass, not knowing what to say.

'Was the water rising much up on the Level?' she said.

'A bit. It'll be worse with the tide.'

'Yes,' she said. 'It'll be worse. And sometimes I wish it would get worse. I wish there'd be a flood. A big, second flood, like the one in the Bible. Like she wants. That'd be the end of it all.'

She had nothing to say after that, and after a moment or two he said good night and went upstairs to bed.

Long afterwards he lay listening to the sound of water. It was falling and rising everywhere about him with tremendous force. He heard it beating on the roof-tiles and the bare branches of the trees and on the raging surface of the river. He heard the constant melancholy beating of the ferry-chain as it struck against the piles of the jetty. He heard the rain roaring across the great level miles of darkness across which the tide too was coming in from the sea. And hearing it and thinking of the woman down below, he felt his heart grow cold.

Time Expired

Miss Burke, who was Irish and at pains to explain that she did not like men, stood on the open airstrip watching the wounded being loaded into the dusty Dakota. Her sunburned face had the deep Irish upper lip; she had square shoulders, and in her khaki drill she did not look like a nurse. She looked rather like a man who has indecisively begun to let his hair grow long and then has become slightly self-conscious of it and tucked it under his cap.

When the wind that churned the soft yellow dust of the airstrip into high smoky clouds came beating under the body of the Dakota it caught the edges of Miss Burke's masculine short back hairs and blew into them sudden small dimples, as into the fur of a cat. The dust had everywhere the fineness of powdered sulphur. It settled like fine sprayed paint on the dark wings of the plane, on the fabric of the ambulance, and even on the bear-brown blankets of the stretchers, whenever for a moment or two a wounded man was set down.

Whenever a plane took off or landed out on the runway, dust rose up into clear air with oppressive insistence in huge yellow smoky columns, and clashed there against the harder, yellower light of sun. It seemed to make even more oppressive the oppressive heat of the shadeless afternoon. Only Miss Burke was not oppressed by it. Miss Burke, who had been nearly three years a nurse on the Burma battlefield, was quite used to most things now.

In about another five minutes all the stretchers were in the body of the plane, strung from the roof traces and ready for take-off, and the crew were pushing past them into the nose. The men on the stretchers did not seem—to Miss Burke–any different from the men on the stretchers of any other day. They were a series of rigid and nameless bodies covered by brown blankets: a couple of Indian boys, turned Chinese yellow by pain and shock, and the rest British boys, pale too, and rather impassive, staring stiffly upward at the dark-green roof of the fuselage. For some reason today's casualties were mostly leg wounds, so that the men, set in plaster, had something of the look of bits of broken statuary. Nobody acutely bad. Nobody screaming, anyway.

Miss Burke got into the stifling plane and sat down on the edge of the iron seat opposite the door. One of the ground boys came almost directly afterwards and shut the door, and in that moment all the dazzling dustiness of the afternoon was shut away. Miss Burke sat with her hands in her pockets, listening to first one and then the other of the engines being started, until both were roaring together. Then as the plane began slowly to move out, away from dispersal tents, to the open runway, she glanced impersonally up at the wounded, suspended like a double row of carcasses in oblong hammocks. They were all quite quiet.

As the plane turned into the runway and then began to move down it, in a moment or two very fast, Miss Burke hung on to the nearest strap. There were no belts in the Dakota, but she liked to hang on to the strap just in case. The runway seemed to bump a little, and it did not occur to her, until she suddenly looked up, that there might be, for men on those slightly swaying stretchers, a feeling of insecurity. Even then she did not move. If anything happened you were all helpless anyway.

It was only when she saw an arm being slowly lifted up and down from the foremost stretcher that she realized something was wrong. The signal annoyed her a little. No sooner airborne than somebody, she thought, starts binding. They were hardly even airborne. That was men, if you like, all over. The plane lifted itself off the earth exactly at the moment that her own impatience lifted her mind, and in the same way: in a slow, unsurprising pull, as of something so often repeated that it had ceased to astonish her.

She walked up the body of the plane, levelled out now, to where the hand was waving limply to beckon her. It was one of the leg cases: an English boy with his left leg entirely encased, like a piece of masonry. His face had once been very brown, but now it had turned, under shock, to the lustreless colour of the dust they had left behind. She saw at once, by trained instinct, that he was very tired.

'Something wrong?' She had trained herself to speak not loudly but visually, with exaggerated movement of her big Irish lips, so that now, at once, the boy was sure what he said. She had trained herself also to record answers, and those also visually, so as not to strain herself against the noise of the plane.

'Are we up?' the boy said.

For crying out loud, Miss Burke thought, where in the name of God does he think we are? Only a man would ask it. She looked out of the window. They had climbed to four or five hundred feet, and down below, already, the tents of the airfield had begun to look like sunbaked seashells on a sandy lake between stunted fringes of palms. Beyond this, in all directions, low jungle was assuming a dark wavy relief, spreading outward in huge monotonous sections, unbroken except by the sulphury veins of tiny roads.

She turned her head and nodded. She did not know if there was anything she could say. Idiotic to ask him if by any chance he thought they weren't going to get up. Idiotic to discuss remote chances against the roar of two engines. She swallowed hard, and the noise of engines changed its note. Idiotic to talk to him, anyway.

'How long shall we be?' the boy said.

'I wouldn't be knowin',' Miss Burke said. 'We'll get there when we'll get there.'

'Where are we going?'

'I wouldn't be knowin' that either,' she said. 'Maybe we're taking you to Comilla. Maybe we're not.'

He moved restlessly, troubled, turned his head towards her, and then, seeing the window, turned it abruptly back again. She knew then that he was afraid of looking out of the plane; she knew that he had never flown before. Of course that was idiotic too, and she wasn't going to have any unprofessional nonsense about it. 'All you have to do is shut your eyes and get some sleep,' she said. 'The other boys are asleep. Now come along.'

'I can't,' the boy said. As he shook his head she saw how deeply the eyes had receded through shock and exhaustion and pure pain.

'What do you mean, you can't?' she said. 'Of course you can. If you can't sleep you can shut your eyes.'

'That's what I can't do,' the boy said. 'I can't shut them. They won't shut. They won't stay shut.'

She swallowed hard and did not answer. Really it was very exhausting talking like this against the noise of engines; it couldn't go on. She looked down with severity at the agitated face, with its dark eyes so sharply impelled by shock that they had become frozenly transfixed, but for some reason or other she did not know what to say. And while she was trying to make up her mind the boy began talking again, this time not exactly to her, not in continuance of anything that had been said before, but simply in pure aimless relief and excitement. She had sense enough to let him go on. And after a moment or two, hearing all the time less than half he said, she sat down on the seat again and rested her head back against the metal of the fuselage, in a pretence of listening. She realized then that all he needed was an object of reception for the things he had to say, and that its identity did not matter much, nor what it said in answer. And so she let him go on, while the plane flew steadily on its level course at about four thousand feet, over the green-encrusted contours of jungle and palm-fenced strips of water glittering in the white heat of afternoon.

For the next half hour she caught at intervals some intelligible phrase in the jumble of things he had to say, and now and then she would nod automatically in reply, as if to indicate that she was still listening. She was not so much bored as very sleepy herself. She expected him at any moment to talk about his mother. For God's sake, she thought, they're just like babies.

The more you sympathize with them the more you may. She was determined not to hear any nonsense like that; she never did. But twice in quick succession the aircraft suddenly gave a violent bump in the heat. It was nothing serious, but it threw her about the seat with a jerk, and she saw the boy's hand flung out as if to save himself from falling. She stretched up and caught it and held it in hers. The palm was clammy with sweat.

'We'll be all right when we're over the sea,' she said. 'It's just the heat. That's all.'

He turned to her and gave her a slow and possibly apathetic smile. For God's sake, she thought, I hope he's not going to be sick. Not that I ought to pander to any of this emotional nonsense at all. Not that I should be doing it. I shouldn't be doing it. What in the name o' God would Johnson say if she could see me? Johnson was a sister up at Comilla. They shared a tent and called each other Johnson and Burke, as if Christian names were a soft concession not to be tolerated. In three years they had watched a constant stream of mutilated men come down from the front, in heat and in rain, at all times of the year, from every quarter from Imphal down to Akyab and Mandalay. It was one of her ambitions to see Mandalay.

'Did you come down from Mandalay?' she said to the boy.

'That's where I got it,' he said, and pointed down to the leg.

'Ah,' she said.

'Two days ago.' His face was restless with fresh anxiety, the lids of the eyes stiffly held open. And then suddenly he came to the point of it all; he made a sudden wild grab as it were at the hot core of his own personal catastrophe: the thing that had been troubling him all the time. 'I was time-expired,' he said. 'Time-expired. Three more days and I'd have had this bloody country.' He grew for a moment or two pathetically excited. 'I'd have had it. I was going home.'

Weak and immobile, his eyes held in them the smallest of solitary tears, so that even Miss Burke was for a moment or two touched by them in spite of herself. Now she knew why he could not shut his eyes. She did not know what to say, and suddenly the boy was silent too. She waited for some moments for him to speak again, but he was still quiet, and at last she said: 'Well, you'll be going home now. It's all the same. You'll be going home, anyway.'

He did not answer even that. Now that at last he had been able to disclose the pain that really bothered him, it was as if it had never existed. It was not the wound but the circumstances that seemed to be destroyed by the wound that troubled him. He seemed quite at rest because of Miss Burke's understanding.

Miss Burke looked out of the small round window of the plane. Below, the jungle was breaking up, and rivers in which she could see shadows of pale brown sand-like muscles under the transparent blue skin of water were beginning to appear and broaden among the mass of trees. She knew that they were coming to the sea.

She sat thinking about the boy being time-expired. Yes, she understood that. There was no one in the whole country who would not understand it. To be going home, to be at the end of exile: for God's sake who didn't know? One day she would be time-expired too. It was only at the rarest moments that she could think of it. But one day it would happen. She would be time-expired and there would be an end for her of the heat and sweat and the dust of summer and the miserable steaming nights of the monsoon, and the callous clash of death in every part of her life. There would be an end of the grey vultures feeding on the dead. They said time went quickly in the East, and that after a while you could not separate the memory of one individual day from another. But what happened really was that time built itself up into a mass of hard white light behind you, like an impersonal and glittering wall that cut you off from the shadowy remembrances of all your life behind it. That was what she hated; she knew that that was what the soldier hated, what they all hated. To be time-expired meant that you were going to break down that wall, break through it, break out into the resurrected memory of a sort of life that mattered.

She had worked through the heat of the plains for three steaming summers without trying to think of it too much. They used to say that it was not the climate for white women—no, it was certainly not the climate. Nor was war exactly their destiny either. But there you are: in time you took the heat and the dust and the war and the blood and all the lunatic filth of India because there was nothing else you could do. You were caught in a violent trap. You had to stay. And your only hope of escape from it was that somewhere, some time, if you were lucky, and if you could outlive the heat and the cancer of your unshed tears, you would become, at last, time-expired. You would be going home.

She looked down out of the window and there now, breaking in a series of glistening lines of white contour that seemed transfixed against the strip of yellow stand, was the sea. Did anyone at home, she thought, understand what it meant?

There were times when she thought that the whole front—all of them, the men, the pilots, the nurses—had been forgotten. They had sometimes said it themselves: a forgotten army of forgotten men. They had been overshadowed—oh yes, she knew that; but the shadow of it did not darken the heat or diminish the glassy impact of their time in exile.

For God's sake there was no use thinking about it. 'We are over the sea now,' she said to the boy. 'Going up the coast.'

He smiled. 'First time I've flown,' he said.

And God knows, she thought, you're a lucky man to be able to fly. Do you know where you'd be if it weren't for the Daks, coming to fetch you out? You'd be time-expired all right. You'd be rotting forgotten somewhere up in that God-forsaken jungle because there'd be no way of getting you out. You, and the Lord knew how many more—you'd have just died up there, wherever you lay. You should all of you go down, she thought, on your bended knees and thank the stars of heaven there were enough Daks to feed and water and supply you, and then when you were wounded bring you out again.

She rested her head against the fuselage and shut her eyes for the first time. Her ears had become slightly blocked by the noise of engines and she had forgotten to swallow and it was quite quiet in her head. Shut away into her own world, she gave herself up to a momentary contemplation of things that were not real. She began to allow herself to think that she, too, was going home. There were no longer any blistering dusty airstrips, no longer any hordes of vultures pouring like bloated grey beetles over the carcasses of the dead, no longer any savage steaming days when you hated the sun. There was no longer any exile, no longer any of that arid female life in transit camps, or of a life with men who, because they were fighting or tired or occupied elsewhere, did not want you. There was an end of all the callous futility of war. She was going home to a place where rain fell deeply and quietly on green grass, not with the madness of the monsoon, and where the pure light and penetration of it would wash the dust for ever out of her bones.

She held on to these thoughts for the remaining half hour of the flight. The wounded all about her were very quiet. The boy made no more attempt to speak to her until the aircraft, banking, began to make its circuit of the field. Even then she did not open her eyes, but clung on a little longer to an inner world remote from everything she knew to be real. She even shut her eyes a little tighter and held her hands painfully on the edges of the metal seat and thought: 'God, how much longer? How much longer? How much, much longer?'

And then her eyes were open. She made them open with brutal suddenness. She stood up on her feet and saw that the boy's stretcher was swaying slightly as the aircraft turned. She held it still again, with instinctive efficiency.

'Coming in to land,' she said, and stood looking down at him. Once again he smiled, and once again she was aware of his helplessness: that same childish masculine helplessness that was always drawing forth her contempt. But she was not contemptuous now.

'Where's your home?' she said.

'Shropshire,' he said.

'Nice there?'

He nodded and smiled, but did not speak. She saw a small glint of tears in his eyes again and thought: 'For God's sake, any moment now, and he'll be asking me for my address.'

And I am not, she thought, having any of that.

She turned away and looked out of the window and saw the landscape below coming to life: palms beyond the black runway, bright fronds of banana trees drooping in the heat, a mass of crimson bougainvillea flaming by a long cane basha, some coolies running. In a few moments it was all flattening out and seeming suddenly to take on its own speed, and presently she knew by the bump of the wheels that they were down.

As the Dakota taxied to dispersal she turned for the last time to look at the boy. He was relieved and glad that the flight was over. It would be a long time before he was well, but before long, if he were lucky, he would be going home. He at last was really time-expired.

'Shropshire for you,' she said, and then walked briskly back through the aircraft just as the pilot cut the engines. There was no sense waiting for an answer.

She stood by the big double doors of the Dakota, and in a moment or two, when they were opened, all the heat and glare of the afternoon rushed in and oppressingly dazzled her face. She helped get the steps out herself, and was the first person to go down them.

She jumped down on the hot sandy concrete and looked about her. For God's sake, nothing but men. All helpless as usual. All standing about and gaping as if they'd never seen a man on a stretcher before. Two clots of Indian drivers were propping up the two ambulances, and two British boys, bare to the waist and brown as burnt butter, were not much better.

'Come on, come on,' Miss Burke said. 'Come on!'

She stood in the fierce sunlight waiting for the stretchers to come out of the plane. To her they came out as they had gone in: a series of anonymous oblongs, plaster-encased, like lumps of nameless statuary. She did not even know which of them differed from another. Even when the boy from Shropshire was brought out, last but one, eyes fixed upon her as if either searching for a sign of friendliness or as if she were something very wonderful, she did not glance at him in return.

Instead she walked deliberately away from the plane to where, by the ambulances, there was some confusion now. The clots couldn't count the ambulance capacity and were trying to get in more men than the vehicles would hold. For the love of God, for God's sake, she thought, just like men. As helpless as babies. Just like men.

'Can't you count now?' she said, raising her voice. 'It's the bunch of wetheads you are, isn't it? You clots, you deadbeats! Can't you see there's a man lying in the sun? Is it round the damn bend all of you are? Get that man out of the sun!'

She marched about among the men and the waiting stretchers with intense impatience, her voice hard and strong and her eyes impersonal as last again in the deadly glare of light.

'Do you think we've got the whole of life to spend here?' she said. 'Do you think we've nothing else to do?'

A Christmas Song

She gave lessons in voice-training in the long room above the music shop. Her pupils won many examinations and were afterwards very successful at local concerts and sometimes in giving lessons in voice-training to other pupils. She herself had won many examinations and everybody said how brilliant she was.

Every Christmas, as this year, she longed for snow. It gave a transfiguring gay distinction to a town that otherwise had none. It lifted up the squat little shops, built of red brick with upper storeys of terra-cotta; it made the roofs down the hill like glistening cakes; it even gave importance to the stuffy gauze-windowed club where local gentlemen played billiards and solo whist over meagre portions of watered whisky. One could imagine, with the snow, that one was in Bavaria or Vienna or the Oberland, and that horse-drawn sleighs, of which she read in travel guides, would glide gracefully down the ugly hill from the gasworks. One could imagine Evensford, with its many hilly little streets above the river, a little Alpine town. One could imagine anything. Instead there was almost always rain and long columns of working-class mackintoshes floating down a street that was like a dreary black canal. Instead of singing Mozart to the snow she spent long hours selling jazz sheet-music to factory workers and earned her reward, at last, on Christmas Eve, by being bored at the Williamsons' party.

Last year she had sung several songs at the Williamsons' party. Some of the men, who were getting hearty on mixtures of gin and port wine, had applauded in the wrong places, and Freddy Williamson had bawled out 'Good old Clara!'

She knew the men preferred Effie. Her sister was a very gay person although she did not sing; she had never passed an examination in her life, but there was, in a strange way, hardly anything you felt she could not do. She had a character like a chameleon; she had all the love affairs. She laughed a great deal, in rippling infectious scales, so that she made other people begin laughing, and she had large violet-blue eyes. Sometimes she laughed so much that Clara herself would begin weeping.

This year Clara was not going to the Williamsons' party; she had made up her mind. The Williamsons were in leather; they were very successful and had a large early Edwardian house with bay-windows and corner cupolas and bathroom windows of stained glass overlooking the river. They were fond of giving parties several times a year. Men who moved only in Rotarian or gold circles turned up with wives whose corset suspenders could be seen like bulging pimples under sleek dresses. About midnight Mrs Williamson grew rowdy and began rushing from room to room making love to other men. The two Williamson boys, George and Freddy, became rowdy too, and took off their jackets and did muscular and noisy gymnastics with the furniture.

At four o'clock she went upstairs to close the windows of the music-room and pull the curtains and make up the fire. It was raining in misty delicate drops and the air was not like Christmas. In the garden there were lime trees and their dark red branches, washed with rain, were like glowing veins in the deep blue air.

As she was coming out of the room her sister came upstairs.

'Oh! there you are. There's a young man downstairs who wants a song and doesn't know the name.'

'It's probably a Danny Kaye. It always is.'

'No it isn't. He says it's a Christmas song.'

'I'll come,' she said. Then half-way downstairs she stopped; she remembered what it was she was going to say to Effie. 'By the way, I'm not coming to the party,' she said.

'Oh! Clara, you promised. You always come.'

'I know; but I'm tired, and I don't feel like coming and there it is.'

'The Williamsons will never let you get away with it,' her sister said. 'They'll drag you by force.'

'I'll see about this song,' she said. 'What did he say it was?'

'He says it's a Christmas song. You'll never get away with it. They'll never let you.'

She went down into the shop. Every day people came into the shop for songs whose names they did not know. 'It goes like this,' they would say, 'or it goes like that.' They would try humming a few notes and she would take it up from them; it was always something popular, and in the end, with practice, it was never very difficult.

A young man in a brown overcoat with a brown felt hat and an umbrella stood by the sheet-music counter. He took off his hat when she came up to him.

'There was a song I wanted—'

'A carol?' she said.

'No, a song,' he said. 'A Christmas song.'

He was very nervous and kept rolling the ferrule of the umbrella on the floor linoleum. He wetted his lips and would not look at her.

'If you could remember the words?'

'I'm afraid I can't.'

'How does it go? Would you know that?'

He opened his mouth either as if to begin singing a few notes or to say something. But nothing happened and he began biting his lip instead.

'If you could remember a word or two,' she said. 'Is it a new song?'

'You see, I think it's German,' he said.

'Oh,' she said. 'Perhaps it's by Schubert?'

'It sounds awfully silly, but I simply don't know. We only heard it once,' he said.

He seemed about to put on his hat. He ground the ferrule of the umbrella into the linoleum. Sometimes it happened that people were too shy even to hum the notes of the song they wanted, and suddenly she said:

'Would you care to come upstairs? We might find it there.'

Upstairs in the music room she sang the first bars of one or two songs by Schubert. She sat at the piano and he stood respectfully at a distance, leaning on the umbrella, too shy to interrupt her. She sang a song by Brahms and he listened hopefully. She asked him if these were the songs, but he shook his head, and finally, after she had sung another song by Schubert, he blurted out:

'You see, it isn't actually a Christmas song. It is, and it isn't. It's more that it makes you think of Christmas—'

'Is it a love song?'

'Yes.'

She sang another song by Schubert; but it was not the one he wanted; and at last she stood up. 'You see, there are so many love songs—'

'Yes, I know, but this one is rather different somehow.'

'Couldn't you bring her in?' she said. 'Perhaps she would remember?'

'Oh! no,' he said. 'I wanted to find it without that.'

They went downstairs and several times on the way down he thanked her for singing. 'You sing beautifully,' he said. 'You would have liked this song.'

'Come in again if you think of it,' she said. 'If you can only think of two or three bars.'

Nervously he fumbled with the umbrella and then quickly put on his hat and then as quickly took it off again. He thanked her for being so kind, raising his hat a second time. Outside the shop he put up the umbrella too sharply, and a breeze, catching it, twisted him on the bright pavement and bore him out of sight.

Rain fell gently all evening and customers came in and shook wet hats on bright pianos. She walked about trying to think of the song the young man wanted. Songs by Schubert went through her head and became mixed with the sound of carols from gramophone cubicles and she was glad when the shop had closed.

Effie began racing about in her underclothes, getting ready for the party. 'Clara, you can't mean it that you're not coming.'

'I do mean it. I'm always bored and they really don't want me.'

'They love you.'

'I can't help it. I made up my mind last year. I never enjoy it, and they'll be better without me.'

'They won't let you get away with it,' Effie said. 'I warn you they'll come and fetch you.'

At eight o'clock her father and mother drove off with Effie in the Ford. She went down through the shop and unbolted the front door and let them out into the street. 'The stars are shining,' her mother said. 'It's getting colder.' She stood for a second or two in the doorway, looking up at the stars and thinking that perhaps, after all, there was a touch of frost in the air.

'Get ready!' Effie called from the car. 'You know what the Williamsons are!' and laughed with high infectious scales so that her mother and father began laughing too.

After the car had driven away she bolted the door and switched off the front shop bell. She went upstairs and put on her dressing-gown and tried to think once again of the song the young man had wanted. She played over several songs on the piano, singing them softly.

At nine o'clock something was thrown against the side street window and she heard Freddy Williamson bawling:

'Who isn't coming to the party? Open the window.'

She went to the window and pulled back the curtain and stood looking down. Freddy Williamson stood in the street below and threw his driving gloves at her.

'Get dressed! Come on!'

She opened the window.

'Freddy, be quiet. People can hear.'

'I want them to hear. Who isn't coming to whose party? I want them to hear.'

He threw the driving gloves up at the window again.

'Everybody is insulted!' he said. 'Come on.'

'Please,' she said.

'Let me in then!' he bawled. 'Let me come up and talk to you.'

'All right,' she said.

She went downstairs and let him in through the shop and he came up to the music room, shivering, stamping enormous feet.

'Getting colder,' he kept saying. 'Getting colder.'

'You should put on an overcoat,' she said.

'Never wear one.' he said. 'Can't bear to be stuffed up.'

'Then don't grumble because you're starved to death.'

He stamped up and down the room, a square-bonded young man with enormous lips and pink flesh and small poodle-like eyes, pausing now and then to rub his hands before the fire.

'The Master sends orders you're to come back with me,' he said, 'and she absolutely won't take no for an answer.'

'I'm not coming,' she said.

'Of course you're coming! I'll have a drink while you get ready.'

'I'll pour you a drink,' she said, 'but I'm not coming. What will you have?'

'Gin,' he said. 'Clara, sometimes you're the most awful bind.'

She poured the drink, not answering. Freddy Williamson lifted the glass and said:

'Sorry, didn't mean that. Happy Christmas. Good old Clara.'

'Happy Christmas.'

'Good old Clara. Come on, let's have one for Christmas.'

Freddy Williamson put clumsy hands across her shoulders, kissing her with lips rather like those of a heavy wet dog.

'Good old Clara,' he said again. 'Good old girl.'

Songs kept crossing and recrossing her mind, bewildering her into moments of dreamy distraction. She had the feeling of trying to grasp something that was floating away.

'Don't stand there like a dream,' Freddy Williamson said. 'Put some clothes on. Come on.'

'I'm going to tie up Christmas presents and then go to bed.'

'Oh! Come on, Clara, come on. Millions of chaps are there, waiting.'

She stood dreamily in the centre of the room, thinking of the ardent shy young man who could not remember the song.

'You're such a dream,' Freddy Williamson said. 'You just stand there. You've got to snap out of yourself.'

Suddenly he pressed himself against her in attitudes of muscular, heavier love, grasping her about the waist, partly lifting her from the floor, his lips wet on her face.

'Come on, Clara,' he kept saying, 'let the blinds up. Can't keep the blinds down for ever.'

'Is it a big party?'

'Come on, let the blinds up.'

'How can I come to the party if you keep holding me here?'

'Let the blinds up and come to the party too,' he said. 'Eh?'

'No.'

'Well, one more kiss,' he said. He smacked at her lips with his heavy dog-like mouth, pressing her body backwards. 'Good old Clara. All you got to do is let yourself go. Come on—let the blinds up. Good old Clara.'

'All right. Let me get my things on,' she said. 'Get yourself another drink while you're waiting.'

'Fair enough. Good old Clara.'

While she went away to dress he drank gin and stumped about the room. She came back in her black coat with a black and crimson scarf on her head and Freddy Williamson said: 'Whizzo. That's better. Good old Clara,' and kissed her again, running clumsy ruffling hands over her face and neck and hair.

When they went downstairs someone was tapping lightly on the glass of the street door. 'Police for the car,' Freddy Williamson said. 'No lights or some damn thing,' but when she opened the door it was the young man who could not remember the song. He stood there already raising his hat:

'I'm terribly sorry. Oh! you're going out. Excuse me.'

'Did you remember it?' She said.

'Some of it,' he said. 'The words.'

'Come in a moment,' she said.

He came in from the street and she shut the door. It was dark in the shop, and he did he did not seem so nervous. He began to say: 'It goes rather like this—I can't remember it all. But something like this—*Leise flehen meine Lieder—Liebchen, komm zu mir—*'

'It is by Schubert,' she said.

She went across the shop and sat down at one of the pianos and began to sing it for him. She heard him say, 'That's it. That's the one,' and Freddy Williamson fidgeted with the latch of the shop door as he kept one hand on it, impatient to go.

'It's very beautiful,' the young man said. 'It's not a Christmas song, but somehow—'

Freddy Williamson stamped noisily into the street, and a second or two later she heard him start up the car. The door catch rattled where he had left it open and a current of cold air blew into the dark shop.

She had broken off her singing because, after the first verse, she could not remember the words. *Softly fly my songs—Loved one, come to me*—she was not sure how it went after that.

'I'm sorry I can't remember the rest,' she said.

'It's very kind of you,' he said. The door irritated her by banging on its catch. She went over and shut it and out in the street Freddy Williamson blew impatiently on the horn of the car.

'Was it the record you wanted?' she said. 'There is a very good on—'

'If it's not too much trouble.'

'I think I can find it,' she said. 'I'll put on the light.'

As she looked for the record and found it, she sang the first few bars of it again. 'There is great tenderness in it,' she began to say. 'Such a wonderful tenderness,' but suddenly it seemed as if the young man was embarrassed. He began fumbling in his pocket-book for his money, but she said, 'Oh! no. Pay after Christmas. Pay any time,' and at the same moment Freddy Williamson opened the door of the shop and said:

'What goes on? After hours, after hours. Come on.'

'I'm just coming,' she said.

'I'll say good might,' the young man said. 'I'm very grateful. I wish you a Happy Christmas.'

'Happy Christmas.' she said.

Outside the stars were green and sharp in a sky without wind; the street had dried except for dark prints of frost on pavements.

'Damn cool,' Freddy Williamson kept saying. 'Damn cool.'

He drove rather fast, silent and a little sulky, out towards the high ground overlooking the river. Rain had been falling everywhere through all the first weeks of December and now as the car came out on the valley edge she could see below her a great pattern of winter floodwater, the hedgerows cutting it into rectangular lakes glittering with green and yellow lights from towns on the far side.

'I'd have told him to go to hell,' Freddy Williamson said. 'I call it damn cool. Damn cool.'

'See the floods,' she said. 'There'll be skating.'

'The damn cheek people have,' Freddy Williamson said. 'Damn cheek.'

He drove the car with sulky abandon into the gravel drive of the big Edwardian house. Dead chestnut leaves swished away on all sides, harsh and brittle, and she could see frost white on the edges of the big lawn.

'One before we go in,' Freddy Williamson said. She turned away her mouth but he caught it with clumsy haste, like a dog seizing a brid. 'Good old Clara. Let the blinds up. It's Christmas Eve.'

'Put the car away and I'll wait for you,' she said.

'Fair enough,' he said. 'Anything you say. Good old Clara. Damn glad you come.'

She got out of the car and stood for a few moments looking down the valley. She bent down and put her hands on the grass. Frost was crisp and had already, and she could see it sparkling brightly on tree branches and on rain-soaked stems of dead flowers. It made her breath glisten in the house-lights coming across the lawn. It seemed to be glittering even on the long wide floodwaters, so that she almost persuaded herself the valley was one great river of ice already, wonderfully transformed.

Standing there, she thought of the young man, with his shy ardent manner, his umbrella and his raised hat. The song he had not been able to remember began to go through her head again—*Softly fly my songs*—*Loved one, come to me*—; but at that moment Freddy Williamson came blundering up the drive and seized her once again like a hungry dog.

'One before we go in,' he said. 'Come on. Good old Clara. One before we go in. Good show.'

Shrieks of laughter came suddenly from the house as if some one, perhaps her sister, had ignited little fires of merriment that were crackling at the windows.

'Getting worked up!' Freddy Williamson said. 'Going to be good!'

She felt the frost crackling under her feet. She grasped at something that was floating away. *Leise flehen meine Lieder*—*Oh! my loved one*—how did it go?

The Evolution of Saxby

I first met him on a black wet night towards the end of the war, in one of those station buffets where the solitary spoon used to be tied to the counter by a piece of string.

He stood patiently waiting for his turn with this spoon, spectacled and undemonstrative and uneager, in a shabby queue, until at last the ration of sugar ran out and nobody had any need for the spoon any longer. As he turned away he caught sight of me stirring my coffee with a key. It seemed to impress him, as if it were a highly original idea he had never thought of, and the thickish spectacles, rather than his own brown kidney-like eyes, gave me an opaque glitter of a smile.

'That's rather natty,' he said.

As we talked he clutched firmly to his chest a black leather brief-case on which the monogram of some government department had been embossed in gilt letters that were no longer clear enough to read. He wore a little homberg hat, black, neat, the fraction of a size too small for him, so that it perched high on his head. In peace-time I should have looked for a rose in his buttonhole, and in peace-time, as it afterwards turned out, I often did; and I always found one there.

In the train on which we travelled together he settled himself down in the corner, under the glimmer of those shaded bluish lights we have forgotten now, and opened his brief-case and prepared, as I thought, to read departmental minutes or things of that sort.

Instead he took out his supper. He unfolded with care what seemed to be several crackling layers of disused wallpaper. He was evidently very hungry, because he took out the supper with a slow relish that was also wonderfully eager, revealing the meal as consisting only of sandwiches, rather thickly cut.

He begged me to take one of these, saying: 'I hope they're good. I rather think they should be. Anyway they'll make up for what we didn't get at the buffet.' His voice, like all his actions, was uneager, mild and very slow.

I remembered the spoon tied to the counter at the buffet and partly because of it and partly because I did not want to offend him I took one of his sandwiches. He took one too. He said something about never getting time to eat at the department and how glad he would be when all this was over, and then he crammed the sandwich eagerly against his mouth.

The shock on his face was a more powerful reflection of my own. His lips suddenly suppurated with revulsion. A mess of saffron yellow, repulsively mixed with bread, hung for a few moments on the lips that had previously been so undemonstrative and uneager. Then he ripped out his handkerchief and spat.

'Don't eat it,' he said. 'For God's sake don't eat it.' He tore the sandwich apart, showing the inside of it as nothing but a vile mess of meatless, butterless mustard spread on dark war-time bread. 'Give it to me, for God's sake,' he said. 'Give it to me. Please don't have that.'

As he snatched the sandwich away from me and crumpled it into the paper his hands were quivering masses of tautened sinew. He got up so sharply that I thought he would knock his glasses off. The stiff wallpaper-like package cracked in his hands. His handkerchief had fallen to the seat and he could not find it again and in a spasm of renewed revulsion he spat in air.

The next thing I knew was the window-blind going up like a pistol shot and the window clattering down. The force of the night wind blew his hat off. The keen soapy baldness of his head sprang out with an extraordinary effect of nakedness. He gave the revolting yellow-oozing sandwiches a final infuriated beating with his hands and then hurled them far out of the window into blackness, spitting after them. Then he came groping back for his lost handkerchief and having found it sat down and spat into it over and over again, half-retching, trembling with rage.

He left it to me to deal with the window and the black-out blind. I had some difficulty with the blind, which snapped out of my hands before I could fix it satisfactorily.

When I turned round again I had an impression that the sudden snap of the blind had knocked his spectacles off. He was sitting holding them in his hands. He was breathing very heavily. His distraction was intolerable because without the spectacles he really looked like a person who could not see. He seemed to sit there groping blindly, feeble and myopic after his rush of rage.

His sense of caution, his almost fearsome correctness, returned in an expression of concern about the black-out blind. He got up and went, as it were, head-first into his spectacles, as a man dives into the neck of his shirt. When he emerged with the glasses on he realised, more or less sane now, his vision corrected, that I had put up the blind.

'Oh! You've done it,' he said.

A respectable remorse afflicted him.

'Do you think it was seen?' he said. 'I hate doing that sort of thing. I've always felt it rather a point to be decent about the regulations.'

I said it was probably not serious. It was then nearly March, and I said I thought the war was almost over.

'You really think so?' he said. What makes you think that? I've got a sort of ghastly feeling it will last for ever. Sort of tunnel we will never get out of.'

I said that was a feeling everyone got. His spectacles had grown misty again from the sweat of his eyes. He took them off again and began slowly polishing them and, as if the entire hideous episode of the mustard had never happened, stared down into them and said:

'Where do you live? Have you been able to keep your house on?'

I told him where I lived and he said:

'That isn't awfully far from us. We live at Elham Street, by the station. We have a house that practically looks on the station.'

He put on his spectacles and with them all his correctness came back.

'Are you in the country?' he said. 'Really in the country?' and when I said yes he said that was really what he himself wanted to do, live in the country. He wanted a small place with a garden— a garden he could see mature.

'You have a garden?' he said.

'Yes.'

'Nice one?'

'I hope it will be again when this is over.'

'I envy you that,' he said.

He picked up his hat and began brushing it thoughtfully with his coat sleeve. I asked him if he had a garden too and he said:

'No. Not yet. The war and everything—you know how it is.'

He put on his hat with great care, almost reverently.

'Not only that. We haven't been able to find anywhere that really suits my wife. That's our trouble. She's never well.'

'I'm sorry—'

'They can't find out what it is, either,' he said. He remembered his handkerchief and as he folded it up and stuck it in his breast-pocket the combination of handkerchief and homberg and his own unassertive quietness gave him a look that I thought was unexpressibly lonely and grieved.

'We move about trying to find something,' he said, 'but—'

He stopped, and I said I hoped she would soon be well again.

'I'm afraid she never will,' he said. 'It's no use not being frank about it.'

His hands, free now of handkerchief and homberg, demonstrated her fragility by making a light cage in the air. His spectacles gave an impervious glint of resignation that I thought was painful.

'It's one of those damnable mysterious conditions of the heart,' he said. 'She can do things of course. She can get about. But one of these days—'

His hands uplifted themselves and made a light pouf! of gentle extermination.

'That's how it will be,' he said.

I was glad at that moment to hear the train slowing down. He heard it too and got up and began to grope about along the hatrack.

'I could have sworn I had my umbrella,' he said.

'No,' I said.

'That's odd.' His face tightened. An effort of memory brought back to it a queer dry little reflection of the anger he had experienced about the sandwiches of mustard. He seemed about to be infuriated by his own absent-mindedness and then he recovered himself and said:

'Oh! no. I remember now.'

Two minutes later, as the train slowed into the station, he shook me by the hand, saying how pleasant it had been and how much he had enjoyed it all and how he hoped I might one day, after the war, run over and see him if it were not too far.

'I want to talk to you about gardens,' he said.

He stood so smiling and glassy-eyed and uneager again in final goodbye that I began too to feel that his lapse of frenzy about the mustard sandwiches was like one of those episodic sudden bomb-explosions that caught you unawares and five minutes later seemed never to have happened.

'By the way my name is Saxby,' he said. 'I shall look for you on the train.'

Trains are full of men who wear homberg hats and carry brief-cases and forget their umbrellas, and soon, when the war was over, I got tired of looking for Saxby.

Then one day, more than a year later, travelling on a slow train that made halts at every small station on the long high gradient below hills of beech-wood and chalk, I caught sight of a dark pink rose floating serenely across a village platform under a homberg hat.

There was no mistaking Saxby. But for a few seconds, after I had hailed him from the carriage window, it seemed to me that Saxby might have mistaken me. He stared into me with glassy preoccupation. There was a cool and formidable formality about him. For one moment it occurred to me to remind him of the painful episode of the mustard sandwiches, and then a second later he remembered me.

'Of course.' His glasses flashed their concealing glitter of a smile as he opened the carriage door. 'I always remember you because you listen so well.'

This was a virtue of which he took full advantage in the train.

'Yes, we've been here all summer,' he said. 'You can very nearly see the house from the train.' This time he had his umbrella with him and with its crooked malacca handle he pointed south-westward through the open window, along the chalk hillside. 'No. The trees are rather too dense. In the early spring you could see it. We had primroses then. You know, it's simply magnificent country.'

'How is your wife?' I said.

The train, charging noisily into the tunnel, drowned whatever he had to say in answer. He rushed to shut the window against clouds of yellow tunnel fumes and suddenly I was reminded of his noisy and furious charge at the window in the black-out, his nauseated frenzy about the sandwiches. And again it seemed, like an episodic explosion, like the war itself, an unreality that had never happened.

When we emerged from the tunnel black-out into bright summer he said:

'Did you ask me something back there?'

'Your wife,' I said. 'I wondered how she was.'

The railway cutting at that point is a high white declivity softened by many hanging cushions of pink valerian and he stared at it with a sort of composed sadness before he answered me.

'I'm afraid she's rather worse if anything,' he said. 'You see, it's sort of progressive—an accumulative condition if you understand what I mean. It's rather hard to explain.'

He bent his face to the rose in his buttonhole and seemed to draw from it, sadly, a kind of contradictory inspiration about his wife and her painfully irremediable state of health.

It was rather on the lines of what diabetics had, he said. The circle was vicious. You got terribly hungry and terribly thirsty and yet the more you took in the worse it was. With the heart it was rather the same. A certain sort of heart bred excitement and yet was too weak to take it. It was rather like over-loading an electric circuit. A fuse had to blow somewhere and sometime.

Perhaps my failure to grasp this was visible in my stare at the railway cutting.

'You see, with electricity it's all right. The fuse blows and you put in another fuse. But with people the heart's the fuse. It blows and—'

Once again he made the light pouf! of extermination with his hands.

I said how sorry I was about all this and how wretched I thought it must be for him.

'I get used to it,' he said. 'Well, not exactly used to it if you understand what I mean. But I'm prepared. I live in a state of suspended preparation.'

That seemed to me so painful a way of life that I did not answer.

'I'm ready for it,' he said quietly and without any sort of detectable desire for sympathy at all. 'I know it will just happen at any moment. Any second it will all be over.'

There was something very brave about that, I thought.

'Well anyway the war's over,' he said cheerfully. 'That at least we've got to be thankful for. And we've got this house, which is awfully nice, and we've got the garden, which is nicer still.'

'You must be quite high there,' I said, 'on the hill.'

'Nearly five hundred feet,' he said. 'It's a stiffish climb.'

I said I hoped the hills were not too much for his wife and he said:

'Oh! she hardly ever goes out. She's got to that stage.'

But the garden, it seemed, was wonderful. He was settling down to the garden. That was his joy. Carnations and phloxes did awfully well there and, surprisingly enough, roses. It was a *Betty Uprichard*, he said, in his buttonhole. That was one of his favourites and so were *Etoile d' Hollande* and *Madame Butterfly*. They were the old ones and on the whole he did not think you could beat the old ones.

'I want gradually to have beds of them,' he said. 'Large beds of one sort in each. But you need time for that of course. People say you need the right soil for roses—but wasn't there someone who said that to grow roses you first had to have roses in your heart?'

'There was someone who said that,' I said.

'It's probably right,' he said, 'but I think you probably need permanence more. Years and years in one place. Finding out what sorts will do for you. Settling down. Getting the roots anchored—you know?'

The sadness in his face was so peculiar as he said all this that I did not answer.

'Have you been in your house long?' he said.

'Twenty years,' I said.

'Really,' he said. His eyes groped with diffused wonder at this. 'That's marvellous. That's a lifetime.'

For the rest of the way we talked—or rather he did, while I did my virtuous act of listening—about the necessity of permanence in living, the wonder of getting anchored down.

'Feeling your own roots are going deeper all the time. Feeding on the soil underneath you,' he said. 'You know? Nothing like it. No desk stuff can ever give you that.'

And then, as the train neared the terminus, he said:

'Look. You must come over. I'd love you to see the place. I'd love to ask you things. I know you're a great gardener. There must be lots you could tell me. Would you come? I'd be awfully grateful if you'd care to come.'

I said I should be delighted to come.

'Oh! good, oh! good,' he said.

He produced from his vest-pocket the inevitable diary with a silver pencil and began flicking over its leaves.

'Let's fix it now. There's nothing like fixing it now. What about Saturday?'

'All right,' I said.

'Good. Saturday's a good day,' he said.

He began to pencil in the date and seemed surprised, as he suddenly looked up, that I was not doing the same.

'Won't you forget? Don't you put it down?'

'I shall remember,' I said.

'I have to put everything down,' he said. 'I'm inclined to forget. I get distracted.'

So it would be two-thirty or about that on Saturday, he said, and his enthusiasm at the prospect of this was so great that it was, in fact, almost a distraction. He seemed nervously uplifted. He shook hands with energetic delight, repeating several times a number of precise and yet confusing instructions as to how to get to the house, and I was only just in time to save him from a spasm of forgetfulness.

'Don't forget your umbrella,' I said.

'Oh! Good God, no,' he said. 'You can't miss it,' he said, meaning the house. 'It's got a sort of tower on the end of it. Quite a unique affair. You can't miss it. I shall look out for you.'

The house was built of white weatherboard and tile and it hung on the steep chalk-face with the precise and arresting effect of having been carved from the stone. The tower of which Saxby had spoken, and which as he said was impossible to miss, was nothing more than a railed balcony that somebody had built on the roof of a stable, a kind of look-out for a better view. That day it was crutched with scaffolding. In the yard below it there were many piles of builders' rubble and sand and broken timber and beams torn from their sockets. A bloom of cement dust lay thick on old shrubberies of lilac and flowing currant, and in the middle of a small orchard a large pit had been dug. From it too, in the dry heat of summer, a white dust had blown thickly, settling on tall yellow grass and apple leaves and vast umbrellas of seeding rhubarb.

There was nowhere any sign of the garden of which Saxby had spoken so passionately.

It took me some time, as he walked with me to and fro between the derelict boundaries of the place, to grasp that this was so. He was full of explanations: not apologetic, not in the form of excuses but, surprisingly, very pictorial. He drew for me a series of pictures of the ultimate shapes he planned. As we walked armpit deep through grass and thistle—the thistle smoking with dreamy seed in the hot air as we brushed it—he kept saying:

'Ignore this. This is nothing. This will be lawn. We'll get round to this later.' Somebody had cut a few desultory swathes through the jungle with a scythe, and a rabbit got up from a seat in a swathe that crackled like tinder as it leapt away. 'Ignore this—imagine this isn't here.'

Beyond this jungle we emerged to a fence-line on the crest of the hill. The field beyond it lay below us on a shelf and that too, it seemed, belonged to him.

Spreading his hands about, he drew the first of his pictures. There were several others, later, but that was the important one. The farther you got down the slope, it seemed, the better the soil was, and this was his rose garden. These were his beds of *Upichard* and *Madame Butterfly* and *Sylvia* and all the rest. He planned them in the form of a fan. He had worked it out on an arc of intensifying shades of pink and red. Outer tones of flesh would dissolve with graded delicacy through segments of tenderer, deeper pink until they mounted to an inverted pinnacle of rich sparkling duskiness.

'Raher fine,' he said, 'don't you think?' and I knew that as far as he was concerned it actually lay there before him, superbly flourishing and unblemished as in a catalogue.

'Very good,' I said.

'You really think so?' he said. 'I value your opinion terrifically.'

'I think it's wonderful,' I said.

We had waded some distance back through the jungle of smouldering thistle before I remembered I had not seen his wife; and I asked him how she was.

'I fancy she's lying down,' he said. 'She feels the hot weather quite a bit. I think we shall make quite a place of it, don't you?'

He stopped at the point where the grass had been partially mown and waved his hand at the wilderness. Below us lay incomparable country. At that high point of summer it slept for miles in richness. In the hotter, moister valley masses of meadow-sweet spired frothily above its hedgerows, and in its cleared hayfields new-dipped sheep grazed in flocks that were a shade mellower and deeper in colour than the flower.

'It's a marvellous view,' I said.

'Now you get what I mean,' he said. 'The permanence of the thing. You get a view like that and you can sit and look at it for ever.'

Through a further jungle of grass and thistle, complicated at one place by an entire armoury of horseradish, we went into the house.

'Sit down,' Saxby said. 'Make yourself comfortable. My wife will be here in a moment. There will be some tea.'

For the first time since knowing Saxby I became uneasy. It had been my impression for some time that Saxby was a man who enjoyed—rather than suffered from—a state of mild hallucination. Now I felt suddenly that I suffered from it too.

What I first noticed about the room was its windows, shuttered with narrow Venetian blinds of a beautiful shade of grey-rose. They only partially concealed long silk curtains pencilled with bands of fuchsia purple. Most of the furniture was white, but there were a few exquisite Empire chairs in black and the walls were of the same grey-rose tint as the blinds. An amazing arrangement of glass walking-sticks, like rainbows of sweetmeats, was all the decoration the walls had been allowed to receive with the exception of a flower-spangled mirror, mostly in tones of rose and magenta, at the far end. This mirror spread across the entire wall like a lake, reflecting in great width the cool sparkle of the room in which, on the edge of an Empire chair, I sat nervously wondering, as I had done of Saxby's mustard sandwiches, whether what I saw had the remotest connection with reality.

Into this beautiful show-piece came, presently, Mrs Saxby.

Mrs Saxby was an immaculate and disarming woman of fifty with small, magenta-clawed hands. She was dressed coolly in grey silk, almost as if to match the room, and her hair was tinted to the curious shade of blue-grey that you see in fresh carnation leaves. I did not think, that first day, that I had ever met anyone quite so instantly charming, so incessantly alive with compact vibration—or so healthy.

We had hardly shaken hands before she turned to Saxby and said:

'They're coming at six o'clock.'

Saxby had nothing to say in answer to this. But I thought I saw, behind the flattering glasses, a resentful hardening bulge of the kidney-brown eyes.

Not all beautiful women are charming, and not all charming women are intelligent, but Mrs Saxby was both intelligent and charming without being beautiful. We talked a great deal during tea—that is, Mrs Saxby and I talked a great deal, with Saxby putting in the afterthought of a phrase or two here and there.

She mostly ignored this. And of the house, which I admired again and again, she said simply:

'Oh! it's a sort of thing with me. I like playing about with things. Transforming them.'

When she said this she smiled. And it was the smile, I decided, that gave me the clue to the fact that she was not beautiful. Her grey eyes were like two hard pearl buttons enclosed by the narrow dark buttonholes of her short lashes. As with the house, there was not a lash out of place. The smile too came from teeth that were as regular, polished and impersonal as piano keys.

It seemed that tea was hardly over before we saw a car draw up among the rubble outside. In the extraordinary transition to the house I had forgotten the rubble. And now as I became aware of it again it was like being reminded of something unpleasantly chaotic. For some uneasy reason I got to thinking that the inside of the house was Mrs Saxby's palace and that the outside, among the wilderness of plaster and thistle and horse-radish, was Saxby's grave.

The visitors turned out to be a man and wife, both in the sixties, named Bulfield. The woman was composed mainly of a series of droops. Her brown dress drooped from her large shoulders and chest and arms like a badly looped curtain. A treble row of pearls drooped from her neck, from which, in turn, drooped a treble bagginess of skins. From under her eyes drooped pouches that seemed once to have been full of something but that were now merely punctured and drained and flabby. And from her mouth, most of the time, drooped a cigarette from which she could not bother to remove the drooping ashes.

Of Bulfield I do not remember much except that he too was large and was dressed in a tropical suit of white alpaca, with colossal buckskin brogues.

'Would you like a drink first?' Mrs Saxby said, 'or would you like to see the house first?'

'I'd like a drink,' Mrs Bulfield said, obviously speaking for both of them. 'If all the house is as terrific as this it will do me. It's terrific, isn't it, Harry?'

Harry said it was terrific.

Perhaps because of something disturbing about Saxby's silence—he sat defiantly, mutinously sipping glasses of gin for almost an hour with scarcely a word—it came to me only very slowly that the Bulfields had come to buy the place.

It came to me still more slowly—again because I was troubled and confused about Saxby's part in it all—that the reason the Bulfields wanted to buy the house was because they were rising in the world. They sought—in fact desired—to be injected with culture: perhaps not exactly culture, but the certain flavour that they thought culture might bring. After the first World War Bulfield would have been called a profiteer. During the second World War it was, of course, not possible to profiteer; Bulfield had merely made money. Mrs Bulfield must have seen, in magazines and books, perhaps scores of times, pictures of the kind of house Mrs Saxby had created. She must have seen it as a house of taste and culture and she had come to regard these virtues as she might have regarded penicillin. Injected with them, she would be immunised from the danger of contact with lower circumstances. Immunised and elevated, she could at last live in the sort of house she wanted without being able to create for herself but which Mrs Saxby—the sick, slowly expiring Mrs Saxby—had created for her.

This was as much an hallucination as Saxby's own belief that his rose-garden was already there in the wilderness. But all dreams, like fires, need stoking, and for an hour the Bulfields sat stoking theirs. They drank stodgily, without joy, at a sort of unholy communion of whisky. And by seven o'clock Mrs Bulfield was loud and stupefied.

Whether it was the moment Mrs Saxby had been waiting for I don't know, but she suddenly got up from her chair, as full of immaculate and sober charm and vibration as ever, and said:

'Well, would you like to see the rest of the house now?'

'It it's all like this it's as good as done,' Mrs Bulfield said. 'It's absolutely terrific. I think it's perfect—where do you keep the coal?'

Bulfield let out thunderclaps of laughter at this, roaring:

'That's it!—we got to see the coal-hole. We must see that. And the whatsit!—we got to see the whatsit too.'

'I'm sorry, Mrs Bulfield,' Mrs Saxby said. 'Forgive me—perhaps you'd like to see it in any case?'

'Not me. I'm all right,' Mrs Bulfield said. 'I'm like a drain.'

'Coal-hole!' Bulfield said. 'Come on, Ada. Coal-hole! Got to see the coal-hole!'

'You'll excuse us, won't you?' Mrs Saxby said to me, and once again the eyes were buttoned-up, grey and charming as the walls of the house, so pale as to be transparent, so that I could look right through them and see nothing at all beyond.

It must have been a quarter of an hour before Saxby spoke again. He drank with a kind of arithmetical regularity: the glass raised, three sips, the glass down. Then a pause. Then the glass up again, three sips, and the glass down. It seemed to me so like a man determined to drink himself silly that I was intensely relieved when he said:

'Let's get a spot of air. Eh? Outside?'

So we wandered out through the back of the house, and his first act there was to point out to me three or four rose trees actually growing on a wall. A bloom of cement dust covered the scarlet and cream and salmon of the flowers. He regarded them for a few moments with uncertainty, appeared about to say something else about them and then walked on.

His evident determination to say nothing more about one halucination, that of the rose-garden, prepared me for his reluctance to elaborate or surrender another. This was his illusion of the sick, the expiring Mrs Saxby.

'She'll kill herself,' he said. 'She can't stand up to it. She'll just wear herself down to the bone.'

I refrained from saying anything about how healthy I thought Mrs Saxby seemed to be.

'You know how many houses, she's done this to?' he said. 'You want to know?'

I encouraged him and he said:

'Fifteen. We've lived in fifteen houses in twenty years.'

He began to speak of these houses wrathfully, with jealousy and sadness. He spoke with particular bitterness of a house called *The Croft*. I gathered it was a big crude mansion of stone in post-Edwardian style having large bay-windows of indelicate pregnant massiveness pushing out into shrubberies of laurel and a vast plant called a gunnera, a kind of giant's castle rhubarb. 'Like fat great paunches they were, the windows,' he said, 'like great fat commissionaires,' and I could see that he hated them as he might have hated another man.

On one occasion the Saxbys had lived in a windmill. Saxby had spent a winter carrying buckets of water up and down the stairway, eating by the light of hurricane lamps, groping across a dark, stark hillside every morning to catch his train to the office in Whitehall. Then there had been a coastguard's house by the sea. The shore was flat and wind-torn and unembellished by a single feather of tamarisk or sea-holly or rock or weed. Then, because the war came, there were smaller houses: accessible, easy to run, *chic* and clever, sops to the new avidity of war, the new, comfortless servantless heaven for which men were fighting. She roamed restlessly about, looking for, and at, only those places that to other people seemed quite impossible: old Victorian junkeries, old stables, old warehouses, old cart-sheds, a riverside boat-house, bringing to all of them the incessant vibration, the intense metamorphosis of her charm. Her passion for each house was, I gathered, a state of nervous and tearing exultancy. She poured herself into successive transformations with an absorption that was violent. She was like a woman rushing from one amorous orgy to another: hungry and insatiable and drained away.

She had in fact been unfaithful to him for a series of houses; it amounted to that. She had taken love away from him and had given it with discriminate wantonness to bricks and mortar. I do not say she could help this; but that was how I looked at it. She and Saxby had been married rather late. He was reaching the outer boundaries of middle-aged comfort when he first met her. He had wanted, as men do, a place of his own. He had wanted to come home at night to a decent meal, unassertive kindliness and some sense of permanency. Above all the sense of permanency. He had a touching desire to get his roots down: to plant things, invest in earth, reap the reward of sowing and nurturing things in one place.

He came home instead to that quivering febrile vibration of hers that was so astonishing and charming to other poeple—people like me—until he could stand it no longer and could only call it a disease. He was really right when he said there was something wrong with her heart. The profundity of its wrongness was perhaps visible only to him. Case-books had no name for her condition or its symptoms or anything else about her—but he had, and he knew it had turned him into a starved wanderer without a home.

That was the second of his pictures: of Mrs Saxby constantly sick with the pressure of transforming another house, too sick to eat, distraught by builders and decorators and electricians and above all by the ferocious impact of herself. 'She's really ill. You don't see it today. She's really ill. She'll kill herself. She lives at that awful pace—'

The third was of himself.

Did I remember the sandwiches, that first night we had met in the train? That was the sort of thing he had to put up with. Could I imagine anything more hideous than that awful bread and mustard? That had been her idea of his supper.

I thought he might well be sick as he spoke of it. And I even thought for a moment I might be sick too. We had again wandered beyond the house into the wilderness of horse-radish and smoking thistle. In the hot late afternoon a plague of big sizzling flies, a fierce blackish emerald turquoise, had settled everywhere on leaves and thistle-heads, in grass mown and unmown. Our steps exploded them. He swung at these repulsive insect-clouds with his hands, trying to beat them off in futile blasphemies that I felt must be directed, really, in their savagery, against Mrs Saxby. I could not help feeling that, in his helpless fury, he wanted to kill her and was taking it out on the flies.

But he was not taking it out on the flies: not his feelings for Mrs Saxby anyway. He took an enormous half-tipsy swipe at a glittering and bloated mass of files and spat at them:

'Get out, you sickening creepers, get out! You see,' he said to me, 'I wouldn't care so much if it wasn't for the people. She makes all the houses so lovely—she always does it so beautifully—and then she sells them to the most ghastly people. Always the most bloody awful ghastly people. That's what gets me.'

From the house, a moment later, came the sound of Mr Bulfield triumphantly playing with the appurtenances of the whatsit and of Mrs Bulfield, drooping drunkenly from an upstairs window, trumpeting hoarsely in the direction of the rose-garden that was not there:

'Now you've started something. Now you've set him off! He'll spend his life in there.'

And I knew, as Saxby did, that another house had gone.

We met only once more: in the late autumn of that year.

On that occasion we travelled down together, into the country, by the evening train. He seemed preoccupied and did not speak much. I imagined, perhaps, that another house had been begun, that he was off again on his homeless, bread-and-mustard wanderings. But when I spoke of this he simply said:

'The Bulfields haven't even moved in yet. We had some difficulty about another licence for an extension over the stable.'

'How is your wife?' I said.

'She's—'

The word dying was too painful for him to frame. Yet I knew that it was the word he was trying to say to me; because once again, as when I had first met him, he lifted his hands in that little pouf! of sad and light extermination.

'She started another house on the other side of the hill,' he said. 'It was too much for her. After all she can't go on like it for ever—'

After he had got out at the little station I could not help feeling very sorry for him. He had left behind him a queer air of sadness that haunted me—and also, as if in expression of his great distraction, his umbrella.

And because I did not know when I should see him again I drove over, the following afternoon, to the house on the chalk hillside, taking the umbrella with me.

The house stood enchanting in its wilderness of perishing grass and weeds, yellow with the first burning of frost on them, and a maid in a uniform of pale grey-rose—to match, evidently, the exquisite walls of that room in which Belfield had roared his joy over the coal-hole and the whatsit—opened the door to me.

'Is Mr Saxby in?' I said. 'I have brought the umbrella he left in the train.'

'No, sir,' she said. 'But Mrs Saxby is in. Would you care to see Mrs Saxby?'

'Yes,' I said.

I went in and I gave the umbrella to Mrs Saxby. The day was coolish, with clear fresh sunlight. As I came away she stood for a moment or two at the door, talking to me, the light filling her eyes with delicate illumination, giving her once again that look of being full of charm, of being very alive with an effect of compact vibration—and as healthy as ever.

'I am glad you came over once more,' she said. 'We are moving out on Saturday.'

The dead grasses, scorched by summer and now blanched by frost, waved across the white hillside where the rose-garden should have been.

'I'm afraid it's an awful wilderness,' she said. 'But we never touch gardens. That's the one thing people prefer to do for themselves.'

I drove slowly down the hill in cool sunshine. The country was incomparable. The fires of autumn were burning gold and drowsy in the beeches.

If they seemed sadder than usual it was because I thought of Saxby. I wondered how long he had wanted to be free of her and how long he had wanted her to die. I wondered how many times he had wanted to kill her and if ever he would kill her— or if he would remain, as I fancied he would do, just bound to her for ever.

Go, Lovely Rose

'He is the young man she met on the aeroplane,' Mrs Carteret said. 'Now go to sleep.'

Outside the bedroom window, in full moonlight, the leaves of the willow tree seemed to be slowly swimming in delicate but ordered separation, like shoals of grey-green fish. The thin branches were like bowed rods in the white summer sky.

'This is the first I heard that there was a young man on the aeroplane,' Mr Carteret said.

'You saw him,' Mrs Carteret said. 'He was there when we met her. You saw him come with her through the customs.'

'I can't remember seeing her with anybody.'

'I know very well you do because you remarked on his hat. You said what a nice colour it was. It was a sort sage-green one with a turn-down brim—'

'God God,' Mr Carteret said. 'That fellow? He looked forty or more. He was as old as I am.'

'He's twenty-eight. That's all. Have you made up your mind which side you're going to sleep?'

'I'm going to stay on my back for a while,' Mr Carteret said. 'I can't get off. I heard it strike three a long time ago.'

'You'd get off if you'd lie still,' she said.

Sometimes a turn of humid air, like the gentlest of currents, would move the entire willow tree in one huge soft fold of shimmering leaves. Whenever it did so Mr Carteret felt for a second or two that it was the sound of an approaching car. Then when the breath of wind suddenly changed direction and ran across the night landscape in a series of leafy echoes, stirring odd trees far away, he knew always that there was no car and that it was only, once again, the quiet long gasp of midsummer air rising and falling and dying away.

'Where are you fussing off to now?' Mrs Carteret said.

'I'm going down for a drink of water.'

'You'd better by half shut your eyes and lie still in one place,' Mrs Carteret said. 'Haven't you been off at all?'

'I can never sleep in moonlight,' he said. 'I don't know how it is. I never seem to settle properly. Besides it's too hot.'

'Put something on your feet,' Mrs Carteret said, 'for goodness sake.'

Across the landing, on the stairs and down in the kitchen the moonlight and the white starkness of a shadowless glare. The kitchen floor was warm to his bare feet and the water warmish as it came from the tap. He filled a glass twice and then emptied it into the sink and then filled it again before it was cold enough to drink. He had not put on his slippers because he could not remember where he had left them. He had been too busy thinking of Sue. Now he suddenly remembered that they were still where he had dropped them in the coal-scuttle by the side of the stove.

After he had put them on he opened the kitchen door and stepped outside and stood in the garden. Distinctly, with astonishingly pure clearness, he could see the colours of all the roses, even those of the darkest red. He could even distinguish the yellow from the white and not only in the still standing blooms but in all the fallen petals, thick everywhere on dry earth after the heat of the July day.

He walked until he stood in the centre of the lawn. For a time he could not discover a single star in the sky. The moon was like a solid opaque electric bulb, the glare of it almost cruel, he thought, as it poured down on the green darkness of summer trees.

Presently the wind made its quickening watery turn of sound among the leaves of the willow and ran away over the nightscape, and again he thought it was the sound of a car. He felt the breeze move coolly, almost coldly, about his pyjama legs and he ran his fingers in agitation once or twice through the pillow tangles of his hair.

Suddenly he felt helpless and miserable.

'Sue,' he said. 'For God's sake where on earth have you got to? Susie, Susie—this isn't like you.'

His pet term for her, Susie. In the normal way, Sue. Perhaps in rare moments of exasperation, Susan. He had called her Susie a great deal on her nineteenth birthday, three weeks before, before she had flown to Switzerland for her holiday. Everyone thought, that day, how much she had grown, how firm and full she was getting, and how wonderful it was that she was flying off alone. He only thought she looked more delicate and girlish than ever, quite thin and childish in the face in spite of her lipstick, and he was surprised to see her drinking what he thought were too many glasses of sherry. Nor, in contrast to himself, did she seem a bit nervous about the plane.

Over towards the town a clock struck chimes for a half hour and almost simultaneously he heard the sound of a car. There was no mistaking it this time. He could see the swing of its headlights too as it made the big bend by the packing station down the road, a quarter of a mile away.

'And quite time too, young lady,' he thought. He felt sharply vexed, not miserable any more. He could hear the car coming fast. It was so fast that he began to run back to the house across the lawn. He wanted to be back in bed before she arrived and saw him there. He did not want to be caught like that. His pyjama legs were several inches too long and were wet with the dew of the grass and he held them up, like skirts, as he ran.

What a damn ridiculous situation, he thought. What fools children could make you look sometimes. Just about as exasperating as they could be.

At the kitchen door one of his slippers dropped off and as he stopped to pick it up and listen again for the sound of the car he discovered that now there was no sound. The headlights too had disappeared. Once again there was nothing at all but the enormous noiseless glare, the small folding echoes of wind dying away.

'Damn it, we always walked home from dances,' he thought. 'That was part of the fun.'

Suddenly he felt cold. He found himself remembering with fear the long bend by the packing station. There was no decent camber on it and if you took it the slightest bit too fast you couldn't make it. Every week there were accidents there. And God, anyway what did he know about this fellow? He might be the sort who went round making pick-ups. A married man or something. Anybody. A crook.

All of a sudden he had a terrible premonition about it all. It was exactly the sort of feeling he had had when he saw her enter the plane, and again when the plane lifted into sky. There was an awful sense of doom about it: he felt sure she was not coming back. Now he felt in come curious way that his blood was separating itself into single drops. The drops were freezing and dropping with infinite systematic deadliness through the veins, breeding cold terror inside him. Somehow he knew that there had been a crash.

He was not really aware of running down through the rose-garden to the gate. He simply found himself somehow striding up and down in the road outside, tying his pyjamas cord tighter in agitation.

My God, he thought, how easily the thing could happen. A girl travelled by plane or train or even bus or something and before you knew where you were it was the beginning of something ghastly.

He began to walk up the road, feeling the cold precipitation of blood take drops of terror down to his legs and feet. A pale yellow suffusion of the lower sky struck into him the astonishing fact that it was almost day. He could hardly believe it and he broke miserably into a run.

Only a few moments later, a hundred yards away, he had the curious impression that from the roadside a pair of yellow eyes were staring back at him. He saw then that they were the lights of a stationary car. He did not know what to do about it. He could not very well go up to it and tap on the window and say, in tones of stern fatherhood, 'Is my daughter in there? Susan, come home.' There was always the chance that it would turn out to be someone else's daughter. It was always possible that it would turn out to be a daughter who liked what she was doing and strongly resented being interrupted in it by a prying middle-aged stranger in pyjamas.

He stopped and saw the lip of daylight widening and deepening its yellow on the horizon. It suddenly filled him with the sobering thought that he ought to stop being a damn fool and pull himself together.

'Stop acting like a nursemaid,' he said. 'Go home and get into bed. Don't you trust her?' It was always when you didn't trust them, he told himself, that trouble really began. That was when you asked for it. It was a poor thing if you didn't trust them.

'Go home and get into bed, you poor sap,' he said. 'You never fussed this much even when she was little.'

He had no sooner turned to go back than he heard the engine of the car starting. He looked round and saw the lights coming towards him down the road. Suddenly he felt more foolish than ever and there was no time for him to do anything but press himself quickly through a gap in the hedge by the roadside. The hedge was not very tall at that point and he found himself crouching down in a damp jungle of cow parsley and grass and nettle that wetted his pyjamas as high as the chest and shoulders. By this time the light in the sky had grown quite golden and all the colours of day were becoming distinct again and he caught the smell of honeysuckle rising from the dewiness of the hedge.

He lifted his head a second or so too late as the car went past him. He could not see whether Susie was in it or not and he was in a state of fresh exasperation as he followed it down the road. He was uncomfortable because the whole of his pyjamas were sopping with dew and he knew that now he would have to change and get himself a good rub-down before he got back into bed.

'God, what awful fools they make you look,' he thought, and then, a second later, 'hell, it might not be her. Oh! hell, supposing it isn't her?'

Wretchedly he felt his legs go weak and cold again. He forgot the dew on his chest and shoulders as the slow freezing precipitation of his blood began. From somewhere the wrenching thought of a hospital made him feel quite faint with a nausea that he could not fight away.

'Oh! Susie, for Jesus' sake don't do this any more to us. Don't do it any more—'

Then he was aware that the car had stopped by the gates of the house. He was made aware of it because suddenly, in the fuller dawn, the red rear light went out.

A second or two later he saw Susie. She was in her long heliotrope evening dress and she was holding it up at the skirt, in her delicate fashion, with both hands. Even from that distance he could see how pretty she was. The air too was so still in the bird-less summer morning silence that he heard her distinctly, in her nice fluty voice, so girlish and friendly, call out:

'Goodbye. Yes: lovely. Thank you.'

The only thing now, he thought, was not to be seen. He had to keep out of sight. He found himself scheming to get in by the side gate. Then he could slip up to the bathroom and get clean pyjamas and perhaps even a shower.

Only a moment later he saw that the car had already turned and was coming back towards him up the road. This time there was no chance to hide and all he could do was to step into the verge to let it go past him. For a few wretched seconds he stood there as if naked in full daylight, trying with nonchalance to look the other way.

In consternation he heard the car pull up a dozen yards beyond him and then a voice called:

'Oh! sir. Pardon me. Are you Mr Carteret, sir?'

'Yes,' he said.

There was nothing for it now, he thought, but to go back and find out exactly who the damn fellow was.

'Yes, I'm Carteret,' he said and he tried to put into his voice what he thought was a detached, unstuffy, coolish sort of dignity.

'Oh! I'm Bill Jordan, sir.' The young man had fair, smooth-brushed hair that looked extremely youthful against the black of his dinner jacket. 'I'm sorry we're so late. I hope you haven't been worried about Susie?'

'Oh! no. Good God, no.'

'It was my mother's fault. She kept us.'

'I thought you'd been dancing?'

'Oh! no, sir. Dinner with my mother. We did dance a few minutes on the lawn but then we played canasta till three. My mother's one of those canasta fanatics. It's mostly her fault, I'm afraid.'

'Oh! that's all right. So long as you had a good time.'

'Oh! we had a marvellous time, sir. It was just that I thought you might be worried about Susie—'

'Oh! great heavens, no.'

'That's fine, then, sir.' The young man had given several swift looks at the damp pyjamas and now he gave another and said: 'It's been a wonderfully warm night, hasn't it?'

'Awfully close. I couldn't sleep.'

'Sleep—that reminds me.' He laughed with friendly, expansive well-kept teeth that made him look more youthful than ever and more handsome. 'I'd better get home or it'll be breakfast-time. Good night, sir.'

'Good night.'

The car began to move away. The young man lifted one hand in farewell and Carteret called after him:

'You must come over and have dinner with us one evening—'

'Love to. Thank you very much, sir. Good night.'

Carteret walked down the road. Very touching, the sir business. Very illuminating and nice. Very typical. It was touches like that which counted. In relief he felt a sensation of a extraordinary self-satisfaction.

When he reached the garden gate the daylight was so strong that it showed with wonderful freshness all the roses that had unfolded in the night. There was one particularly beautiful crimson one, very dark, almost black, that he thought for a moment of picking and taking upstairs to his wife. But finally he decided against it and left it where it grew.

By that time the moon was fading and everywhere the birds were taking over the sky.

The Watercress Girl

The first time he ever went to that house was in the summer, when he was seven, and his grandfather drove him down the valley in a yellow trap and all the beans were in flower, with skylarks singing so high above them in the brilliant light that they hung trembling there like far-off butterflies.

'Who is it we're going to see?' he said.

'Sar' Ann.'

'Which one is Sar' Ann?'

'Now mek out you don' know which one Sar' Ann is,' his grandfather said, and then tickled the flank of the pony with the end of the plaited whip—he always wanted to plait reeds like that himself but he could never make them tight enough—so that the brown rumps, shorn and groomed for summer, quivered like firm round jellies.

'I don't think I've ever seen her,' he said.

'You seen her at Uncle Arth's,' his grandfather said. 'Mek out you don't remember that, and you see her a time or two at Jenny's.' He pronounced it Jinny, but even then the boy couldn't remember who Jinny was and he knew his grandfather wouldn't tell him until he remembered who Sar' Ann was and perhaps not even after that.

He tried for some moments longer to recall what Sar' Ann was like and remembered presently a square old lady in a porkpie lace cap and a sort of bib of black jet beads on a large frontal expanse of shining satin. Her eyes were watering. She sat on the threshold of a house that smelled of apples and wax polish. She was in the sun, with a lace-pillow and bone bobbins in a blue and ivory fan

173

on her knees. She was making lace and her hands were covered with big raised veins like the leaves of cabbages when you turned them upside down. He was sure that this was Sar' Ann. He remembered how she had touched his hands with her big cold cabbagy ones and said she would fetch him a cheese-cake, or if he would rather have it a piece of toffee, from the cupboard in her kitchen. She said the toffee was rather sugary and that made him say he preferred the cheese-cake, but his grandfather said:

'Now don't you git up. He's ettin' from morn to night now. His eyes are bigger'n his belly. You jis sit still,' and he felt he would cry because he was so fond of cheese-cake and because he could hardly bear his disappointment.

'She's the one who wanted to give me cheese-cake,' he said, 'isn't she?'

'No, she ain't,' his grandfather said. 'That's your Aunt Turvey.'

'Then is she the one who's married to Uncle Arth? Up the high steps?' he said.

'Uncle Arth ain't married,' his grandfather said. 'That's jis the widder-woman who looks after him.'

His Uncle Arth was always in a night-shirt, with a black scarf round his head. He lived in bed all the time. His eyes were very red. Inside him, so his grandfather said, was a stone and the stone couldn't go up or down but was fixed, his grandfather said, in his kitney, and it was growing all the time.

The stone was an awful nightmare to him, the boy. How big was it? What sort of stone was it? he would say, a stone in the kitney?

'Like a pibble,' his grandfather said. 'Hard as a pibble. And very like as big as a thresh's egg. Very like bigger'n that by now. Very like as big as a magpie's.'

'How did it get there?'

'You're arstin' on me now,' his grandfather said. 'It'd be a puzzle to know. But it got there. And there it is. Stuck in his kitney.'

'Has anybody ever seen it?'

'Nobody.'

'Then if nobody's ever seen it how do they know it's there?'

'Lean forward,' his grandfather said. 'We're gittin' to Long Leys hill. Lean forward, else the shafts'll poke through the sky.'

It was when they climbed slowly up the long wide hill, already white with the dust of early summer, that he became aware of the beans in flower and the skylarks singing so loftily above them. The scent of beans came in soft waves of wonderful sweetness. He saw the flowers on the grey sunlit stalks like swarms of white, dark-throated bees. The hawthorn flower was nearly over and was turning pink wherever it remained. The singing of the skylarks lifted the sky upward, farther and farther, loftier and loftier, and the sun made the blue of it clear and blinding. He felt that all summer was pouring down the hill, between ditches of rising meadowsweet, to meet him. The cold quivering days of coltsfoot flower, the icy-sunny days of racing cloud-shadow over drying ploughland, the dark-white days of April hail, were all behind him, and he was thirsty with summer dust and his face was hot in the sun.

'You ain't recollected her yit, have you?' his grandfather said.

They were at the top of the hill now and below them, in its yellow meadows, he could see a river winding away in broad and shining curves. He knew that that river was at the end of the earth; that the meadows, and with them the big woods of oak and hornbeam and their fading dusty spangles of flower, were another world.

'Take holt o' the reins a minute,' his grandfather said. He put on the brake a notch and the brake shoes scraped on the metal tyres. The boy held the thin smooth reins lightly between his fingers, the way he had been taught to do. He sat forward on the high horse-hair cushions and looked down the long black tramlines of the dead level reins to the brown pony's ears and felt himself, for one moment, high on the hill, to be floating in air, level with all the skylarks above the fields below.

'I'll jis git me bacca going,' his grandfather said. 'We'll be there in about a quartern of hour. You keep holt on her steady.'

He wanted to say to his grandfather that that was a funny word, quartern; his schoolteacher never used that word; and then as he turned he saw the brown, red-veined face softened by the first pulls of tobacco. All the mystery of it was dissolved in a blue sweet cloud. Then his grandfather began coughing because the bacca, he said, had gone down wrong way and was tiddling his gills. His eyes were wet from coughing and he was laughing and saying:

'You know who she is. She's the one with the specs like glarneys.'

Then he knew. She was a little woman, he remembered clearly now, with enormous spy-glass spectacles. They were thick and round like the marbles he played with. She was always whisking about like a clean starched napkin. He had seen her at Uncle Arth's and she had jolted Uncle Arth about the bed with a terrible lack of mercy as she re-made his pillows, smacking them with her lightning hands as if they were disobedient bottoms. The colossal spectacles gave the eyes a terrible look of magnification. They wobbled sometimes like masses of pale floating frog-spawn. He didn't like her; he was held in the spawn-like hypnotism of the eyes and dared not speak. She had a voice like a jackdaw's which pecked and mocked at everybody with nasty jabs. He knew that he had got her mixed up somehow and he said:

'I thought the one with the glass eye was Aunt Prunes.'

'Prudence!' his grandfather said. 'They're sisters. She's the young 'un, Prudence.' He spat in a long liquid line, with off-hand care, over the side of the trap. 'Prunes?—that was funny. How'd you come to git holt o' that?'

'I thought everybody else called her Prunes.'

'Oh! You did, simly? Well, it's Prudence. Prudence—that's her proper name.'

Simly was another funny word. He would never understand that word. That was another word his schoolteacher never used.

'Is she the one with the moustache?'

'God alive,' the man said. 'Don't you say moustache. You'll git me hung if you say moustache. That's your Aunt Prudence you're talking about. Females don't have moustaches—you know that.'

He knew better than that because Aunt Prunes had a moustache. She was a female and it was quite a long moustache and she had, what was more, a few whiskers on the central part of her chin.

'Why doesn't she shave it off?' he said.

'You watch what you're doing,' his grandfather said. 'You'll have us in the duck-pond.'

'How do you spell it?' he said. 'Her name—Prunes?'

'Here, you gimme holt o' the reins now,' his grandfather said. 'We'll be there in five ticks of a donkey's tail.'

His grandfather took the reins and let the brake off, and in a minute the pony was trotting and they were in a world of high green reeds and grey dropping willows by the river.

'Is it the house near the spinney?' he said.

'That's it,' his grandfather said. 'The little 'un with the big chimney.'

He was glad he remembered the house correctly: not because he had ever seen it but because his grandfather always described it with natural familiarity, as if taking it for granted that he had seen it. He was glad too about Aunt Prunes. It was very hard to get everyone right. There were so many of them, Aunt Prunes and Sar' Ann and Aunt Turvey and Uncle Arth and Jenny and Uncle Ben Newton, who kept a pub, and Uncle Olly, who was a fat man with short black leggings exactly like polished bottles. His grandfather would speak of these people as if they were playmates who had always been in his life and were to be taken for granted naturally and substantially like himself. They were all very old, terribly old, and he never knew, even afterwards, if they were ordinary aunts or great ones or only cousins some stage removed.

The little house had two rooms downstairs with polished red bricks for floors and white glass vases or dried reeds from the river on the mantelpiece. His grandfather and Aunt Prunes and Sar' Ann and himself had dinner in the room where the stove was, and there were big dishes of potatoes, mashed with thick white butter sauce. Before dinner he sat in the other room with his grandfather and Aunt Prunes and looked at a large leather book called *Sunday at Home*, a prize Aunt Prunes had won at Bible Class, a book in which there were sandwiched, between steel-cuts of men in frock coats and sailors in sailing ships and ladies in black bonnets, pressings of dried flowers thin as tissue from the meadows and the riverside. His contemplation of the flat golden transparencies of buttercup and the starry eyes of bull-daisy and the woolly feathers of grass and reed was ravaged continually by the voice of Sar' Ann, the jackdaw, pecking and jabbing from the kitchen:

'There's something there to keep you quiet. That's a nice book, that is. You can look at that all afternoon.'

'You tell me,' Aunt Prunes said softly, 'when you want another.'

He liked Aunt Prunes. She was quiet and tender. The moustache, far from being forbidding, brushed him with friendly softness, and the little room was so hot with sun and cooking that there were beads of sweat on the whiskers which he made the mistake of thinking, for some time, were drops of the cowslip wine she was drinking. His grandfather had several glasses of cowslip wine and after the third or fourth of them he took off his coat and collar.

At the same time Aunt Prunes bent down and took the book away from him and said:

'You can take off your coat too. That's it. That's better. Do you want to go anywhere?'

'Not yet.'

'When you do it's down the garden and behind the elderberry tree.' Her eyes were a modest brown colour, the same colour as her moustache, and there were many wrinkles about them as she smiled. He could smell the sweetish breath, like the yeast his grandmother used for baking, of the fresh wine on her lips, and she said:

'What would you like to do this afternoon? Tell me what you'd like to do.'

'Read this book.'

'I mean really.'

'I don't know.'

'You do what you like,' she said. 'You go down to the back-brook or in the garden or into the spinney and find snails or sticklebacks or whatever you like.'

She smiled delicately, creating thousands of wrinkles, and then from the kitchen Sar' Ann screeched:

'I'm dishing up in two minutes, you boozers. You'd guzzle there till bulls'-noon if I'd let you.'

Bulls'-noon was another word, another strange queer thing he didn't understand.

For dinner they had Yorkshire pudding straight out of the pan and on to the plate, all by itself, as the opening course. Sometimes his grandfather slid slices of the creamy yellow pudding into his mouth on the end of his knife and said he remembered the days when all pudden was eaten first and you had your plate turned upside down, so that you could turn it over when the meat came. Sar' Ann said she remembered that too and she said they were the days and she didn't care what anybody said. People were happier. They didn't have so much of everything but they were happier. He saw Aunt Prunes give a little dry grin whenever Sar' Ann went jabbing on and once he thought he saw her wink at his grandfather. All the time the door of the little room was open so that he could see into the garden with its white pinks and stocks and purple iris flags and now and then he could hear the cuckoo, sometimes near, sometimes far off across the meadows, and many blackbirds singing in endless call and answer in the oak-trees at the end of the garden, where rhubarb and elderberry were in foaming flower together.

'You can hear nightingales too,' Aunt Prunes said. 'Would you like more pudding? You can have more pudding if you want it.'

But his grandfather said again that his eyes were always bigger than his belly and the pudding was put away. 'Ets like a thacker,' his grandfather said and Aunt Prunes said, 'Let him eat then. I like to see boys eat. It does your heart good,' and she smiled and gave him cloudy piles of white potatoes and white sauce from a blue china boat and thin slices of rich beef with blood running out and washing against the shores of his potatoes like the little waves of a delicate pink sea.

'How's Nance and Granny Houghton?' Sar' Ann said, and his grandfather said they were fair-to-mid and suddenly there was great talk of relatives, of grown-ups, of people he didn't know, of Charley and a man he thought was named Uncle Fuggles and Cathy and Aunt Em and Maude Rose and two people called Liz and Herbert from Bank Top. His grandfather, who had begun the meal with three or four glasses of cowslip wine and a glass of beer, now helped himself to another glass of beer and then dropped gravy down his waistcoat. Aunt Prunes had beer too and her eyes began to look warm and sleepy and beautifully content.

Afternoon, cuckoo-drowsy, very still and full of sun, seemed to thicken like a web about him long before the meal was over. He thought with dread of the quietness when all of them would be asleep and he himself in the little room with a big boring book and its rustling transparencies of faded flowers. He knew what it was like to try to move in the world of grown-up sleep. The whisper of the thinnest page would wake them. Night was the time for sleeping and it was one of the mysteries of life that people could also sleep by day, in chairs, in summertime, in mouth-open attitudes, and with snorting noises and legs suddenly jumping like the legs of horses when the flies were bad.

Then to his joy Aunt Prunes remembered and said:

'You know what I said. You run into the garden and have a look in the spinney for nests. Go down as far as the back-brook if you like.'

'That's it,' his grandfather said. 'You'll very like see a moorhen's or a coot's or summat down there. Else a pike or summat. Used to be a rare place for pike, a-layin' there a-top o' the water—'

'Don't you git falling in,' Sar' Ann said. 'Don't you git them feet wet. Don't you git them gooseberries—they'll give you belly-ache summat chronic—'

'You bring me some flowers,' Aunt Prunes said. 'Eh?—how's that? You stay a long time, as long as you like, and bring me some flowers.'

There were no nests in the spinney except a pigeon's high up in a hazel-tree that was too thin to climb. He was not quite sure about the song of a nightingale. He knew the blackbird's, full and rich and dark like the bird itself and deep like the summer shadow of the closing wood, and with the voices of thrushes the blackbirds' song filled all the wood with bell-sounds and belling echoes.

Beyond the wood the day was clear and hot. The grass was high to his knees and the ground, falling away, was marshy in places, with mounds of sedge, as it ran down towards the backbrook and the river. He walked with his eyes on the ground, partly because of oozy holes among the sedge, partly because he hoped to see the brown ring of a moorhen's nest in the marshier places.

It was because of his way of walking that he did not see, for some time, a girl standing up to her knees in red-ochre mud, among half-floating beds of dark-green cresses. But suddenly he lifted his head and saw her standing there, bare-legged and bare-armed, staring at him as if she had been watching him for a long time. Her brown osier cress-basket was like a two-bushel measure and was slung over her shoulder with a strap.

'You don't live here,' she said.

'No,' he said. 'Do you?'

'Over there,' she said. 'In that house.'

'Which house?' He could not see a house.

'You come here and you can see it,' she said.

When he had picked his way through tufts of sedge to where she was standing in the bed of cresses he still could not see a house, either about the wood or across the meadows on the rising ground beyond.

'You can see the chimney smoking,' she said.

'It's not a house. It's a hut,' he said.

'That's where we live.'

'All the time?'

'Yes,' she said. 'You're sinking in.'

The toes of his boots were slowly drowning in red-ochre water.

'If you're coming out here you'd better take your shoes and stockings off,' she said.

A moment or two later his bare feet were cool in the water. She was gathering cresses quickly, cutting them off with an old shoe-knife, leaving young sprigs and trailing skeins of white root behind. She was older than himself, nine or ten, he thought, and her hair hung ribbonless and uncombed, a brown colour, rather like the colour of the basket, down her back.

'Can I gather?' he said, and she said, yes, if he knew what brook-lime was.

'I know brook-lime,' he said. 'Everybody knows brook-lime.'

'Then which is it? Show me which it is. Which is brook-lime?'

That was almost as bad, he thought, as being nagged by Sar' Ann. The idea that he did not know brook-lime from cress seemed to him a terrible insult and a pain. He snatched up a piece in irritation but it did not break and came up instead from the mud-depths in a long rope of dripping red-black slime, spattering his shirt and trousers.

She laughed at this and he laughed too. Her voice, he thought, sounded cracked, as if she were hoarse from shouting or a cold. The sound of it carried a long way. He heard it crack over the meadows and the river with a coarse broken sort of screech that was like the slitting of rag in the deep oppressive afternoon.

He never knew till long afterwards how much he liked that sound. She repeated it several times during the afternoon. In the same cracked voice she laughed at questions he asked or things he did not know. In places the water, shallower, was warm on his feet, and the cresses were a dark polished green in the sun. She laughed because he did not know that anyone could live by gathering cresses. He must be a real town boy, she said. There was only she and her father, she told him, and she began to tell what he afterwards knew were beautiful lies about the way they got up every other day at two in the morning and tramped out to sell cresses in Evensford and Bedford and towns about the valley.

'But the shops aren't open then,' he said and that made her laugh again, cracked and thin, with that long slitting echo across the drowsy meadows.

'It's not in the shops we sell them,' she said. 'It's in the streets—don't you know that?—in the streets—'

And suddenly she lifted her head and drew back her throat and yelled the cry she used in the streets. He had heard that cry before, high and long and melancholy, like a call across lonely winter marshes in its slow fall and dying away, and there was to be a time in his life when it died for ever and he never heard it again:

'Watercree-ee-ee-ee-ee-s! Fresh cre-ee-ee-ee-ee-ee-s! Lovely fresh watercre-ee-ee-ee-ee-ee-s!'

Standing up to his knees in water, his hands full of wet cresses and slimy skeins of roots dripping red mud down his shirt and trousers, he listened to that fascinating sound travelling like a bird-cry, watery and not quite earthly, down through the spinney and the meadows of buttercup and the places where the pike were supposed to lie.

His eyes must have been enormous and transfixed in his head as he listened, because suddenly she broke the note of the cry and laughed at him again and then said:

'You do it. You see if you can do it—'

What came out of his mouth was like a little soprano trill compared with her own full-throated, long-carrying cry. It made her laugh again and she said:

'You ought to come with us. Come with us tomorrow—how long are you staying here?'

'Only today.'

'I don't know where we'll go tomorrow,' she said. 'Evensford, I think. Sometimes we go forty or fifty miles—miles and miles. We go to Buckingham market sometimes—that's forty miles—'

'Evensford,' he said. 'That's where I come from. I could see you there if you go.'

'All right,' she said. 'Where will you be? We come in by *The Waggon and Horses*—down the hill, that way.'

'I'll be at *The Waggon and Horses* waiting for you,' he said. 'What time?'

'You be there at five o'clock,' she said. 'Then I'll learn you how to do it, like this—watercree-ee-ee-ee-ee-ee-ee-s! Fresh cree-ee-ee-ee-ee-ee-ee-s! Lovely fresh watercree-ee-ee-ee-ee-s!'

As the sound died away it suddenly seemed to him that he had been there, up to his knees in water, a very long time, perhaps throughout the entire length of the sultry, sun-flushed afternoon. He did not know what time it was. He was cut off from the world of Aunt Prunes and Sar' Ann and his grandfather, the little house and the white pinks and the gooseberry trees, the big boring book whose pages and dead flowers turned over in whispers.

He knew that he ought to go back and said:

'I got to go now. I'll see you tomorrow though—I'll be there. Five o'clock.'

'Yes, you be there,' she said. She wiped a may-fly from her face with her forearm, drawing water and mud across it, and then remembered something. 'You want some cresses for tea? You can take some.'

She plunged her hands into the basket and brought them out filled with cresses. They were cool and wet; and he thought, not only then but long afterwards, that they were the nicest things perhaps anyone had ever given him.

'So long,' she said.

'So long.' That was another funny expression, he thought. He could never understand people who said so long when they seemed to mean, as he did, soon.

She waved her hands, spilling arcs of water-drops in the sun, as he climbed the stile into the spinney and went back. He did his best to wave in answer, but his shoes and stockings were too wet to wear and his hands were full with them and the cresses. Instead he simply stood balanced for a moment on the top bar of the stile, so that she could see him well and then call to him for the last time:

'Cree-ee-ee-ee-ee-es! Lovely fresh cree-ee-ee-ee-es!'

It was only Aunt Prunes who was not angry with him. His grandfather called him 'A young gallus,' and kept saying, 'Where the Hanover've you bin all the time? God A'mighty, you'll git me hung. I'll be burned if I don't git hung,' and Sar' Ann flew about the kitchen with the squawks of a trapped hen, telling him:

'You know what happens to little boys what git wet-foot? And look at your shirt! They git their death, they catch their death. And don't you know who them folks are? Gyppos—that's all they are. Gyppos—they nick things, they live on other folks. That's the sort of folks they are. Don't you go near such folks again—they'll very like keep you and take you away and you'll never see nobody who knows you again. Then we'll find you in the bury-hole.'

But he was not afraid of that and Aunt Prunes only said:

'You didn't bring me my flowers, did you? I like watercress though. I'm glad you brought the watercress. I can have it with my tea.'

It was late before they could start for home again. That was because his socks and shirt took a long time to dry and his shirt had to have an iron run over it several times in case, Sar' Ann kept saying, his mother had a fit. Before getting up into the trap he had to kiss both Sar' Ann and Aunt Prunes, and for some moments he was lost in the horror of the big globular spectacles reflecting and magnifying the evening sun, and then in the friendliness of the dark moustaches below which the warm mouth smiled and said:

'How would you like to stay with me one day? Just you and me in the summer. Would you?'

'Yes,' he said.

'Then you come and see me again, won't you, soon?'

He said Yes, he would see her soon. But in fact he did not see her soon or later or at any time again. He did not go to that house again until he was grown up. That was the day they were burying her and when the cork of silence that passed over the grave had blown out again he felt he could hear nothing but the gassy voice of Sar' Ann, who was old by then but still with the same fierce roving globular eyes, shrilly reminding him of the day he had gathered cresses.

'I'll bet you would never know her now,' she said, 'that girl, would you? Would you ever know that this was her?'

Then she was by his side and he was talking to her: the girl who had gathered the cresses, the same girl who had called with that screeching, melancholy, marshy cry across the summer afternoon. She was all in black and her hat had a purple feather in the crown. He remembered the little hut and the brown osier basket on her lithe thin shoulders and he asked her where she lived and what she was doing now. 'In the new houses,' she said. 'I'm Mrs Corbett now.' She took him to the garden hedge and pointed out to him blocks of bricks, like the toys of gigantic children, red and raw and concrete fenced, lining the road above the valley. That was the road where he and his grandfather had driven down on that distant summer morning, when the beans were in flower and he had got so mixed with his relatives and had wondered how Aunt Prunes had spelled her name.

'That's us,' she said. She pointed with stout and podgy finger, a trifle nervously but with pride, across the fields. 'The second one. The one with the television. Have you got television?'

'No.'

'You ought to have it,' she said. 'It's wonderful to see things so far away. Don't you think it's wonderful?'

'Wonderful,' he said.

But on the night he drove home as a boy, watching the sky of high summer turn from blue to palest violet and then more richly to purple bronze and the final green-gold smokiness of twilight, he did not know these things. He sat still on the cushions of the trap, staring ahead. The evening was full of the scent of bean flowers and he was searching for early stars.

'Shall we light the lamps?' he said.

And presently they lit the lamps. They too were golden. They seemed to burn with wonderful brightness, lighting the grasses of the roadside and the flowers of the ditches and the crowns of fading may. And though he did not know it then they too were fading, for all their brightness. They too were dying, along with the things he had done and seen and loved: the little house, the cuckoo day, the tender female moustaches and the voice of the watercress girl.

Love in a Wych Elm

When I was a boy the Candleton sisters, seven of them, lived in a large gabled house built of red brick that gave the impression of having been muted by continual sunlight to a pleasant shade of orange-rose. The front face of it had a high, benign open appearance and I always felt that the big sash windows actually smiled down on the long gravel terrace, the iron pergola of roses and the sunken tennis lawn. At the back were rows of stables, all in the same faded and agreeable shade of brick, with lofts above them that were full of insecure and ancient bedsteads, fire-guards, hip-baths, tennis rackets, croquet hammers, rocking horses, muscle-developers, Indian clubs, travelling trunks and things of that sort thrown out by Mr and Mrs Candleton over the course of their fruitful years.

I was never very sure of what Mr Candleton did in life; I was not even sure in fact if he did anything at all except to induce Mrs Candleton, at very regular intervals, to bear another daughter. In a town like Evensford there were at that time very few people of independent means who lived in houses that had stables at the back. The Candletons were, or so it seemed to me, above our station. There was at one time a story that Mr Candleton was connected with wine. I could well believe this. Like his house, Mr Candleton's face had toned to a remarkably pleasant shade of inflammable rose. This always seemed perhaps brighter than it really was because his eyes were so blue. They were of that rare shade of pale violet blue that always seems about to dissolve, especially in intoxication. This effect was still further heightened by hair of a most pure distinguished shade of yellow:

a thick oat-straw yellow that was quite startling and remarkable in a male.

All the Candleton sisters too had their father's pale violet dissolving eyes and that exceptional shade of oat-straw hair.

At first, when they were very small children, it was white and silky. Then as they grew up its characteristic shining straw-colour grew stronger. A stranger seeing them for the first time would have said that they were seven dolls who had been dipped in a solution of something several shades paler than saffron. The hair was very beautiful when brushed and as children they all wore it long.

On hot days in summer Mr Candleton wore cream flannel trousers with a blue pin stripe in them, a blazer with red and orange stripes, and a straw hat with a band of the same design. Round his waist he wore a red silk cummerbund. All his shirts were of silk and he always wore them buttoned at the neck. In winter he wore things like Donegal tweeds: roughish, sporting, oatmeal affairs that were just right for his grained waterproof shooting brogues. He wore smart yellow gloves and a soft tweed hat with a little feather in the band. He always seemed to be setting off somewhere, brisk and dandyish and correct, a man of leisure with plenty of time to spare.

It was quite different with Mrs Candleton. The house was big and rambling and it might well have been built specially to accommodate Mrs Candleton, who was like a big, absent-minded, untidy, roving bear. My mother used to say that she got up and went to bed in a pinafore. It wasn't a very clean pinafore either. Nor were her paper hair-curlers, which were sometimes still in her rough unruly black hair at tea-time. She always seemed to be wearing carpet-slippers and sometimes her stockings would be slipping down. She was a woman who always seemed to be catching up with life and was always a day and a half behind.

The fact was, I suppose, that with seven children in something like a dozen years Mrs Candleton was still naturally hazy in some of her diurnal calculations. Instead of her catching up with life, life was always catching up with her.

Meals, for example, made the oddest appearances in the Candleton household. If I went on a school-less day to call on Stella—she was the one exactly of my own age, the one I knew best—it was either to find breakfast being taken at eleven-thirty, with Mr Candleton always immaculate behind the silver toast-rack and Mrs Candleton looking like the jaded mistress of a rag-and-bone man, or dinner at half-past three or tea at seven. In a town like Evensford everybody was rigidly governed by factory hours and the sound of factory hooters. At various times of the day silences fell on the town that were a hushed indication that all honest people were decently at work. All this meant that breakfast was at seven, dinner at twelve-thirty and tea at half-past five. That was how everybody ate and lived and ran their lives in Evensford: everybody, that is, except the Candletons.

These characteristics of excessive and immediate smartness on the one hand and the hair-curler and pinafore style on the other had been bequeathed by him and Mrs Candletown in almost exactly equal measure to their children. The girls were all beautiful, all excessively dressy as they grew up and, as my mother was fond of saying, not over clean.

'If they get a cat-lick once a week it's about as much as they do get,' was one of her favourite sayings.

But children do not notice such things very acutely and I can not say that I myself was very interested in the virtues of soap and water. What I liked about the Candletons was not only a certain mysterious quality of what I thought was aristocracy but a feeling of untamed irresponsibility. They were effervescent. When the eldest girl, Lorna, was seventeen she ran off with a captain in the Royal Artillery who turned out to be a married man. I thought it might well have been the sort of thing that would have ruined a girl, temporarily at least, in Evensford, but Stella simply thought it a wild joke and said:

'She had a wonderful time. It was gorgeous. They stayed at a marvellous hotel in London. She told us all about it. I thought Mother would die laughing.'

Of laughing, not shame: that was typical of the Candleton standard, the Candleton approach and the Candleton judgement on such things.

The four eldest girls, two of them twins, were called Lorna, Hilda, Rosa and Freda. This habit of giving names ending in the same letter went on to Stella, with whom I played street-games in winter in front of the gas-lit windows of a pork-pie and sausage shop and games in summer in the Candleton garden and among the muscle-developers and bedsteads of the Candleton loft, and then on to the two youngest, who were mere babies as I knew them, Wanda and Eva. Mrs Candleton's Christian name was Blanche, which suited her perfectly.

It was a common tendency in all the Candleton girls to develop swiftly. At thirteen they were filling out; at fifteen they were splendidly and handsomely buxom and were doing up their hair. Hilda appeared to me to be a goddess of marbled form long before she was eighteen and got engaged to a beefy young farmer who bred prize cattle and called for her in a long open sports car.

Hilda had another characteristic not shared by any of the rest of the family except her mother. She sang rather well. At eighteen she began to have her pleasant, throaty, contralto voice trained. Mr Candleton was a strict Sunday morning churchgoer in pin-stripe trousers, bowler hat and spats, and Hilda went with him to sing in the choir. Her voice was trained by a Mr Lancaster, a rather bumptious pint-size tenor who gave her lessons three evenings a week. It was generally known that Mr Lancaster was, as a singer at any rate, past his best, but it was not long before the engagement between Hilda and the farmer was broken.

At that time Stella and I were nine. I, at least, was nine and Stella, physically, was twelve or thirteen. What I liked about her so much in those days was her utter freedom to come and go as she pleased. Other children had errands to run, confirmation classes to attend, catechisms to learn, aunts to visit, restrictive penances like shoes to clean or knives to rub up with bath-brick.

In the Candleton way she had never anything to do but play, enjoy herself, indulge in inconsequential make-believe and teach me remarkable things about life and living.

'What shall we do? Let's be married. Let's go up to the loft and be married.'

'We were married the day before yesterday.'

'That doesn't matter. You can be married over and over again. Hilda's going to be. Come on, let's be married.'

'All right. But not in the loft. Let's have a new house this time.'

'All right. Let's be married in the wych-elm.'

The Candleton garden extended beyond the stables into a rough orchard of old damson trees, with a few crooked espalier pears. A pepper-pot summer house in rustic work with a thatched roof stood in one corner, almost obliterated by lilac trees. In summer damsons and pears fell into the deep grass and no one picked them up. A sense of honeyed rotting quietness spread under the lurching trees and was compressed and shut in by a high boundary line of old, tapering wych-elms.

Rooks nested in the highest of the elms and when summer thickened the branches the trees were like a wall. The house was hidden and shut away. On a heavy summer day you would hear nothing there but the sound of rooks musing and croaking and fruit falling with a squashy mellow plop on the grass and paths.

Up in the wych-elms the peculiar structure of boughs made a house for us. We could walk about it. We crawled, like monkeys, from tree to tree. In this paradise we stayed for entire afternoons, cocooned with scents, hidden away in leaves. We made tea in ancient saucepans on flameless fires of elm twigs and prepared dinners of potatoes and gravy from fallen pears. And up here, on a soft August afternoon, we were married without witnesses and Stella, with her yellow hair done up for the first time, wore a veil of lace curtains and carried a bunch of cow-parsley.

But before that happened I had caught, only the day before, another glimpse of the Candleton way of living.

I had called about six o'clock in the evening for Stella but although the door of the house was open nobody, for some time at any rate, answered my ring at the bell. That was not at all unusual at the Candleton household. Although it never seemed possible for nine such unmistakable people to disappear without trace it was frequently happening and often I went to the door and rang until I was tired of ringing and then went away without an answer.

I remember once ringing the bell and then, tired of it, peeping into the kitchen. It was one of those big old-fashioned kitchens with an enormous iron cooking range with plate racks above it and gigantic dressers and vast fish-kettles and knife-cleaners everywhere. In the middle of it all Mrs Candleton sat asleep. Not normally asleep, I could see. A quarter-full bottle of something for which I had no definition stood on the table in front of her, together with a glass and, beside the glass, most astonishing thing of all, her false teeth.

Blowsily, frowsily, comfortably, toothlessly, Mrs Candleton was sleeping away the afternoon in her hair-curlers and her pinafore.

But on the evening I called for Stella the kitchen was empty. I rang the bell four or five times and then, getting no answer, stepped into the hall.

'Hullo,' someone said.

That very soft, whispered throaty voice was Hilda's. She was standing at the top of the stairs. She was wearing nothing but her petticoat and her feet were bare. In her hands she was holding a pair of stockings, which she had evidently been turning inside out in readiness to put on.

'Oh! it's you,' she said. 'I thought I heard someone.'

'Is Stella here?'

'They're all out. They've all gone to the Robinsons' for tea. It's Katie's birthday.'

'Oh! I see,' I said. 'Well, I'll come again tomorrow—'

'I'm just going to a dance,' she said. 'Would you like to see my dress? Would you?—come on, come up.'

Standing in the bedroom, with the August sunlight shining on her bare shoulders, through the lace of her slip and on her sensational yellow Candleton hair, she was a magnificent figure of a girl.

'Just let me put my stockings on and then you can see my dress.'

She sat down on the bed to put on her stockings. Her legs were smooth and heavy. I experienced an odd sensation as the stockings unrolled up her legs and then were fastened somewhere underneath the petticoat. Then she stood up and looked at the back of her legs to see if her stockings were straight. After that she smoothed the straps of her petticoat over her shoulders and said:

'Just wait till I give my hair one more brush.'

I shall never forget how she sat before the dressing mirror and brushed her hair. I was agreeably and mystically stunned. The strokes of the brush made her hair shine exactly, as I have said before, like oat-straw. Nothing could have been purer and more shining. It was marvellously burnished and she laughed at me in the mirror because I stood there so staring and speechless and stunned.

'Well, do I look nice? You think I shall pass in a crowd?'

'Yes.'

'That's good. It's nice to have a man's opinion.'

She laughed again and put on her dress. It was pure white, long and flouncy. I remember distinctly the square low collar. Then she put on her necklace. It was a single row of pearls and she couldn't fasten it.

'Here, you can do this,' she said.

She sat on the bed and I fastened the necklace. The young hair at the nape of her neck was like yellow chicken down. I was too confused to notice whether she had washed her neck or not and then she said:

'That's it. Now just a little of this and I'm ready.'

She sprayed her hair, her arms and the central shadow of her bosom with scent from a spray.

'How about a little for you?'

She sprayed my hair and in a final moment of insupportable intoxication I was lost in a wave of wallflowers.

'That's the most expensive scent there is,' she said. 'The most difficult to make. Wallflowers.'

Perhaps it was only natural, next day, as I came to be married to Stella high at the altar of the wych-elms, that I found myself oppressed by a sensation of anticlimax. Something about Stella, I felt, had not quite ripened. I had not the remotest idea as to what it could be except that she seemed, in some unelevating and puzzling way, awkward and flat.

'What do you keep staring at me for?'

'I'm just going to spray you with scent,' I said. 'There—piff! pish! piff—'

'Whatever made you think of that?'

I was afraid to speak of Hilda and I said:

'All girls have to have scent on when they're married.'

'Do I look nice?'

She didn't really look nice. The lace curtain was mouldy in one corner and had holes down one side. I didn't like the odour of cow-parsley. But the soft golden oat-straw hair was as remarkable as ever and I said:

'You look all right.'

Then we were married. After we were married she said:

'Now you have to make love to me.'

'Why?'

'Everybody has to make love when they're married.'

I looked at her in utter mystification. Then suddenly she dropped the cow-parsley and pushed back her veil and kissed me. She held me in an obliterating and momentary bondage by the trunk of the wych-elm, kissing me with such blistering force that I lost my cap. I was rather upset about my cap as it fell in the nettles below but she said:

'Sit down. We're in bed now. We have to be in bed now we're married. It's the first thing people do.'

'Why?'

'Don't you know?'

I did not know; nor, as it happens, did she. But one of the advantages of being born one of a family of seven sisters is that you arrive much earlier at the approximation of the more delicate truths than you do if you are a boy. Perhaps in this respect I was a backward boy, but I could only think it was rather comfortless trying to make love in a wych-elm and after a time I said:

'Let's go and play in the loft now.'

'What with?'

'I don't know,' I said. 'Let's have a change. We've been married an awful lot of times—'

'I know,' she said. 'We'll play with the chest-developers.'

While we played in the loft with the chest-developers she had an original thought.

'I think if I practise a lot with these I shall get fat up top more quickly.'

'You will?'

'I think I shall soon anyway.'

Like Hilda, I thought. A renewed sensation of agreeable and stupefying delight, together with a scent of wallflowers, shot deliciously through me and I was half-way to the realisation of the truth that girls are pleasant things when she said:

'One day, when we're big, let's be really married, shall us?'

'All right.'

'Promise?'

'Yes,' I said.

'You know what you'll be when you're married to me, don't you?' she said.

I couldn't think.

'You'll be a viscount,' she said.

'What's a viscount?'

'It's the husband of a viscountess.'

'How shall I come to be that?'

'Because a viscountess is the daughter of a lord.'

'But,' I said, 'your father isn't a lord.'

'No,' she said, 'but his brother is. He lives in a castle in Bedfordshire. It has a hundred and forty rooms in it. We go there every summer. And when he dies my father will be a lord.'

'Is he going to die?'

'Soon.'

'Supposing your father dies before he does?'

'Oh! he won't,' she said. 'He's the youngest son. The oldest always die first.'

She went on to tell me many interesting things about our life together. Everything in that life would be of silk, she said, like her father's shirts. Silk sheets on the bed, silk pillows, silk tablecloths, silk cushions. 'And I shall always wear silk drawers,' she said. 'Even on week-day.'

Altogether, it seemed, we should have a marvellous life together.

'And we shall drink port wine for supper,' she said. 'Like my father does. He always drinks port wine for supper.'

'Is it nice?'

'Yes,' she said. 'I'm allowed to have it sometimes. You'll like it. You can get drunk as often as you like then. Like my father does.'

'Does he get drunk?'

'Not as often as my mother does,' she said; 'but quite a lot.'

I suppose I was shocked.

'Oh! that's all right,' she said. 'Lords always get drunk. That's why people always say "drunk as a lord." That's the proper thing to do.'

Armed with the chest-developers, we spent an ecstatic afternoon. I was so filled with the golden snobbery of being a viscount that it was a cold and dusty sort of shock when she told me that anyway we couldn't be married for years and years, not until she was fatter; like Hilda was.

The recollection of Hilda, all burnished and magnificent and intoxicating and perfumed, inflamed and inspired me to greater efforts with the chest-developers.

'We must work harder,' I said.

I wanted so much to be a lord, to live in a castle, to drink port wine and to be married to someone with silk drawers that I was totally unprepared for the shock my mother gave me.

'The little fibber, the little story-teller, the little liar,' she said.

'But she said, so,' I said. 'She told me.'

'I went to board school with Reggie Candleton,' she said. 'He was in my class. They came from Gas Street.'

Nothing in the world was worse than coming from Gas Street. You could not go lower than Gas Street. The end of the respectable world was Gas Street.

'It's she who had the money,' my mother said. 'Mrs Candleton. Her father was a brewer and Reggie Candleton worked there. He was always such a little dandy. Such a little masher. Always the one for cutting such a dash.'

I decided it was wiser to say nothing about the prospect of marrying, or about Stella's urgent efforts with the chest-developers, or the silk drawers.

'All top show,' my mother said. 'That's what it is. All fancy fol-di-dols on top and everything dropping into rags underneath. Every one of them with hair like a ten-guinea doll and a neck you could sow carrots in.'

I don't suppose for a moment that Stella remembers me; or that, on an uncomfortable, intimate occasion, we were married in a wych-elm. It is equally unlikely that Hilda remembers me; or that, with her incomparable yellow hair, her white dance dress, her soft blonde flesh and her rare scent of wallflowers, she once asked me to give her my opinion as a man. I believe Stella is married to a bus-conductor. The rest of the Candletons have faded from my life. With the summer frocks, the summer strawhats and the summer flannels, the cummerbunds, the silk shirts, the elegant brogues, the chest-developers and the incomparable yellow hair they have joined Mr Candleton in misty, muted, permanent bankruptcy.

Love in a wych-elm is not an easy thing; but like the Candletons it is unforgettable.

Now Sleeps the Crimson Petal

Clara Corbett, who had dark brown deeply sunken eyes that did not move when she was spoken to and plain brown hair parted down the middle in a straight thin line, firmly believed that her life had been saved by an air warden's anti-gas cape on a black rainy night during the war.

In a single glittering, dusty moment a bomb had blown her through the window of a warden's post, hurling her to the wet street outside. The wind from the bomb had miraculously blown the cape about her face, masking and protecting her eyes. When she had picked herself up, unhurt, she suddenly knew that it might have been her shroud.

'Look slippy and get up to Mayfield Court. Six brace of part-ridges and two hares to pick up—'

'And on the way deliver them kidneys and the sirloin to Paxton Manor. Better call in sharp as you go out. They're having a lunch party.'

Now, every rainy day of her life, she still wore the old camouflaged cape as she drove the butcher's van, as if half fearing that some day, somewhere, another bomb would blow her through another window, helplessly and for ever. The crumpled patterns of green-and-yellow camouflage always made her look, in the rain, like a damp, baggy, meditating frog.

Every day of his life, her husband, Clem, wore his bowler hat in the butcher's shop, doffing it obsequiously to special customers, revealing a bald, yellow suet-shining head. Clem had a narrow way of smiling and argued that war had killed the meat trade.

Almost everyone else in that rather remote hilly country, where big woodlands were broken by open stretches of chalk heathland covered with gorse and blackthorn and occasional yew trees, had given up delivering to outlying houses. It simply didn't pay. Only Clem Corbett, who doffed his hat caressingly to customers with one hand while leaving the thumb of his other on the shop scales a fraction of a second too long, thought it worth while any longer.

'One day them people'll all come back. The people with class. Mark my words. The real gentry. They're the people you got to keep in with. The pheasant-and-partridge class. The real gentry. Not the sausage-and-scragenders.'

Uncomplainingly, almost meekly, Clara drove out, every day, in the old delivery van with a basket or two in the back and an enamel tray with a few bloody, neatly-wrapped cuts of meat on it, into wooded, hilly countryside. Sometimes in winter, when the trees were thinned of leaves, the chimneys of empty houses, the mansions of the late gentry, rose starkly from behind deep thick beechwoods that were thrown like vast bearskins across the chalk. In summer the chalk flowered into a hill garden of wild yellow rock-rose, wild marjoram, and countless waving mauve scabious covered on hot afternoons with nervous darting butterflies.

She drove into this countryside, winter and summer, camouflaged always by the gas-cape on days of rain, without much change of expression. Her meek sunken eyes fixed themselves firmly on the winter woods, on the narrow lanes under primroses or drifts of snow, and on the chalk flowers of summer as if the seasons made no change in them at all. It was her job simply to deliver meat, to rap or ring at kitchen doors, to say good morning and thank you and then to depart in silence, camouflaged, in the van.

If she ever thought about the woods, about the blazing open chalkland in which wild strawberries sparkled, pure scarlet, in hot summers, or about the big desolate mansions standing empty among the beechwoods, she did not speak of it to a soul. If the mansions were on day to be opened up again, then they would, she supposed, be opened up. If people with money and class were to come back again, as Clem said they would, once more to order barons of beef and saddles of lamb and demand the choicest cuts of vension, then she supposed they would come back. That was all.

In due course, if such things happened, she supposed Clem would know how to deal with them. Clem was experienced, capable and shrewd, a good butcher and a good business man. Clem knew how to deal with people of class. Clem, in the early days of business, had been used to supplying the finest of everything, as his father and grandfather had done before him, for house parties, shooting luncheons, ducal dinners, and regimental messes. The days of the gentry might, as Clem said, be under a temporary cloud. But finally, one day, class would surely triumph again and tradition would be back. The war might have half killed the meat trade, but it couldn't kill those people. They were there all the time, as Clem said, somewhere. They were the backbone, the real people, the gentry.

'Didn't I tell you?' he said one day. 'Just like I told you. Belvedere's opening up. Somebody's bought Belvedere.'

She knew about Belvedere. Belvedere was one of those houses, not large but long empty, whose chimneys rose starkly, like tombs, above the beechwoods of winter-time. For six years the army had carved its ashy, cindery name on Belvedere.

'See, just like I told you,' Clem said two days later, 'the gentleman from Belvedere just phoned up. The right people are coming back. We got an order from Belvedere.'

By the time she drove up to Belvedere, later that morning, rain was falling heavily, sultrily warm, on the chalk flowers of the hillsides. She was wearing the old war-time cape, as she always did under rain, and in the van, on the enamel tray, at the back, lay portions of sweetbreads, tripe, and liver.

High on the hills, a house of yellow stucco frontage, with thin iron balconies about the windows and green iron canopies above them, faced the valley.

'Ah, the lady with the victuals! The lady with the viands. The lady from Corbett, eh?' A man of forty-five or fifty, in shirtsleeves, portly, wearing a blue-striped apron, his voice plummy and soft, answered her ring at the kitchen door.

'Do come in. You are from Corbett, aren't you?'

'I'm Mrs Corbett.'

'How nice. Come in, Mrs Corbett, come in. Don't stand there. It's loathsome and you'll catch a death. Come in. Take off your cape. Have a cheese straw.'

The rosy flesh of his face was smeared with flour dust. His fattish soft fingers were stuck about with shreds of dough.

'You arrived in the nick, Mrs Corbett. I was about to hurl these wretched things into the stove, but now you can pass judgment on them for me.'

With exuberance he suddenly put in front of her face a plate of fresh warm cheese straws.

'Taste and tell me, Mrs Corbett. Taste and tell.'

With shyness, more than usually meek, her deep brown eyes lowered, she took a cheese straw and started to bite on it.

'Tell me,' he said, 'if it's utterly loathsome.'

'It's very nice, sir.'

'Be absolutely frank, Mrs Corbett,' he said. 'Absolutely frank. If they're too revolting say so.'

'I think—'

'I tell you what, Mrs Corbett,' he said, 'they'll taste far nicer with a glass of sherry. That's it. We shall each have a glass of pale dry sherry and see how it marries with the cheese.'

Between the sherry and the cheese straws and his own conversation she found there was not much chance for her to speak. With bewilderment she watched him turn away, the cheese straws suddenly forgotten, to the kitchen table, a basin of flour, and a pastry board.

With surprising delicacy he pressed with his fingers at the edges of thin pastry lining a brown shallow dish. Beside it lay a pile of pink peeled mushrooms.

'This I know is going to be delicious,' he said. 'This I am sure about. I adore cooking. Don't you?'

Speechlessly she watched him turn to the stove and begin to melt butter in a saucepan.

'*Croûte aux champignons,*' he said. 'A kind of mushroom pie. There are some things one knows one does well. This I love to do, It's delicious—you know it, of course, don't you? Heavenly.'

'No, sir.'

'Oh, don't call me sir, Mrs Corbett. My name is Lafarge. Henry Lafarge.' He turned to fill up his glass with sherry, at the same time fixing her with greyish bulbous eyes. 'Aren't you terribly uncomfortable in that wretched mackintosh? Why don't you throw it off for a while?'

The voice, though not unkindly, shocked her a little. She had never thought of the cape as wretched. It was a very essential, useful, hard-wearing garment. It served its purpose very well, and with fresh bewilderment she pushed it back from her shoulders.

'Do you think I'm a fool?' he said. 'I mean about this house? All my friends say I'm a fool. Of course it's in a ghastly state, one knows, but I think I can do things with it. Do you agree? Do you think I'm a fool?'

She could not answer. She felt herself suddenly preoccupied, painfully, with the old brown dress she was wearing under the gas-cape. With embarrassment she folded her hands across the front of it, unsuccessfully trying to conceal it from him.

To her relief he was, however, staring at the rain. 'I think it's letting up at last,' he said. 'In which case I shall be able to show you the outside before you go, You simply must see the outside, Mrs Corbett. It's a ravishing wilderness. Ravishing to the point of being sort of almost Strawberry Hill. You know?'

She did not know, and she stared again at her brown dress, frayed at the edges.

Presently the rain slackened and stopped and only the great beeches overshadowing the house were dripping. The sauce for the *croûte aux champignons* was almost ready, and Lafarge dipped a little finger into it and then thoughtfully licked it, staring at the same time at the dripping summer trees.

'I'm going to paint most of it myself,' he said. 'It's more fun, don't you think? More creative. I don't think we're half creative enough, do you? Stupid to allow menials and lackeys to do all the nicest things for us, don't you think?'

Pouring sauce over the mushrooms, he fixed on her an inquiring, engaging smile that did not need an answer.

'Now, Mrs Corbett, the outside. You must see the outside.'

Automatically she began to draw on her cape.

'I can't think why you cling to that wretched cape, Mrs Corbett,' he said. 'The very day war was over I had a simply glorious ceremonial bonfire of all those things.'

In a cindery garden of old half-wild roses growing out of matted tussocks of grass and nettle, trailed over by thick white horns of convolvulus, he showed her the southern front of the house with its rusty canopies above the windows and its delicate iron balconies entwined with blackberry and briar.

'Of course at the moment the plaster looks frightfully leprous,' he said, 'but it'll be pink when I've done with it. The sort of pink you see in the Mediterranean. You know?'

A Virginia creeper had enveloped with shining tendrilled greed the entire western wall of the house, descending from the roof in a dripping curtain of crimson-green.

'The creeper is coming down this week,' he said. 'Ignore the creeper.' He waved soft pastry-white hands in the air, clasping and unclasping them. 'Imagine a rose there. A black one. An enormous deep red-black one. A hat rose. You know the sort?'

Again she realised he did not need an answer.

'The flowers will glow,' he said, 'like big glasses of dark red wine on a pink tablecloth. Doesn't that strike you as being absolute heaven on a summer's day?'

Bemused, she stared at the tumbling skeins of creeper, at the rising regiments of sow-thistle, more than ever uncertain what to say. She began hastily to form a few words about it being time for her to go when he said: 'There was something else I had to say to you, Mrs Corbett, and now I can't think what it was. Terribly important too. Momentously important.'

A burst of sunshine falling suddenly on the wet wilderness, the rusting canopies and Clara's frog-like cape seemed abruptly to enlighten him. 'Ah—hearts,' he said. 'That was it.'

'Hearts?'

'What's today? Tuesday. Thursday,' he said, 'I want you to bring me one of your nicest hearts.'

'One of my hearts?'

He laughed, again not unkindly. 'Bullock's,' he said.

'Oh! Yes, I see.'

'Did you know,' he said, 'that hearts taste like goose? Just like goose-flesh?' He stopped, laughed again, and actually touched her arm. 'No, no. That's wrong. Too rich. One can't say that. One can't say hearts like goose-flesh. Can one?'

A stir of wind shook the beech boughs, bringing a spray of rain sliding down the long shafts of sunlight.

'I serve them with cranberry sauce,' he said. 'With fresh peas and fresh new potatoes I defy anyone to tell the difference.'

They were back now at the kitchen door, where she had left her husband's basket on the step.

'We need more imagination, that's all,' he said. 'The despised heart is absolutely royal, I assure you, if you treat it properly—'

'I think I really must go now, Mr Lafarge,' she said, 'or I'll never get done. Do you want the heart early?'

'No,' he said, 'afternoon will do. It's for a little evening supper party. Just a friend and I. Lots of parties, that's what I shall have. Lots of parties, little ones, piggy ones in the kitchen, first. Then one big one, an enormous house-warmer, a cracker, when the house is ready.'

She picked up her basket, automatically drawing the cape round her shoulders and started to say, 'All right, sir. I'll be up in the afternoon—'

'Most kind of you, Mrs Corbett,' he said. 'Goodbye. So kind. But no "sir"—we're already friends. Just Lafarge.'

'Goodbye, Mr Lafarge,' she said.

She was halfway back to the van when he called, 'Oh, Mrs Corbett! If you get no answer at the door you'll probably find me decorating.' He waved soft, pastry-white hands in the direction of the creeper, the canopies, and the rusting balconies. 'You know—up there.'

When she came back to the house late on Thursday afternoon, not wearing her cape, the air was thick and sultry. All along the stark white fringes of chalk, under the beechwoods, yellow rock-roses flared in the sun. Across the valley hung a few high bland white clouds, delicate and far away.

'The creeper came down with a thousand empty birds' nests,' Lafarge called from a balcony. 'A glorious mess.'

Dressed in dark blue slacks, with yellow open shirt, blue silk muffler, and white panama, he waved towards her a pink-tipped whitewash brush. Behind him the wall, bare of creeper, was drying a thin blotting-paper pink in the sun.

'I put the heart in the kitchen,' she said.

Ignoring this, he made no remark about her cape, either. 'The stucco turned out to be in remarkably good condition,' he said. 'Tell me about the paint. You're the first to see it. Too dark?'

'I think it's very nice.'

'Be absolutely frank,' he said. 'Be as absolutely frank and critical as you like, Mrs Corbett. Tell me exactly how it strikes you. Isn't it too dark?'

'Perhaps it is a shade too dark.'

'On the other hand one has to picture the rose against it,' he said. 'Do you know anyone who grows that wonderful black-red rose?'

She stood staring up at him. 'I don't think I do.'

'That's a pity,' he said, 'because if we had the rose one could judge the effect—However, I'm going to get some tea. Would you care for tea?'

In the kitchen he made tea with slow, punctilious ritual care.

'The Chinese way,' he said. 'First a very little water. Then a minute's wait. Then more water. Then another wait. And so on. Six minutes in all. The secret lies in the waits and the little drops of water. Try one of these. It's a sort of sourmilk tart I invented.'

She sipped tea, munched pastry, and stared at the raw heart she had left in a dish on the kitchen table.

'Awfully kind of you to stop and talk to me, Mrs Corbett,' he said. 'You're the first living soul I've spoken to since you were here on Tuesday.'

Then, for the first time, she asked a question that had troubled her.

'Do you live here all alone?' she said.

'Absolutely, but when the house is done I shall have masses of parties. Masses of friends.'

'It's rather a big house for one person.'

'Come and see the rooms,' he said. 'Some of the rooms I had done before I moved in. My bedroom for instance. Come upstairs.'

Upstairs a room in pigeon grey, with a deep green carpet and an open french window under a canopy, faced across the valley.

He stepped out on the balcony, spreading enthusiastic hands.

'Here I'm going to have big plants. Big plushy ones. Petunias. Blowzy ones. Begonias, fuchsias, and that sort of thing. Opulence everywhere.'

He turned and looked at her. 'It's a pity we haven't got that big black rose.'

'I used to wear a hat with a rose like that on it,' she said, 'but I never wear it now.'

'How nice,' he said, and came back into the room, where suddenly, for the second time, she felt the intolerable dreariness of her brown woollen dress.

Nervously she put her hands in front of it again and said:

'I think I ought to be going now, Mr Lafarge. Was there something for the weekend?'

'I haven't planned,' he said. 'I'll have to telephone.'

He stood for a moment in the window, looking straight at her with a expression of sharp, arrested amazement.

'Mrs Corbett,' he said, 'I saw the most extraordinary effect just now. It was when I was on the ladder and we were talking about the rose. You were standing there looking up at me and your eyes were so dark that it looked as if you hadn't got any. They're the darkest eyes I've even seen. Didn't anyone ever tell you so?'

No one, as she remembered it, had ever told her so.

The following Saturday morning she arrived at the house with oxtail and kidneys. 'I shall have the kidneys with *sauce madère*,' he said. 'And perhaps even *flambés*.'

He was kneading a batch of small brown loaves on the kitchen table, peppering them with poppy seeds, and he looked up from them to see her holding a brown-paper bag.

'It's only the rose off my hat,' she said. 'I thought you might like to try—'

'Darling Mrs Corbett,' he said. 'You dear creature.'

No one, as she remembered it, had ever called her darling before. Nor could she ever remember being, for anyone, at any time, a dear creature.

Some minutes later she was standing on the balcony outside his bedroom window, pressing the dark red rose from her hat against the fresh pink wall. He stood in the cindery wilderness below, making lively, rapturous gestures.

'Delicious, my dear. Heavenly. You must see it. You simply must come down!'

She went down, leaving the rose on the balcony. A few seconds later he was standing in her place while she stood in the garden below, staring up at the effect of her dark red rose against the wall.

'What do you feel?' he called.

'It seems real,' she said. 'It seems to have come alive.'

'Ah! but imagine it in another summer,' he said. 'When it will be real. When there'll be lots of them, scores of them, blooming here.'

With extravagant hands he tossed the rose down to her from the balcony. Instinctively she lifted her own hands, trying to catch it. It fell instead into a forest of sow-thistle.

He laughed, again not unkindly, and called, 'I'm so grateful, darling Mrs Corbett. I really can't tell you how grateful I am. You've been so thoughtful. You've got such taste.'

With downcast eyes she picked the rose out of the mass of sow-thistle, not knowing what to say.

Through a tender August, full of soft light that seemed to reflect back from dry chalky fields of oats and wheat and barley just below the hill, the derelict house grew prettily, all pink at first among the beeches. By September, Lafarge had begun work on the balconies, painting them a delicate seagull grey. Soon the canopies were grey, too, hanging like half sea-shells above the windows. The doors and windows became grey also, giving an effect of delicate lightness to the house against the background of arching, massive boughs.

She watched these transformations almost from day to day as she delivered to Lafarge kidneys, tripe, liver, sweetbreads, calves' heads, calves' feet, and the hearts that he claimed were just like goose-flesh.

'Offal,' he was repeatedly fond of telling her, 'is far too under-rated. People are altogether too superior about offal. The eternal joint is the curse. What could be more delicious than sweetbreads? Or calf's head? Or even chitterlings? There is a German recipe for chitterlings, Mrs Corbett, that could make you think you were eating I don't know what—some celestial, melting manna. You must bring me chitterlings one day soon, Mrs Corbett dear.'

'I have actually found the rose too,' he said one day with excitement. 'I have actually ordered it from a catalogue. It's called *Château Clos de Vougeot* and it's just like the rose on your hat. It's like a deep dark red burgundy.'

All this time, now that the weather had settled into the rainless calm of late summer, she did not need to wear her cape. At the same time she did not think of discarding it. She thought only with uneasiness of the brown frayed dress and presently replaced it with another, dark blue, that she had worn as second-best for many years.

By October, when the entire outside of the house had become transformed, she began to feel, in a way, that she was part of it. She had seen the curtains of creeper, with their thousand bird's nests, give way to clean pink stucco. The canopies had grown from bowls of rusty green tin to delicate half seashells and the balconies from mere paintless coops to pretty cages of seagull grey. As with the fields, the beechwoods, the yellow rock-roses running across the chalk and the changing seasons she had hardly any way of expressing what she felt about these things. She could simply say, 'Yes, Mr Lafarge, I think it's lovely. It's very nice, Mr Lafarge. It's sort of come alive.'

'Largely because of you, dear,' he would say. 'You've inspired the thing. You've fed me with your delicious viands. You've helped. You've given opinions. You brought the rose for the wall. You've got such marvellous instinctive taste, Mrs Corbett dear.'

Sometimes too he would refer again to her eyes, that were so dark and looked so straight ahead and hardly moved when spoken to. 'It's those wonderful eyes of yours, Mrs Corbett,' he would say. 'I think you have a simply marvellous eye.'

By November the weather had broken up. In the shortening rainy days the beeches began to shed continuous golden-copper showers of leaves. Electric light had now been wired to the outer walls of the house, with concealed lamps beneath the balconies and windows.

She did not see these lights-switched on until a darkening afternoon in mid November, when Lafarge greeted her with an intense extravagance of excitement.

'Mrs Corbett, my dear, I've had an absolute storm of inspiration. I'm going to have the house-warmer next Saturday. All my friends are coming and you and I have to talk of hearts and livers and delicious things of that sort and so on and so on. But that isn't really the point. Come outside, Mrs Corbett dear, come outside.'

In the garden, under the dark, baring trees, he switched on the lights. 'There, darling!'

Sensationally a burst of electric light gave to the pink walls and feather-grey canopies, doors, windows, balconies, a new, uplifting sense of transformation. She felt herself catch her breath.

The house seemed to float for a moment against half-naked trees, in the darkening afternoon, and he said in that rapturously plummy voice of his, 'But that isn't all, dear, that isn't all. You see, the rose has arrived. It came this morning. And suddenly I had this wild surmise, this wonderful on-a-peak-in-Darien sort of thing. Can you guess?'

She could not guess.

'I'm going to plant it,' he said, 'at the party.'

'Oh yes, that will be nice,' she said.

'But that's not all, dear, that's not all,' he said. 'More yet. The true, the blushful has still to come. Can't you guess?'

Once again she could not guess.

'I want you to bring that rose of yours to the party,' he said. 'We'll fix it to the tree. And then in the electric light, against the pink walls—'

She felt herself catch her breath again, almost frightened.

'Me?' she said. 'At the party?'

'Well, of course, darling. Of course.'

'Mr Lafarge, I couldn't come to your party—'

'My dear,' he said, 'if you don't come to my party, I shall be for ever mortally, dismally, utterly offended.'

She felt herself begin to tremble. 'But I couldn't, Mr Lafarge, not with all your friends—'

'Darling Mrs Corbett. You are my friend. There's no argument about it. You'll come. You'll bring the rose. We'll fix it to the tree and it will be heaven. All my friends will be here. You'll love my friends.'

She did not protest or even answer. In the brilliant electric light she stared with her dark diffident eyes at the pink walls of the house and felt as if she were under an arc-light, about to undergo an operation, naked, transfixed, and utterly helpless.

It was raining when she drove up to the house on Saturday evening, wearing her cape and carrying the rose in a paper bag. But by the time she reached the hills she was able to stop the windscreen-wipers on the van and presently the sky was pricked with stars.

There were so many cars outside the house that she stood for some time outside, afraid to go in. During this time she was so nervous and preoccupied that she forgot that she was still wearing the cape. She remembered it only at the last moment, and then took it off and rolled it up and put it in the van.

Standing in the kitchen, she could only think that the house was a cage, now full of gibbering monkeys. Bewildered, she stood staring at trays of glasses, rows of bottles, many dishes of decorated morsels of lobster, prawns, olives, nuts, and sausages.

As she stood there a woman came in with a brassy voice, a long yellow cigarette holder, and a low neckline from which melon-like breasts protruded white and hard, and took a drink from a tray, swallowing it quickly before taking the entire tray back with her.

'Just float in, dear. It's like a mill-race in there. You just go with the damn stream.'

Cautiously Mrs Corbett stood by the door of the drawing-room, holding the rose in its paper bag and staring at the gibbering, munching, sipping faces swimming before her in smoky air.

It was twenty minutes before Lafarge, returning to the kitchen for plates of food, accidentally found her standing there, transfixed with deep immobile eyes.

'But darling Mrs Corbett! Where have you been? I've been telling everyone about you and you were not here. I want you to meet everyone. They've all heard about you. Everyone!'

She found herself borne away among strange faces, mute and groping.

'Angela darling, I want you to meet Mrs Corbett. The most wonderful person. The dearest sweetie. I call her my heart specialist.'

A chestless girl with tow-coloured hair, cut low over her forehead to a fringe, as with a basin, stared at her with large, hollow, unhealthy eyes. 'Is it true you're a heart specialist? Where do you practise?'

Before Clara could answer a man with an orange tie, a black shirt and a stiff carrot beard came over and said, 'Good lord, what a mob. Where does Henry get them from? Let's whip off to the local. That woman Forbes is drooling as usual into every ear.'

Excuseless, the girl with hollow eyes followed him away. Lafarge too had disappeared.

'Haven't I seen you somewhere before? Haven't we met? I rather fancied we had.' A young man with prematurely receding, downy yellow hair and uncertain reddish eyes, looking like a stoat, sucked at a glass, smoked a cigarette, and held her in a quivering, fragile stare.

'Known Henry long? Doesn't change much, does he? How's the thing getting on? The opus, I mean. The great work. He'll never finish it, of course. Henry's sort never do.'

It was some time before she realised what was wrong with the fragile uncertain eyes. The young man spilt the contents of his glass over his hands, his coat, and his thin, yellow snake of a tie. He moved away with abrupt unsteadiness and she heard a crash of glass against a chair. It passed unnoticed, as if a pin had dropped.

Presently she was overwhelmed by hoglike snorts of laughter followed by giggling, and someone said, 'What's all this about a rose?'

'God knows.'

'Some gag of Henry's.'

A large man in tweeds of rope-like thickness stood with feet apart, laughing his hoglike laugh. Occasionally he steadied himself as he drank and now and then thrust his free hand under a heavy shirt of black-and-yellow check, scratching the hairs on his chest.

Drinking swiftly, he started to whisper, 'What's all this about Henry and the grocer's wife? They say she's up here every hour of the day.'

'Good lord, Henry and what wife?'

'Grocer's, I thought—I don't know. You mean you haven't heard?'

'Good lord, no. Can't be. Henry and girls?'

'No? You don't think so?'

'Can't believe it. Not Henry. He'd run from a female fly.'

'All females are fly.'

Again, at this remark, there were heavy, engulfing guffaws of laughter.

'Possible, I suppose, possible. One way of getting the custom.'

She stood in a maze, only half hearing, only half awake. Splinters of conversation sent crackling past her bewildered face like scraps of flying glass.

'Anybody know where the polly is? Get me a drink while I'm gone, dear. Gin. Not sherry. The sherry's filthy.'

'Probably bought from the grocer.'

Leaning against the mantelpiece, a long arm extended, ash dropping greyly and seedily down her breast, the lady with the yellow cigarette holder was heard, with a delicate hiss, to accuse someone of bitchiness.

'But then we're all bitches, aren't we,' she said, 'more or less? But she especially.'

'Did she ever invite you? She gets you to make up a number for dinner and when you get there a chap appears on the doorstep and says they don't need you any more. Yes, actually!'

'She's a swab. Well, poor Alex, he knows it now.'

'That's the trouble, of course—when you do know, it's always too bloody late to matter.'

Everywhere the air seemed to smoke with continuous white explosions. Soon Clara started to move away and found herself facing a flushed eager Lafarge, who in turn was pushing past a heavy woman in black trousers, with the jowls of a bloodhound and bright blonde hair neatly brushed back and oiled, like a man.

'There you are, Mrs Corbett. You've no drink. Nothing to eat. You haven't met anybody.'

A man was edging past her and Lafarge seized him by the arm.

'Siegfried. Mrs Corbett, this is my friend Siegfried Pascoe. Siegfried, dear fellow, hold her hand. Befriend her while I get her a drink. It's our dear Mrs Corbett, Siegfried, of heart fame.' He squeezed Mrs Corbett's arm, laughing. 'His mother called him Siegfried because she had a Wagner complex,' he said. 'Don't move!'

An object like an unfledged bird, warm and boneless, slid into her hand. Limply it slid out again and she looked up to see a plump creaseless moon of a face, babyish, almost pure white under carefully curled brown hair, staring down at her with pettish, struggling timidity. A moment later, in a void, she heard the Pascoe voice attempting to frame its syllables like a little fussy machine misfiring, the lips loose and puffy.

'What do you f-f-f-feel about Eliot?' it said.

She could not answer; she could think of no one she knew by the name of Eliot.

To her relief Lafarge came back, bearing a glass of sherry and a plate on which were delicate slices of meat rolled up and filled with wine-red jelly. 'This,' he told her, 'is the heart. Yes, your heart, Mrs Corbett. The common old heart. Taste it, dear. Take the fork. Taste it and see if it isn't absolute manna. I'll hold the sherry.'

She ate the cold heart. Cranberry sauce squeezed itself from the rolls of meat and ran down her chin and just in time she caught it with a fork.

The heart, she thought, tasted not at all unlike heart and in confusion she heard Lafarge inquire, 'Delicious?'

'Very nice.'

'Splendid. So glad—'

With a curious unapologetic burst of indifference he turned on his heel and walked away. Five seconds later he was back again, saying, 'Siegfried, dear boy, we shall do the rose in five minutes. Could you muster the spade? It's stopped raining. We'll fling the doors open, switch on the lights, and make a dramatic thing of it. Everybody will pour forth—'

He disappeared a second time into the mass of gibbering faces, taking with him her glass of sherry, and when she turned her eyes she saw that Siegfried Pascoe too had gone.

'What on earth has possessed Henry? They say she's the butcher's wife. Not grocer's after all.'

'Oh, it's a gag, dear. You know how they hot things up. It's a gag.'

She set her plate at last on a table and began to pick her way through the crush of drinkers, seeking the kitchen. To her great relief there was no one there. Suddenly tired, hopelessly bewildered and sick, she sat down on a chair, facing a wreckage of half-chewed vol-au-vents, canapés, salted biscuits and cold eyes of decorated egg. The noise from the big drawing-room increased like the hoarse and nervous clamour rising from people who, trapped, lost, and unable to find their way, were fighting madly to be free.

Out of it all leapt a sudden collective gasp, as if gates had been burst open and the trapped, lost ones could now mercifully find their way. In reality it was a gasp of surprise as Lafarge switched on the outside lights, and she heard it presently followed by a rush of feet as people shuffled outwards into the rainless garden air.

Not moving, she sat alone at the kitchen table, clutching the rose in the paper bag. From the garden she heard laughter bursting in excited taunting waves. A wag shouted in a loud voice, 'Forward the grave-diggers! On with the spade-work!' and there were fresh claps of caterwauling laughter.

From it all sprang the sudden petulant voice of Lafarge, like a child crying for a toy, 'The rose! On, my dear, the rose! Where *is* the rose? We can't do it without the rose.'

Automatically she got up from the table. Even before she heard Lafarge's voice, nearer now, calling her name, she was already walking across the emptied drawing-room, towards the open french windows, with the paper bag.

'Mrs Corbett! Mrs Corbett! Oh, there you are, dear. Where did you get to? What a relief—and oh, you poppet, you've got the rose.'

She was hardly aware that he was taking her by the hand. She was hardly aware, as she stepped into the blinding white light of electric lamps placed about the bright pink walls, that he was saying, 'Oh, but Mrs Corbett, you must. After all, it's your rose, dear. I insist. It's all part of the thing. It's the nicest part of the thing—'

Vaguely she became aware that the rose tree, spreading five fanlike branches, was already in its place by the wall.

'Just tie it on, dear. Here's the ribbon. I managed to get exactly the right-coloured ribbon.'

From behind her, as she stood under the naked light, tying the rose to the tree, she was assailed by voices in chattering boisterous acclamation. A few people actually clapped their hands and there were sudden trumpeted bursts of laughter as the wag who had shouted of grave-diggers suddenly shouted again, 'Damn it all, Henry, give her a kiss. Kiss the lady! Be fair.'

'Kiss her!' everyone started shouting. 'Kiss her. Kiss! Kiss, Henry! Kiss, kiss!'

'*Pour encourager les autres!*' the wag shouted. 'Free demonstration.'

After a sudden burst of harsh, jovial catcalls she turned her face away, again feeling utterly naked and transfixed under the stark white lights. A second later she felt Lafarge's lips brush clumsily, plummily across her own.

Everyone responded to this with loud bursts of cheers.

'Ceremony over!' Lafarge called out. He staggered uncertainly, beckoning his guests housewards. 'Everybody back to the flesh-pots. Back to the grain and grape.'

'Henry's tight,' somebody said. 'What fun. Great, the kissing. Going to be a good party.'

She stood for some time alone in the garden, holding the empty paper bag. In an unexpected moment the lights on the pink walls were extinguished, leaving only the light from windows shining across the grass outside. She stood for a few moments longer and then groped to the wall, united the rose and put it back in the paper bag.

Driving away down the hillside, she stopped the van at last and drew it into a gateway simply because she could think of no other way of calming the trembling in her hands. She stood for a long time clutching the side of the van. In confusion she thought of the rose on the wall, of hearts that were like goose-flesh, and of how, as Clem said, the gentry would come back. Then she took her cape and the paper bag with its rose out of the van.

When she had dropped the paper bag and the rose into the ditch she slowly pulled on the old cape and started to cry. As she cried she drew the cape over her head, as if afraid that someone would see her crying there, and then buried her face in it, as into a shroud.

Where the Cloud Breaks

Colonel Gracie, who had decided to boil himself two new-laid eggs for lunch, came into the kitchen from the garden and laid his panama hat on top of the stove, put the eggs into it and then, after some moments of blissful concentration, looked inside to see if they were cooking.

Presently he sensed that something was vaguely wrong about all this and began to search for a saucepan. Having found it, a small blue enamel one much blackened by fire, he gazed at it with intent inquiry for some moments, half made a gesture as if to put it on his head and then decided to drop the eggs into it, without benefit of water. In the course of doing this he twice dipped the sleeve of his white duck jacket into a dish of raspberry jam, originally put out on the kitchen table for breakfast. The jam dish was in fact a candlestick, in pewter, the candle part of which had broken away.

Soon the Colonel, in the process of making himself some toast, found himself wondering what day it was. He couldn't be sure. He had recently given up taking *The Times* and it was this that made things difficult. He knew the month was July, although the calendar hanging by the side of the stove actually said it was September, but that of course didn't help much about the day. He guessed it might be Tuesday; but you never really knew when you lived alone. Still, it helped sometimes to know whether it was Tuesday or Sunday, just in case he ran short of tobacco and walked all the way to the village shop only to find it closed.

Was it Tuesday? The days were normally fixed quite clearly in his mind by a system of colouration. Tuesday was a most distinct shade of raspberry rose. Thursday was brown and Sunday a pleasant yellow, that particularly bright gold you got in sunflowers. Today seemed, he thought, rather a dark green, much more like a Wednesday. It was most important to differentiate, because if it were really Wednesday it would be not the slightest use his walking down to the shop to get stamps after lunch, since Wednesday was early closing day.

There was nothing for it, he told himself, but to semaphore his friend Miss Wilkinson. With a piece of toast in his hand he set about finding his signalling flags, which he always kept in a cupboard under the stairs. As he stooped to unlatch the cupboard door a skein of onions left over from the previous winter dropped from a fragile string on the wall and fell on his neck without alarming him visibly.

One of the flags was bright yellow, the other an agreeable shade of chicory blue. Experience had shown that these two colours showed up far better than all others against the surrounding landscape of lush chestnut copse and woodland. They were clearly visible for a good half mile.

In the army, from which he was now long retired, signalling had been the Colonel's special pigeon. He had helped to train a considerable number of men with extreme proficiency. Miss Wilkinson, who was sixty, wasn't of course quite so apt a pupil as a soldier in his prime, but she had nevertheless been overjoyed to learn what was not altogether a difficult art. It had been the greatest fun for them both; it had whiled away an enormous number of lonely hours.

For the past five weeks Miss Wilkinson had been away, staying on the south coast with a sister, and the Colonel had missed her greatly. Not only had there been no one to whom he could signal his questions, doubts and thoughts; he had never really been quite sure, all that time, what day it was.

After now having had the remarkable presence of mind to put an inch or two of water into the egg saucepan the Colonel set out with the flags to walk to the bottom of the garden, which sloped fairly steeply to its southern boundary, a three foot hedge of hawthorn. Along the hedge thirty or forty gigantic heads of sunflower were in full flower, the huge faces staring like yellow guardians across the three sloping open meadows that lay between the Colonel and Miss Wilkinson, who lived in a small white weatherboard house down on the edge of a narrow stream. Sometimes after torrential winter rains the little stream rose with devastating rapidity, flooding Miss Wilkinson, so that the Colonel had to be there at the double, to bale her out.

In the centre of the hedge was a stile and the Colonel, who in his crumpled suit of white duck looked something like a cadaverous baker out of work, now stood up on it and blew three sharp blasts on a whistle. This was the signal to fetch Miss Wilkinson from the kitchen, the greenhouse, the potting shed, or wherever she happened to be. The system of whistle and flag suited both the Colonel and Miss Wilkinson admirably, the Colonel because he hated the telephone so much and Miss Wilkinson because she couldn't afford to have the instrument installed. For the same reasons neither of them owned either television or radio, the Colonel having laid it down in expressly severe terms, almost as if in holy writ, that he would not only never have such antisocial devices in the house but that they were also, in a sense, degenerate: if not immoral.

Miss Wilkinson having appeared in her garden in a large pink sun hat and a loose summery blue dress with flowers all over it, the Colonel addressed her by smartly raising his yellow flag. Miss Wilkinson replied by promptly raising her blue one. This meant that they were receiving each other loud and clear.

The day in fact was so beautifully clear that the Colonel could actually not only see Miss Wilkinson in detail as she stood on the small wooden bridge that spanned the stream but he could also pick out slender spires of purple loosestrife among the many tall reeds that lined the banks like dark green swords. Both he and Miss Wilkinson, among their many other things in common, were crazy about flowers.

Having given himself another moment to get into correct position, the Colonel presently signalled to Miss Wilkinson that he was frightfully sorry to trouble her but would she very much mind telling him what day it was?

To his infinite astonishment Miss Wilkinson signalled back that it was Thursday and, as if determined to leave no doubt about it, added that it was also August the second.

August? the Colonel replied. He was much surprised. He thought it was July.

No, no, it was August, Miss Wilkinson told him. Thursday the second—the day he was coming to tea.

The Colonel had spent the morning since ten o'clock in a rush of perspiring industry, cleaning out the hens. The fact that he was going to tea with Miss Wilkinson had, like the precise date and month, somehow slipped his mind.

'You hadn't forgotten, had you?'

'Oh! no, no, I hadn't forgotten. Had an awfully long morning, that's all. Would you mind telling me what time it is now?'

In the clear summer air the Colonel could distinctly see the movement of Miss Wilkinson's arm as she raised it to look at her watch. He himself never wore a watch. Though altogether less pernicious than telephone, television and radio, a watch nevertheless belonged, in his estimation, to that category of inventions that one could well do without.

'Ten to four.'

Good God, the Colonel thought, now struck by the sudden realisation that he hadn't had lunch yet.

'I was expecting you in about ten minutes. It's so lovely I thought we'd have tea outside. Under the willow tree.'

Admirable idea, the Colonel thought, without signalling it. What, by the way, had he done with the eggs? Were they on the boil or not? He couldn't for the life of him remember.

'Do you wish any eggs?' he asked. 'I have heaps.'

'No, thank you all the same. I have some.' It might have been a laugh or merely a bird-cry that the Colonel heard coming across the meadows. 'Don't be too long. I have a surprise for you.'

As he hurried back to the house the Colonel wondered, in a dreamy sort of way, what kind of surprise Miss Wilkinson could possibly have for him and as he wondered he felt a sort of whisper travel across his heart. It was the sort of tremor he often experienced when he was on the way to see her or when he looked at the nape of her neck or when she spoke to him in some specially direct or unexpected sort of way. He would like to have put his feeling into words of some kind—signalling was child's play by comparison—but he was both too inarticulate and too shy to do so.

Half an hour later, after walking down through the meadows, he fully expected to see Miss Wilkinson waiting for him on the bank of the stream under the willow-tree, where the tea-table, cool with lace cloth, was already laid. But there was no sign of her there or in the greenhouse, where cucumbers were growing on humid vines, or in the kitchen.

Then, to his great surprise, he heard her voice calling him from some distance off and a moment later he saw her twenty yards or so away, paddling in the stream.

'Just remembered I'd seen a bed of watercress yesterday and I thought how nice it would be. Beautifully cool, the water.'

As he watched her approaching, legs bare and white above emerald skim of water-weed, the Colonel again experienced the tremor that circumvented his heart like a whisper. This time it was actually touched with pain and there was nothing he could say.

'Last year there was a bed much farther upstream. But I suppose the seeds get carried down.'

Miss Wilkinson was fair and pink, almost cherubic, her voice jolly. A dew-lap rather like those seen in ageing dogs hung floppily down on the collar of her cream shantung dress, giving her a look of obese friendliness and charm.

'The kettle's on already,' she said. 'Sit yourself down while I go in and get my feet dried.'

The Colonel, watching her white feet half-running, half-trotting across the lawn, thought again of the surprise she had in store for him and wondered if paddling in the stream was it. No other, he thought, could have had a sharper effect on him.

When she came back, carrying a silver hot water jug and tea-pot, she laughed quite gaily in reply to his query about the surprise. No: it wasn't paddling in the stream. And she was afraid he would have to wait until after tea before she could tell him, anyway.

'Oh! how stupid of me,' she said, abruptly pausing in the act of pouring tea, 'I've gone and forgotten the watercress.'

'I'll get it, I'll get it,' the Colonel said, at once leaping up to go into the house.

'Oh! no, you don't,' she said. 'Not on your life. My surprise is in there.'

Later, drinking tea and munching brown bread and butter and cool sprigs of watercress dipped in salt, the Colonel found it impossible to dwell on the question of the surprise without uneasiness. In an effort to take his mind off the subject he remarked on how good the sunflowers were this year and what a fine crop of seeds there would be. He fed them to the hens.

'I think it's the sunflowers that give the eggs that deep brown colour,' he said.

'You do?' she said. 'By the way did you like the pie I made for you?'

'Pie?'

With silent distress the Colonel recalled a pie of morello cherries, baked and bestowed on him the day before yesterday. He had put it into the larder and had forgotten that too.

'It was delicious. I'm saving half of it for supper.'

Miss Wilkinson, looking at him rather as dogs sometimes look, head sideways, with a meditative glint in her eye, asked suddenly what he had had for lunch? Not eggs again?

'Eggs are so easy.'

'I've told you before. You can't live on eggs all the time,' she said. 'I've been making pork brawn this morning. Would you care for some of that?'

'Yes, I would. Thank you. I would indeed.'

From these trivial discussions on food it seemed to the Colonel that a curious and elusive sense of intimacy sprang up. It was difficult to define but it was almost as if either he or Miss Wilkinson had proposed to each other and had been, in spirit at least, accepted.

This made him so uneasy again that he suddenly said:

'By the way, I don't think I told you. I've given up *The Times*.'

'Oh! really. Isn't that rather rash?'

'I don't think so. I'd been considering it for some time actually. You see, one is so busy with the hens and the garden and all that sort of thing that quite often one gets no time to read until ten o'clock. Which is absurd. I thought that from time to time I might perhaps borrow yours?'

'Of course.'

The Colonel, thinking that perhaps he was talking too much, sat silent. How pretty the stream looked, he thought. The purple loosestrife had such dignity by the waterside. He must go fishing again one day. The stream held a few trout and in the deeper pools there were chub.

'Are you quite sure you won't feel lost without a paper? I think I should.'

'No, no. I don't think so. One gets surfeited anyway with these wretched conferences and ministerial comings and goings and world tension and so on. One wants to be away from it all.'

'One mustn't run away from life, nevertheless.'

Life was what you made it, the Colonel pointed out. He preferred it as much as possible untrammelled.

Accepting Miss Wilkinson's offer of a third cup of tea and another plate of the delicious watercress he suddenly realised that he was ravenously hungry. There was a round plum cake on the table and his eye kept wandering back to it with the poignant voracity of a boy after a game of football. After a time Miss Wilkinson noticed this and started to cut the cake in readiness.

'I'm thinking of going fishing again very soon,' the Colonel said. 'If I bag a trout or two perhaps you might care to join me for supper?'

'I should absolutely love to.'

It was remarks of such direct intimacy, delivered in a moist, jolly voice, that had the Colonel's heart in its curious whispering state again. In silence he contemplated the almost too pleasant prospect of having Miss Wilkinson to supper. He would try his best to cook the trout nicely, in butter, and not burn them. Perhaps he would also be able to manage a glass of wine.

'I have a beautiful white delphinium in bloom,' Miss Wilkinson said. 'I want to show it you after tea.'

'That isn't the surprise?'

Miss Wilkinson laughed with almost incautious jollity.

'You must forget all about the surprise. You're like a small boy who can't wait for Christmas.'

The Colonel apologised for what seemed to be impatience and then followed this with a second apology, saying he was sorry he'd forgotten to ask Miss Wilkinson if she had enjoyed the long visit to her sister.

'Oh! splendidly. It really did me the world of good. One gets sort of ham-strung by one's habits, don't you think? It's good to get away.'

To the Colonel her long absence had seemed exactly the opposite. He would like to have told her how much he had missed her. Instead something made him say:

'I picked up a dead gold-finch in the garden this morning. It had fallen among the sea kale. Its yellow wing was open on one of the grey leaves and I thought it was a flower.'

'The cat, I suppose?'

'No, no. There was no sign of violence at all.'

Away downstream a dove cooed, breaking and yet deepening all the drowsiness of the summer afternoon. What did one want with world affairs, presidential speeches, threats of war and all those things? the Colonel wondered. What had newspapers ever given to the world that could be compared with that one sound, the solo voice of the dove by the waterside?

'No, no. No more tea, thank you. Perhaps another piece of cake, yes. That's excellent, thank you.'

The last crumb of cake having been consumed, the Colonel followed Miss Wilkinson into the flower garden to look at the white delphinium. Its snowy grace filled him with an almost ethereal sense of calm. He couldn't have been, he thought, more happy.

'Very beautiful. Most beautiful.'

'I'm going to divide it in the spring,' Miss Wilkinson said, 'and give you a piece.'

After a single murmur of acceptance for this blessing the Colonel remained for some moments speechless, another tremor travelling round his heart, this time like the quivering of a tightened wire.

'Well now,' Miss Wilkinson said, 'I think I might let you see the surprise if you're ready.'

He was not only ready but even eager, the Colonel thought. 'I'll lead the way,' Miss Wilkinson said.

She led the way into the sitting room, which was beautifully cool and full of the scent of small red carnations. The Colonel, who was not even conscious of being a hopelessly untidy person himself, nevertheless was always struck by the pervading neatness, the laundered freshness, of all parts of Miss Wilkinson's house. It was like a little chintz holy-of-holies, always embalmed, always the same.

'Well, what do you say? There it is.'

The Colonel, with customary blissful absent-mindedness, stared about the room without being able to note that anything had changed since his last visit there.

'I must say I don't really see anything in the nature of a surprise.'

'Oh! you do. Don't be silly.'

No, the Colonel had to confess, there was nothing he could see. It was all exactly as he had seen it the last time.

'Over there. In the corner. Of course it's rather a small one. Not as big as my sister's.'

It slowly began to reach the blissfully preoccupied cloisters of the Colonel's mind that he was gazing at a television set. A cramping chill went round his heart. For a few unblissful moments he stared hard in front of him, tormented by a sense of being unfairly trapped, with nothing to say.

'My sister gave it to me. She's just bought herself a new one. You see you get so little allowed for an old one in part exchange that it's hardly worth—'

'You mean you've actually got it permanently?'

'Why, yes. Of course.'

The Colonel found himself speaking with a voice so constricted that it seemed almost to be disembodied.

'But I always thought you hated those things.'

'Well, I suppose there comes a day. I must say it was a bit of a revelation at my sister's. Some of the things one saw were absorbing. For instance there was a programme about a remote Indian tribe in the forests of South America that I found quite marvellous.' The Colonel was stiff, remote-eyed, as if not listening. 'This tribe was in complete decay. It was actually dying out, corrupted—'

'Corrupted by what? By civilisation my guess would be.'

'As a matter of fact they were. For one thing they die like flies from measles.'

'Naturally. That,' the Colonel said, 'is what I am always trying to say.'

'Yes, but there are other viewpoints. One comes to realise that.'

'The parallel seems to me to be an exact one,' the Colonel said. 'I'm afraid I can't agree.'

There was now a certain chill, almost an iciness, in the air. The ethereal calm of the afternoon, its emblem the white delphinium, seemed splintered and blackened. The Colonel, though feeling that Miss Wilkinson had acted in some way like a traitor, at the same time had no way of saying so. It was all so callous, he thought, so shockingly out of character. He managed to blurt out:

'I really didn't think you'd come down to this.'

'I didn't come down to it, as you so candidly put it. It was simply a gift from my sister. You talk about it as if I'd started taking some sort of horrible drug.'

'In a sense you have.'

'I'm afraid I disagree again.'

'All these things are drugs. Cinemas, radio, television, telephone, even newspapers. That's really why I've given up *The Times*. I thought we always agreed on that?'

'We may have done. At one time. Now we'll have to agree to differ.'

'Very well.'

A hard lump rose in the Colonel's throat and stuck there. A miserable sense of impotence seized him and kept him stiff, with nothing more to say.

'I might have shown you a few minutes of it and converted you,' Miss Wilkinson said. 'But the aerial isn't up yet. It's coming this evening.'

'I don't think I want to be converted, thank you.'

'I hoped you'd like it and perhaps come down in the evenings sometimes and watch.'

'Thank you, I shall be perfectly happy in my own way.'

'Very well. I'm sorry you're so stubborn about it.'

The Colonel was about to say with acidity that he was not stubborn and then changed his mind and said curtly that he must go. After a painful silence Miss Wilkinson said:

'Well, if you must I'll get the pork brawn.'

'I don't think I care for the pork brawn, thank you.'

'Just as you like.'

At the door of the sitting room the Colonel paused, if anything stiffer than ever, and remarked that if there was something he particularly wanted he would signal her.

'I shan't be answering any signals,' Miss Wilkinson said.

'You won't be answering any signals?'

An agony of disbelief went twisting through the Colonel, imposing on him a momentary paralysis. He could only stare.

'No: I shan't be answering any signals.'

'Does that mean you won't be speaking to me again?'

'I didn't say that.'

'I think it rather sounds like that.'

'Then you must go on thinking it sounds like that, that's all.'

It was exactly as if Miss Wilkinson had slapped him harshly in the face; it was precisely as if he had proposed and been rudely rejected.

'Goodbye,' he said in a cold and impotent voice.

'Goodbye,' she said. 'I'll see you out.'

'There's no need to see me out, thank you. I'll find my way alone.'

Back in his own kitchen the Colonel discovered that the eggs had boiled black in the saucepan. He had forgotten to close the door of the stove. Brown smoke was hanging everywhere. Trying absentmindedly to clear up the mess he twice put his sleeve in the jam dish without noticing it and then wiped his sleeve across the tablecloth, uncleared since breakfast-time.

In the garden the dead gold-finch still lay on the silvery leaf of sea kale and he stood staring at it for a long time, stiff-eyed and impotent, unable to think one coherent simple thought.

Finally he went back to the house, took out the signalling flags and went over to the stile. Standing on it, he gave three difficult blasts on the whistle but nothing happened in answer except that one of two men standing on the roof of Miss Wilkinson's house, erecting the television aerial, casually turned his head.

Then he decided to send a signal. The three words he wanted so much to send were 'Please forgive me' but after some moments of contemplation he found that he had neither the heart nor the will to raise a flag.

Instead he simply stood immovable by the stile, staring across the meadows in the evening sun. His eyes were blank. They seemed to be groping in immeasurable appeal for something and as if in answer to it the long row of great yellow sunflower faces, the seeds of which were so excellent for the hens, stared back at him, in that wide, laughing, almost mocking way that sunflowers have.